THE DINOSAUR DIARIES

AND OTHER TALES ACROSS SPACE AND TIME

THE DINOSAUR DIARIES

AND OTHER TALES ACROSS SPACE AND TIME

SCOTT WILLIAM CARTER

With a foreword by
Kristine Kathryn Rusch

"The Dinosaur Diaries" originally appeared in *Realms of Fantasy*, April 2008. "Road Gamble" originally appeared in *Ellery Queen*, June 2007. "A Dark Planetarium" originally appeared in *Indy Men's Magazine*, December 2003. "The Liberators" originally appeared in *Analog*, April 2004. "Tommy Top Hat" is published here for the first time. "Shatterboy" originally appeared in *Cicada*, November 2005. "Heart of Stone" originally appeared in HAGS, SIRENS, AND OTHER BAD GIRLS, Daw Books, July 2006. "The Tiger in the Garden" originally appeared in *Asimov's*, June 2006. "Directions to Mourning's Deep" originally appeared in *Weird Tales*, April 2007. "Motivational Speaker" originally appeared in MYSTERY DATE, Daw Books, February 2008. "The Time Traveler's Wife" originally appeared in *Analog*, July 2005. "Epic, The" originally appeared in TWENTY EPICS, All-Star Stories, July 2006. "Happy Time" originally appeared in *Postscripts*, November 2006 "The Grand Mal Reaper" originally appeared in *Realms of Fantasy*, August 2006. "The World in Primary Colors" originally appeared in *Ellery Queen*, September 2007. "Father Hagerman's Dog" originally appeared in *Analog*, June 2007. "With Dignity" originally appeared in BURIED TREASURES, Eugene Professional Writer's Workshops, November 1996. "A Christmas in Amber" originally appeared in *Analog*, December 2005.

For more about Flying Raven Press, please visit our web site at
http://www.flyingravenpress.com

ISBN-10 0692247440
ISBN-13 978-0692247440
Printed in the United States of America
Flying Raven Press paperback edition, August 2014

For Mom and Dad

I'm still that kid who spent all those hours
in his room dreaming up imaginary worlds.
Now I just write them down.

Contents

Foreword

Kristine Kathryn Rusch

THEY ARRIVED IN A GROUP. Three college students from the University of Oregon showed up at G. Willickers Restaurant one night in 1992. G. Willickers, which smelled of grease and fried hamburgers. G. Willickers, whose chicken basket I can still picture as if the restaurant hadn't gone out of business years ago.

We held a workshop in the back room, and it was a hell of a workshop. On any given night, one of four major fiction editors sat at the table. A top game designer came regularly. More than half of the writers were published regularly.

We talked shop, exchanged business tips and—oh, yeah—critiqued stories. The workshop was open to anyone who followed the rules, meaning they had to read the stories before they spoke up, they had to be quiet when someone else spoke, and they had to want to be published not lauded for actually writing something.

College students came in and out. Most of them left after a week or so. We weren't going to tell them how wonderful or talented they were, so they pouted and disappeared. But we started to notice that these three remained.

For a while, they were the Scotts, because all we knew was that two of them were named Scott. Then we figured out that two of them were brothers, and slowly we learned their names.

Scott Totten. Michael Totten. Scott Carter. The brothers looked nothing alike. Over time, we realized the blond was the Carter.

They came and stayed, turning in stories, trying to figure out the career, trying to incorporate it into their college life. They sold some stories—Scott Carter sold some to a magazine my husband edited. Michael Totten got into the prestigious Clarion Writers Workshop. I don't remember if they left before the workshop ended its fantastic life. Those last few years are a bit of a blur.

But I had hope for those three guys. I figured if anyone could make it in this tough writing career, they could.

I didn't hear from any of them for years, even though I edited for at least five years after I met them.

Then Scott Carter showed up. He was older, a bit battered by some bad instruction, somewhat disillusioned by his venture into the world of academic writing. Scott had applied to a short story writing class I was teaching with Gardner Dozois. Gardner and I are both Hugo-award winning editors. Gardner still edits; I'd given it all up for a full-time fiction career years ago.

The applicants had to submit a story to get into the workshop. Turns out that Scott had spent years on it, following the academic approach, instead of the approach he had learned in our earlier workshop. Professional writers don't spend years on a short story. If they did, they wouldn't make a living. In fact, quite often stories that get polished over years are so smooth as to be unmemorable.

But Scott's was so powerful he later sold it to *Cicada*. The story is in this collection. It's called "Shatterboy," and I remember it years after I read it.

Those of you who don't edit don't understand what that last sentence means. I barely remember stories I bought, stories that won awards, stories I thought brilliant at the time. For a story to stand head-and-shoulders over all the other wonderful stories I've read makes it quite special indeed.

I've read most of the stories in this collection long before they saw print. Some came out of workshops. Some Scott sent to me as he was trying to break into print. All are good. Some are spectacular.

Like "A Christmas in Amber," which I can remember damn near word for word. That one, I didn't read in manuscript. I read it in *Analog* the day the issue hit my mailbox. I can still remember sitting on my couch, magazine in hand, thinking Scott had written one of the best stories of the year.

I have other favorites in this book. "Dinosaur Diaries" deserves its place in the title. "The World in Primary Colors" haunts me years after I read it.

Scott is one of those rare writers who can and does cross genres, and do it well. You never know what kind of story you'll get from him, but you do know that it'll be good.

Of the three boys who came to that writing workshop almost two decades ago, two have become professional writers. Michael Totten makes his living writing nonfiction. Scott Carter writes fiction.

So what did Gardner and I teach Scott in that first workshop? Not much. We taught him to trust his instincts. We reminded him that professional writers write more than one story per year. We demanded that he put his stories in the mail to editors who would then buy them.

Scott did all of those things. He trusted his instincts, wrote a lot of stories, and mailed them. Editors bought them.

And now he's collected the stories.

So far only a few of us have been lucky enough to read all of these stories. But as of this printing, the rest of you will get a chance to see how great it is that Scott Carter has decided to follow his college dreams and become a professional fiction writer.

This is his first collection. I know there will be many, many more.

Introduction

THE EIGHTEEN TALES in this collection are a good representation of my short fiction. I'd say *best* short fiction, because that's the way I see them, but I think writers, as a whole, are often poor judges of their own stories. But what I can say without hesitation is that these stories do reflect the scope and variety of my work. They're short and long, dark and light, and published in a broad spectrum of places. Even the lightest, however, have at least a tinge of darkness, because that seems to be my bent as a writer, and nearly all of them have at least some sort of fantastical element—or, at least, the feel of a fantastical story—because that's just the way my mind works. It just seems to be a bit more fun when things get *weird*.

That's not to say all my work is the same. I told someone not too long ago that my writing was a lot like my reading, and that my reading was a lot like my eating—all across the board. Sometimes I'm in the mood for a beer, and sometimes I'm in the mood for a glass of cabernet sauvignon. I like Stephen King and I like William Shakespeare. It's all good.

I used to worry quite a bit about how I should label myself, but in the end, I'm just a writer. I write first to entertain. I write second to move. The only way I can do this is by writing what entertains and moves me, and then by hoping it does the same for you. I write under the desperate fear that you have something more pressing to do—kids to put to bed, dishes to wash, a burning house to flee—and that if I don't make my stories as engaging as possible, you will not only hurl my work across the room, but also curse my mother that she ever gave birth to the fool who would even dare rob you of a few precious moments on this Earth.

My hope is that you're a little like me—that you have a wide appetite, that you sometimes like nachos with melted cheese and other times you want filet mignon, and that it's all good.

Regarding the stories themselves, I don't want to say too much, because I think revealing much about the process behind a story is a bit like seeing that the wizard behind the curtain is a short, bald, frumpy man with glasses. It really does have the potential to ruin the fun.

But I will say that the oldest among them is "With Dignity," which was published in 1996 in a collection called *Buried Treasures*; they were stories that didn't see print when *Pulphouse Magazine* ceased publication and were eventually published by a fine writer named Jerry Oltion. It included work by such luminaries as Kate Wilhelm, Kristine Kathryn Rusch, and Nin Kiriki Hoffman, so though it was published on a very small scale, it certainly put me in rarified company. They were originally bought for the magazine by Dean Wesley Smith, who incidentally was the editor who bought my second story as well, meaning he gave me my start publishing short fiction *twice*—the first time when I was still in college, playing at being a writer, and the second eight years later, when I decided I was going to be one.

The most recent is the novelette "The Dinosaur Diaries," which was published in *Realms of Fantasy*. The fact that the oldest is barely 500 words and the most recent is 13,000 is something I find somewhat symbolic of how my writing has developed over the years. I wrote well over a million words of fiction between the penning of those two tales, some of which has made its way into print, but most of which will never see the light of day. But these eighteen, they are some of my best. At least I think so. You'll have to judge for yourself, of course.

Please don't curse my mother if you disagree.

Beyond that, I'll leave the stories to speak for themselves, which I think is generally the best idea.

Scott William Carter
December 2009

The Dinosaur Diaries

MA FOUND the dinosaur tracks shortly after supper.

Ashley and I were crouching in the cornfields, my hands inching under her bra. The sun was down, but the last remnants of hazy purple light clung to the overcast sky. Ashley was moaning and contorting her body toward me, and I thought maybe this was one of those rare times she would want to go all the way, when Ma's shrill cry silenced the chirping crickets. Normally I would have been pretty p-o'd at having her interrupt my private time with Ash, especially when I had a hard-on the size of a Buick, but her cry was too real to feel anything but dread.

There was only one other time Ma had cried like that—when she found Pa facedown in the barn one winter morning two years ago, stone dead from a heart attack.

I pulled away from Ashley, her long blond hair brushing against my nose. Her eyes were wide. We pushed through the head-high cornstalks back to the road and ran in the twilight toward the old barn. That's where Ma had been doing her night-wandering the last few weeks. The lingering heat of the day still clung to the air, but it was cooling fast, goose bumps prickling my bare arms.

"Ma?" I called.

We had reached the backside of the gray-weathered barn, and there were ominous gaping holes in both the roof and the sides. Big and boxy, the barn looked like a ghostly ship afloat on a sea of corn, a great rolling green sea that stretched up the gentle rise to the horizon. Our house was a quarter mile in the opposite direction, this barn all that was left from the fire that leveled our first home when I was a baby. My oldest brother, Harry, died in that fire. Ma and Pa couldn't find him, and when it was all over the firemen discovered his body in the back of his closet, where he must have gone hiding when he saw the flames. People always tell me Ma was never the same after that.

I was panting from the run—I was on the heavy side, and even a short dash left me winded—and I held my breath so I could listen. She didn't answer. Ashley adjusted her bra underneath her t-shirt. I was about to yell again when Ma cried out a second time. I followed her voice into the stalks, running full tilt, and very nearly plowed right into her. When I skidded to a halt, Ashley crashed into me, and then both of us went down at Ma's feet.

I spat out the dry, bitter dirt. Ma stood with her back to me. She was a big woman, bigger still since Pa died, and her white robe stretched tight across her back. The robe was pretty much all she wore, that and Pa's old army boots. Because she had shaved her head a week earlier, something she did two or three times a month when it struck her fancy, she had only a brown stubble of hair. The underside of her right arm was pink and splotchy in a webbed pattern, like a fleshy imitation of reptile scales. It was the scar that remained from when she ran through a wall of fire into my nursery all those years ago.

"Oh my," I heard her whisper.

"Ma?" I said.

When Ma didn't answer, I stood and helped Ashley do the same, then we both edged on either side of Ma. I saw right away what had so alarmed her.

An area of stalks about the size of a Volkswagen Beetle had been flattened. That wasn't what bugged me out, though. What bugged me out was the indentation in those flattened stalks, an indentation about three feet long and two feet wide with three front claws and a single back one. Anyone could tell right off that it belonged to something larger than an elephant, maybe three or four times as large, but I knew from Pa's books exactly what kind of creature had left those tracks—or at least what kind of creature someone wanted us to *think* had left them. As far as anyone knew, there was only one fossilized track that had ever been found, and this track was nearly an exact match.

A Tyrannosaurus rex.

"Check for others," Ma said, her voice choking.

"Ma—" I began.

"Check! Check!"

She began sobbing and Ashley put an arm around her. In something of a daze, I searched the stalks nearby, but didn't find any other indentations. I returned to the track and knelt beside it. It looked authentic, all right. The indentation was at least six inches deep in the soil at the toes, but only an inch or two deep at the heel. That made sense, because most paleontologists believed the T-Rex walked on its toes like a bird. Somebody had tried real hard to get the details perfect.

A cool breeze made the stalks around us shake and shimmy.

"You find any?" Ma asked in a quiet voice.

"No," I said.

The most obvious person behind the stunt would have been Ma, of course, but it would have taken something heavy, some big oil drums, maybe, and Ma got tired just lifting a jug of milk. But it had to be somebody who knew about Pa's fascination—some would say obsession—with dinosaurs, and Pa hadn't been the socializing type. In fact, I once overheard a hired hand joke to his girlfriend on the phone that Gary B. Dellanger must have been the only known hermit with a family.

So that left Ma, my little sister Harriet, and my older brother Chuck. Since Harriet never left the house unless the power was out, and Chuck, who was in college in Iowa City, told me on the phone he would rather ice skate in hell than come home, Ma was the most likely culprit.

Most likely, maybe, but not really likely at all.

"I think somebody," I said, choosing my words carefully, "is playing a trick on us."

"It's real," Ma said. "I saw it in a dream. It's real. It's a real dinosaur."

"Ma, it's only one track."

"It's your father. I saw this coming. I prayed for it."

She started crying again. Ashley rubbed her shoulders and made shushing sounds as you would to a crying baby. In some ways Ma looked a lot like a baby. There was the lack of hair, of course. She also had a puffy, round face, her features softly defined in that way that all baby's features are softly defined until they grow into toddlers. But with Ma, she *did* have distinctive characteristics (I had seen how she looked in her wedding album), but that face was hard to see under all the insulation "Ma," I said, "you should go inside."

"He's coming," she said. "He wants to help me. He was always there to help me and he wants to help me again."

"Now!" I snapped.

Ashley gave me a look—one of those *how could you talk to your mother that way sort of looks*—and turned Ma toward the house. "Let's go inside, Mrs. D," she said. "I'll make you some nice hot chocolate."

Ma went willingly, but she was mumbling the whole way. I bent down beside the track and impulsively touched the crushed stalks. My hand wasn't there a second before I jerked it back.

The track was cold, much colder than it had a right to be.

It took Ma a good hour to calm down, and by then it was time to put her to bed. We turned off *Wheel of Fortune*—it was better than a sedative for Ma—and Ashley helped me take her upstairs. I had cleaned her room that morning, but Ma had pretty much made a mess of it. That was normal.

Her crayon drawings covered the queen bed, the two dressers, and most of the floor. None of them looked like anything recognizable, just lots of colors and shapes. It was something she started after Pa died. She was still murmuring when I laid her down, but she was asleep by the time I tucked the sheets up to her double chin. I turned off the light, turned on her amber Navaho nightlight, and left the door open three inches just the way she liked it. At the other end of the dark hall, past my bedroom and Chuck's bedroom, both of which were dark, there was a blue strip of flickering light under Harriet's door.

"Should we tell her about it?" Ashley whispered.

"Nah," I said. "I'll tell her later."

After we cleaned up the rest of the dinner dishes, I walked her out to her Ford Ranger. The sky was dark and there was a fine mist in the air. Her tires still didn't have hubcaps. I had given her new ones for her birthday, but she hadn't gotten around to putting them on. I didn't know what to make of that. The truck was white, but you couldn't tell because of how much mud was caked to it. Going mudding—which pretty much consisted of driving around in muddy fields like a mad person—was one of Ashley's favorite activities. It also made her real horny, which of course made it one of my favorite activities, too.

She opened the door and climbed in, looking out at me through the open window. She was eighteen, a few months older than me. Her best feature was her big green eyes—elf eyes, Ma called them—and her face was kinda heart-shaped, with large cheekbones and a pointy chin. She said she was plain looking, but I didn't believe it.

There was no more horniness in her eyes this night, though. What was left was a look of sorrow and sympathy, the way you might look at a three-legged spaniel that's trying to play with the other dogs. And she was looking that way at *me*.

"You think she did it herself?" she asked.

"I don't know," I replied, and I really didn't. I was also thinking about how cold the track had felt when I had touched it.

She gripped the steering wheel, looking out the front window as if she was already on the road. "Who else could have done it? Who else *would* have done it?"

"You got me."

She shook her head. I didn't know if she was shaking her head at Ma or at me. Maybe both.

"You think any more about next month?" she asked.

Next month was when Ashley was moving to California, to start at the University of Santa Barbara in the fall. We had been together for about three years, serious for about two. For the last ten months, she had been trying to convince me to come with her. It irritated her to no end I hadn't even applied for any colleges, especially with my grades and SAT scores. Top of the class. Not that I had really tried. I guess that was one of the things I got from Pa. Book stuff always came easy.

"A little," I said.

"And?"

The breeze picked up and I looked out at the corn. In the near total darkness, I couldn't see much but shadows, but the fields moved as if waves were passing over them. At least that's what I imagined. I had never seen the ocean except on television.

"I want to go," I said, and that was the truth.

"But?"

"It's just . . . well, you know . . ."

"Jerry, you can't put your life on hold."

"Yeah."

"You're smart. Way too smart to stay here. You can't run this place by yourself, anyway. And your Ma's gotten a lot worse since your Pa died."

"Yeah." Our last hired hand, Ben, had left two months earlier when Ma told him to go seek his life's purpose. I had argued with her, but she wouldn't have anything of it. Besides, we wouldn't have been able to afford him anyway, what with her donating most of our money to all of her crazy organizations, another thing she started after Pa died. Harvest was coming up in October, and I was dreading it. "Yeah, I know. I just . . . She won't leave, Ash. And there's Harriet, too. As soon as Chuck comes back to help—"

"That's not happening and you know it."

I nodded. That was one thing that *did* make me mad, Chuck not willing to do his part. The last few months, he hadn't even returned my calls. But what was there to say? It was what it was.

I was leaning against her door, and she reached out and placed both of her hands over mine. Her hands were soft and warm. She didn't work on a farm like me. Her Pa owned the general store where we bought most of our groceries. "Jerry," she said, "you know I want you to come with me. But if you don't . . ."

Her eyes teared up, and I felt a tightening in my chest. She didn't have to say the rest. If I didn't come with her, she wasn't going to sit around pining for me.

Ashley looked away and quickly started the engine. She hated to cry almost as much as she hated to wear a dress. "Let me know how your Ma's doing tomorrow," she said, and then put the truck in gear and drove away.

I WANTED TO LOOK at the track again, but it was too dark. I parked myself on the easy chair in the family room and endured one of Timothy Dalton's unfortunate turns as James Bond, then moseyed upstairs a little before eleven. The hardwood floors were cool under my bare feet. When I saw that the blue light was still under Harriet's door, I felt a sinking feeling in my stomach. I needed to tell her about the dinosaur track, but I was hoping to put it off until the next day. Now there was no reason to wait.

I eased open the door. I could only see her bunk bed and her bureau, awash with the flickering light. The computer was around the corner. Posters of all the Pokemon characters covered the walls. She hadn't played Pokemon in years.

"Harriet?"

I heard a few clicks of the keyboard. "I'm busy."

"Can I just talk to you for a minute?"

"Later."

"It's important."

She sighed. "Fine."

She hunched over her keyboard in the corner, her legs tucked underneath her on the swivel chair. She didn't look up when I entered. Her red hair was braided into a pony tail and stuck out through the back of her black baseball cap. Her ten-year-old body was painfully thin, the Spider-man t-shirt and purple pajama bottoms barely hanging on her body. She had always been thin, but since Pa died she almost never ate, no matter how often I bugged her about it.

A chess game was in progress on her monitor, and only a handful of pieces were left on the board. I watched as the black queen darted diagonally across the board and took the rook. It would be my sister's queen. She always played black.

"Take that," she said.

I stood off to the side of the desk so I could see her face. She had the hollowed-out look you see on the faces of starving Africans in the pages of National Geographic, her eyes deep sockets, her skin stretched tight against her cheekbones. If not for the emaciated look, though, she looked a lot like Ma did back in her yearbook. The hair she had gotten from Pa.

"I gotta tell you something," I said.

She clicked the keyboard a few times. "Bishop to Queen 8. This guy's good."

"It's something you should know," I continued. "I don't know what it means, but . . . well, Ma found this track out in the corn. It looks a lot like a dinosaur track. A T-Rex track, actually."

Her only reaction was to squint more intently at the monitor.

"It's not real, obviously," I said. "Somebody put it there. It may have even been Ma, though I doubt it."

"It wasn't her," Harriet said.

"Well, I don't really think it was her, but it was definitely . . ." I trailed off, her words finally registering. "What do you mean? You know something about this?"

"Knight takes bishop. I got 'em now."

"Harriet."

She bit down on her bottom lip.

"Harriet," I said, more insistently. "Harriet, if you know something . . . *You* didn't do it, did you?"

She snorted and finally looked at me. "Why would I do that?"

"I don't know, but—"

"It's stupid," she said, turning back to the monitor. "I mean, if he wants to talk to her, he should just talk to her. Not do stupid stuff like this."

I felt as if somebody had taken an ice cube and dropped it into the pit of my stomach.

"Who wants to talk to her?"

"Pawn to Rook eight!" she exclaimed. "I never saw that one coming!"

"Who?" I repeated.

"Well, Pa of course. Who else? I think I'll go with a castle move. Yeah, that should be good."

Dumbstruck, I stared at her. "What do you mean? Have you . . . talked to him?"

"Well, duh," she said, typing away.

"How? By phone?"

"Nah. On the computer."

"You can talk to him on the computer?"

She shook her head. "You're messing up my concentration. This guy has already beaten me twice."

"When does he talk to you on the computer?"

"He doesn't talk real talk, stupid. You can't do that in the game."

"You play chess with him?"

"Mostly he just stops by when I'm playing other people, says hi and stuff. People can send messages in the all-chat area." She nodded at the monitor. "Yeah, I figured he'd take my pawn. Asshole."

I looked at the monitor. I was afraid some jerk-off was pretending to be Pa, hoping to seduce my sister. "How do you know it's really him?" I asked.

"Cause he knows stuff."

"What kind of stuff?"

"Just stuff, okay."

"No, it's not okay. I need to know about this, Harriet. This could be somebody dangerous."

She glared at me. "It's him, Jerry. He knows about the time you went swimming at Yankee Pond and knocked your head on the rock. He knows about how I used to have bad nightmares about the corn monsters when I was a little and how he used to sing me to sleep. It's him. He's the one who told me about the track. He said he was going to leave it for Ma to find. I told him it was dumb, but he didn't listen."

I swallowed away the coal-sized lump in my throat. She hadn't convinced me it was Pa. What she *had* convinced me was that this predator knew a lot of stuff about us, which was even weirder.

"When did this start?" I asked.

"A couple weeks ago."

"And you didn't tell me?"

She turned back to her game. "It didn't seem like a big deal."

"Somebody's pretending to be our dead Pa and it didn't seem like a big deal?"

I could see her jaw muscles tightening. "I don't care if you believe me or not. I just want to finish my game, okay?"

"You need to get some sleep."

"After I finish this."

"We'll talk more about this tomorrow."

She waved me away. Angry, I contemplated shutting her computer off, but I knew no good would come of it. I walked to the door, feeling queasy about what she had told me. I didn't want to believe it was Pa, told myself it was impossible, but even then part of me knew that something far stranger than an Internet predator was going on here.

As I was closing the door behind me, she spoke.

"Did you ever play chess with him?"

I looked back at her. She was still gazing at the monitor. "A couple times," I said. "Chuck played with him more often. It wasn't something I liked very much."

"Well, he sucks," she said. "Does dumb things for no reason. It's almost like he's trying to lose. You don't play chess like that. You play to win. Always to win."

She said it fiercely, as if to suggest otherwise was an insult to chess players everywhere. I shut the door, and as I headed back to my dark room, I thought about all the times Pa had lost to Chuck and me. In fact, I could never remember him winning even once. I always assumed it wasn't because he *couldn't* win, but because he couldn't bear to see us lose.

One of my earliest memories of Pa involved dinosaurs. That wasn't unusual. Nearly all of my memories of Pa had to do with dinosaurs in one way or another, since that was one of the few things that he liked to talk about.

It was just after supper, and the sun was creeping its way down to the white-washed horizon. Me and Chuck walked with Pa along our drive, the frozen snow crunching under our boots, our breaths frosting and blowing back hot on our faces. The telephone poles along the main road up ahead were the only thing breaking up all that white.

"My face hurts," Chuck sniveled. He was still nursing a cold. "I want to go inside."

Pa didn't answer, but he did grip my hand more tightly. I was six, Chuck ten. Harriet was not yet born. We had been living in the new house, the house we built after the fire, for just over five years. I remember how tall Pa seemed—tall and gangly like the scarecrow we had out in the vegetable garden. He wasn't really tall at all, hardly even six feet, but he towered over me and my brother. All three of us were bundled in multiple layers of clothing: wool caps, nylon gloves, hand-knitted scarves from Aunt Jeanie, and matching green parkas that Pa had bought on sale from a surplus store in Des Moines. Ice stuck to Pa's eyebrows.

My face hurt, too, but I didn't want to go back. Ma had been screaming and throwing pots all afternoon and it scared me. She just started doing that sometimes and everybody just got out of the way.

"Is it a real dinosaur, Pa?" I asked him.

"It's right up here," he said.

"But is it real?"

"You'll just have to see."

"I want to go back," Chuck said.

When we reached the end of our private road, where it joined up with the single-lane road that we shared with five other farms, I saw what Pa had wanted us to see: a dinosaur made of snow, twice as big as me.

"A T-Rex!" I exclaimed, letting go of his hand and running toward it.

I knew Pa had made it, but it still seemed magical. The details were so precise, right down to the jagged teeth and the flaring nostrils, and the deeper shadows of the low sun accentuated the curves and gave the dinosaur depth. The tail curled around its thick legs and clawed feet. I reached down to touch it.

"Careful," Pa said. "You don't want to break it."

"It's awesome!" I said.

"It's all right," Chuck said. "It's not like it's real or anything." I looked at him. His red bangs stuck out from the end of his hat and partially covered his eyes. The end of his nose, a long beak nose just like Pa's, was red and blistered. I didn't understand why he had to be so mean. He was always saying mean stuff to Pa.

"Well, I like it," I said adamantly. "The T-Rex is my favorite."

"Mine, too," Pa said. He sounded proud.

"I want to go back," Chuck said.

"Then why don't you?" I shot back.

"Boys," Pa admonished.

"I will if Pa lets me," Chuck said.

Pa grimaced. His eyes, already small and recessed under his brow, squinted and nearly disappeared. "Best to give your Ma time," he said.

"Pa, what does the T-Rex eat?" I asked.

A smile creased Pa's face. "Now that's an interesting question," he said. "You see, most people think a Tyrannosaurus rex was a fearsome predator, and he may have been. He was definitely a carnivore. But there are signs he was more of a scavenger than a hunter. They say he was probably too slow to really track down prey, so he probably waited nearby while other more agile carnivores killed the prey, and then he moved in to take what was left. But he could certainly kill if he had to. One look at his teeth and you could see that." He paused. "Most scientists don't think there were ever many dinosaurs in Iowa, but this one here has an interesting story."

"It does?" I said. It was the most Pa had said at one time in as long as I could remember, and I wanted him to keep talking. I liked the sound of his voice.

"This is stupid," Chuck scoffed.

"Oh, yes," Pa continued, ignoring him. "Every dinosaur has an interesting personal history. This one was originally from the Rockies area, but he was a little small for his kind. It forced him to search far and wide for a mate, which was what brought him here. It's a long way to go for a dinosaur. In the end, he showed he was as strong as the rest, just in his own way."

"I'm going," Chuck said defiantly, and turned back toward the house.

"Son," Pa said.

Chuck kept walking, teetering from side to side as his boots sank into the crusty snow.

"Son," Pa said again. Even then he didn't raise his voice. He never raised his voice, even when Ma was saying the most awful stuff to him. "Son, I mean it now."

Chuck swiveled. "Or what? It's not like you're going to do anything."

"You need to give your Ma time," he said pleadingly.

"Time? How much? Harry died over five years ago, and she's still doing all this crap!"

"Son . . . Son, she's doing the best she can."

"She's crazy! She's crazy and you won't stand up to her. Somebody has to stand up to her." Tears streaked his frosted cheeks, leaving tracks in their wake. "Why don't you do something?"

When Pa didn't answer, Chuck stalked away. I watched my Pa's hand rise, reaching for my brother, then drop helplessly to his side. A stiff wind picked up, biting my ears even through the wool cap, and producing a sound I imagined was very much like the roar of a Tyrannosaurus rex.

THE STORM OPENED up late that first night after we found the T-Rex track. The lightning and thunder let up after a few hours, but the rain, tapping against the metal roof, continued for two days. I mostly stayed inside except to go out to feed the animals and milk the cows, but I did venture once over to the track. It was still there, though the well-defined edges had melted away. When I brought Ma her meals, I found her sitting in the rocker by her window, her girth spilling out between the cracks in the chair. She had her drawing pad in one hand and a crayon in the other, but she didn't draw anything. She just sat there and stared out the window, the wan, gray light making her look sad and old.

I tried to talk to Harriet, but she wouldn't have anything to do with me. Finally the storm broke that third morning, and by the time I was up, Ma was already clomping through the soggy fields in her boots, the mud spotting her robe. I wondered how long it would take for me to convince her to wash it.

The air was humid and thick with the smell of moist, fecund earth, but it was a welcome change from air so dry it had left my fingertips chapped. The sky was the color of tinsel, the sun invisible. When I was walking back to the house, the morning chores done and my stomach grumbling, I heard a wheezing truck coming up the lane.

I froze. I knew the sound. It was Pa's brother, Ed.

Sure enough, there was his metallic gray F-150 with the black topper jostling up the road. He honked his horn. I walked to our porch, put the horse brush down on the first step, and turned as he skidded to a stop only a few feet from me. Asshole did that all the time, and once even smashed the first post in the railing with his bumper when he showed up drunk and misjudged the distance.

The rattling, clanking engine chugged and died. He spilled out from the truck, a heavy man with face round and flat like a button, and spit onto the blooming yellow roses bordering the deck. Brown tobacco specks blemished the petals. His straw hat with the red bandana band was tilted back on his head, and I saw the white strip at the top of his forehead where the sun seldom reached. He wore his green and blue plaid shirt untucked, probably hoping it would hide his belly, but it was hard to hide when it was the size of beach ball. Dried mud caked the hem of his overalls.

He grinned at me. I say it was a grin, but it was only my interpretation of a grotesque expression that made an ugly face even uglier: he bit down on his lower lip with his buck teeth and lifted the corners of his mouth just a hair. The chew was split into two and bulged from both cheeks equally. It made me think of Rocky J. Squirrel of Rocky and Bullwinkle.

"Jer," he said.

"Hey there, Uncle Ed."

"Your Ma home?"

There was only one thing Edward Dellanger wanted from Ma, the same thing he had wanted from Pa: the deed to our land. I had gathered from bits of conversations over the years that Uncle Ed was still mad as hell that his father had willed the family land to the oldest brother rather than split it equally among all the brothers. There were four brothers in all, but the other two had gone into dentistry and had no interest in the land. Uncle Ed's bitterness on the matter had finally forced Pa to tell him to stay away, and he had until Pa died. It was the only time I could remember Pa actually getting mad at anyone.

That their father had given all the brothers enough money to buy their own land hadn't made a whit of difference to Uncle Ed. He owned five hundred acres twenty miles away, but he wouldn't rest until he had our measly hundred and twenty-seven acres too.

"She's out, sir," I said. I prayed she was far enough out in the cornfields that she wouldn't come back before he left.

He squinted at me. "Z'at right?"

"Yep. What can I help you with?"

"You know what it's about, boy. It's about doing the right thing."

I knew he had judged me as dumb as a turnip, so I played the part. "Sorry? I reckon I don't know quite what you mean."

He looked at me for a long time. "Well, that's all right, son. That's all right. It's for us adults to worry about anyway. You just go on tell your Ma that I'm still interested. She'll know what I'm talking about."

"Okay, sir," I said meekly. "I'll do that."

"That's right," he said, flashing me another one of his Rocky J. Squirrel smiles. "You be a good boy and tell her that. Hey, how old are you?"

"Seventeen. Almost eighteen, sir."

"Oh, that's plenty old enough. You wanna hear a joke?"

"Well, I've got my chores—"

"How many Mexicans does it take to screw in a light bulb?" "I don't know, sir."

"Ten! But the first nine got electrocuted when they tried to put their peckers in the socket!"

He had barely finished the sentence and he was already breaking into guffaws of laughter. He bent over and slapped his knee, wheezing so hard his face turned red. I tried to laugh, but what came out sounded more like a cough. With his head still bent down, he looked up at me. "Get it? They thought to screw meant to screw! 'Cause that's what . . . they . . know . . . " He squeezed out the last few words before he lost the ability to speak in another fit of laughter.

As he continued to laugh, I saw over his shoulder a bit of white emerging from the stalks. It was one of those moments when you know exactly what's about to happen—and pretty much how awful it's going to be—and yet you're powerless to stop it. Uncle Ed was sobering up, rubbing his eyes and saying "oh, boy, screw, oh boy" over and over, and there came Ma out of the corn, her boots and most of her legs smothered in mud, her robe now looking like a piece of abstract art—brown specks on a white canvas. She took no more than two or three steps before jerking to a halt, looking at Uncle Ed. Her pale face went pink up from the cheeks on down her neck.

"Get off!" she cried.

Uncle Ed jumped as if he had been shot in the back. For just a second, I saw an expression of utter rage on his face before it was quickly replaced with the feigned politeness you get from car salesmen and bible thumpers. He turned, extending his arms as if awaiting a hug.

"Margaret!" he exclaimed. "My, how it's good to see you."

Each of Ma's bulging cheeks looked like ripe tomatoes. "Get off! Get off right now!"

"Now, Margaret—"

"Off!" She charged forward, arms pumping from side to side as if they were powering her body. "You get your filth off my land!"

Because of the angle, I could only see part of Uncle Ed's face, but I was sure I saw fear there. He took a step toward his truck, maybe to climb inside, but ended up leaning over the front tire as Ma cornered him. Her shaved head was speckled with mud. There was a fly perched on her neck that wasn't moving.

"You!" she cried, pointing a finger in his face. "You know you're not supposed to be here! Gary said you was to keep off and he meant it."

Uncle Ed was leaning so far back I thought he was going to fall onto the hood. "Now, Margaret, all that bad blood is behind us. I'm trying to do something nice—"

"Nice!" Ma shouted, spittle flying out of her mouth onto Uncle Ed's shirt. "You're trying to steal my husband's land. Steal it right out from under him! Dead or no, he wouldn't have it. The poison is in you, in you deep. You bring disease and foulness with you. Look at this weather! It's a harbinger of your filth. Filth!"

She spat the last word in his face. He twitched as if she had poked him with a cattle prod, stood absolutely still for a few seconds, then wiped his face with the sleeve of his shirt. Slowly, he slid away, not looking at Ma once, and eased his way around the side mirror to the driver side door. Ma watched him the way she watched me or the other kids when we'd just been told to go to our rooms.

He opened the door, started to climb inside, then looked at Ma. "I'm only asking for what's rightfully mine, and I'm trying to help you in the pro—"

"FILTH!" Ma shouted. "FILTH AND VILENESS!"

Uncle Ed leaped into his truck and slammed the door. I saw mostly whites in his eyes as he fumbled with the key and finally started the engine. Revving the truck, he looked out over the wheel, and just for a moment I thought he was going to mow Ma down. Then he put the car in gear, looked over his shoulder, and peeled away, his tires spitting mud up onto Ma as high as her waist.

She didn't move. When he had the car spun around, he shouted through his open passenger side window.

"You best sell now while the selling's good! Might not be any takers 'fore too long, the way you're running the place!" He shifted into first, squealed forward a few feet, then stopped again. "And get that pot hole out by your mailbox fixed! Damn thing will kill somebody!"

With that, his truck rattled away. Ma watched him go until he had reached the end of our drive, then, muttering to herself, walked past me without so much as a glance. It wasn't more than ten seconds later that the rain started up again—a filthy, vile rain that left me cold to the bone.

WHEN I WAS sure that Uncle Ed was gone, I walked to the end of our drive. It only took a few seconds for the rain to soak my overalls and my hair, but I didn't care. I had to know. When I saw the pothole right there in the middle of the road, and its unmistakable shape, my heart began to pound.

Three feet long. Two feet wide. Three toes, the one in the middle the largest.

The mud was soft, and it only took a moment to use the side of my boot to make the track disappear.

I DIDN'T TELL MA or Harriet about the second track. Harriet stayed in her room with the door locked, surfacing only for infrequent meals, and wouldn't talk again about Pa. Uncle Ed mailed us a long, typewritten letter two days later that sent Ma into a screaming rage. Usually, I managed to get to the mail before she did, but there were days when she saw the mail truck while she was out wandering, and if she did, she went straight for the box. She thrust the letter at me while I was milking one of our cows.

"See this!" she cried. "See this! The man won't leave us alone!"

Her robe was partially open, exposing the tops of her breasts. I had stolen the robe away from her room while she slept the previous night, so at least it was somewhat clean again. I wiped my hands on my pants and took the letter from her. The barn smelled of manure and hay, and the inside was dimly lit by the three fluorescent lamps still working. In the next stall, our horse, Ginny, whinnied. I read the letter quickly. It was nothing new. Just Uncle Ed going on and on about how the farm needed to stay with the brothers, that Ma was running it into the ground, and with interest rates low this was the best time to sell. I handed it back to her.

"Your Pa would be so mad if he saw this," Ma said. "He'd give that man a piece of his mind."

I knew Pa would do no such thing, but I nodded. The truth was, I was getting more nervous about October. I didn't know how I would manage to run the combines by myself, let alone do everything else. We had never made a lot of money from our small production, and with one bad harvest we'd lose everything. I knew it. I had been paying the bills and signing Ma's name.

I didn't want to sell to Uncle Ed no matter what, but something had to be done. Between the farm chores, making meals for the family, and keeping up around the house, I was surviving on four hours sleep a night.

"Ma," I said. "We need to get some help if we're going to do the harvest."

She shook her head. "Can't have no one else on this farm but family. The future is clear."

"But if I don't get help, I can't do it."

"The land will provide."

"It's not the land I'm worried about. It's me."

She smiled. "You're a strong boy. Almost a man. You'll get it done. Your father would be proud."

She turned and walked away, the letter crumpled in her fist. I wanted to strangle her. Later, when Ashley was over helping me with dinner, which she did a couple times a week, she said something that surprised me.

"Maybe you should try to get your brother to help out again," she said.

I paused stirring the sauce, which smelled of mushrooms and garlic, and looked at her to see if she was serious. She was looking down into the pot of boiling noodles, and the steam enveloped her face. She wore a Pearl Jam T-shirt and cut-off jeans, her hair pulled back into a pony tail and tied with a rubber band.

"I thought you said—" I began.

"I know," she said. "But you need help and he's your best bet. Lay the guilt trip on him. It's not fair that he can be in college while you work your tail off here."

"He won't answer the phone."

"Then drive out there."

"Huh? I can't leave Ma and—"

"It'll only take you a couple of hours. You can go tomorrow afternoon. I'll get off early from the store and watch the place for you."

I knew her real reason for me to get Chuck was to try to free me up to go to California, but I didn't say so. I didn't see how that was going to happen. Even with my brother's help, it would still take two of us to run the farm. I also knew that if she really wanted me to join her, she would have just let the farm go under, which meant she was putting my need to save the place above her own interests.

I kissed her on the cheek, a cheek moist from the steam, and she looked at me in surprise.

"What's that for?" she asked.

"For being the best girlfriend a guy can have," I replied.

So the next day, with the skies again clear and blue, I took to the road in Pa's old '79 Thunderbird. It was white with a black top, a top he had replaced after a nasty hailstorm back in the eighties. Flat and rectangular, the car looked like a rather thick playing card, but it drove well. I worked my way north along the smaller web of highways, hit I-80, and then two hours later rolled into Iowa City. The University of Iowa was downtown, and I parked at a pay meter in front of the Iowa Memorial Union, which looked out over the Iowa River. There were plenty of students walking about, which surprised me, because it was summer.

The whole thing was crazy. I didn't even have an address. But I found a student directory, and as luck would have it, Charles L. Dellanger was in there, and even luckier, he was living in Stanley Residence Hall on campus. I walked the short distance to the hall and walked inside as someone was leaving. Just like that, I was standing in front of his second floor room.

He flung the door open on the third knock, shirtless and wearing orange Bermuda shorts. A silver peace symbol on a leather strap hung around his neck. He was taller and skinner than me, plus his once red hair had been bleached blond. He had let it grow to his shoulders in the nine months since I had seen him last. He was also paler than I remembered. No more farmer tan.

"Holy shit," he said.

I smelled marijuana smoke wafting out of his room. The only reason I knew the smell was that Ashley and I had tried it once—tried it and hated it. Behind him I saw that his computer was on, and that there were sticky notes all over the monitor. The shades were closed, only a lamp clipped to his headboard lighting the room. On the rumpled bed on the other side of the room were stacks of comic books. Green Lantern, by the looks of them. He had been collecting them forever.

"Can I come in?" I asked.

"What do you want?"

Chuck was always one to get right to the point. I swallowed, realizing this was most likely not going to go well.

"I just want to talk," I said.

"'Bout what?"

"Just stuff. Can I come in?"

"Well, I was kinda busy."

"Bagging comics and smoking pot?" I said sarcastically. I wondered if his scholarship would be revoked if they knew he was buying weed with the money.

He looked at me, squinting as if there was something on the end of my nose. "I'm taking a break. So sue me. But I got a lot of studying to do."

"Chuck, I came a long way."

"I go by Charlie now."

"Fine, Charlie—"

"My girlfriend likes it better. Says it sounds sexier. Like Charlie Sheen."

"That's great. Think I can have just a few minutes of your time?"

He sighed and walked away from the door, which I realized was the only invitation I was going to get. I followed, closing the door behind me. You could actually see the mist in the air. He launched himself onto his narrow bed, one bare foot draped over the side, and proceeded to leaf through one of his comics. Posters of Superman, Wonder Woman, and the Green Lantern covered the walls. A microwave sat on the small refrigerator in the corner, an empty popcorn bag on the floor next to it.

I look a seat in the swivel chair in front of the computer. "Look, I'll get right to the point," I said. "I need you to come home and help with the farm."

He turned a page. "Uh huh."

"I can't do it by myself. We need you."

"What about the hired hands?

"Ma fired them."

He snorted. "Figures."

"I can't reason with her."

"Big surprise."

"That's why we need you. Harriet needs you. Ma needs you."

His jaw tensed. He flipped a few more pages in silence, then picked up a clear plastic bag from a box on the floor and slipped the comic inside. Finally, he looked at me. There was rage in his eyes for a moment, then it slipped away and he looked sad.

"You came all the way out here to beg for my help?" he asked.

"I don't know what other choice I have."

"Sure you do. You can leave just like I did."

I shook my head. "I can't do that."

"Why not?"

I felt my own rage and resentment bubbling to the surface. "Because I actually care what happens to Ma and Harriet."

"Ah, they'll be fine. Listen, you can't let her drag you down, man. You've got to get out of there. I got out and I ain't ever going back no matter what. When the farm goes under, she'll be forced to come to grips with reality. Until then it's crazy day everyday on the Dellanger farm. Trust me. You leave and you'll be doing her a favor."

I sat there and stewed in my anger. I hated the casual way he talked about our family's problems. I hated how he called me "man" as if he was some kind of New Age hippie. I hated that he didn't have the foggiest notion of what it meant to actually be responsible.

I realized that nothing I said would change his mind about coming back, and that my being there was a mistake.

"Okay," I said, rising, "thanks, then. I best be getting back."

"Back to shoveling cow shit, huh? What a life."

He laughed. He didn't even get up to let me out, just sat there smirking at me with his fingers clasped over his chest. When I was at the door, he spoke again.

"Hey, man," he said.

"Yeah?"

"Look, no hard feelings, you know? I mean, you're my brother, but we've all got to do what's in our best interest. If Pa had done that, he'd still be alive today. Seriously. He should've put Ma in a home. Sold the farm and done something he really wanted to do. A million things. But he did nothing. He just let life happen to him because he was too scared to make something happen on his own, and then all of Ma's crazy shit just wore him down and killed him. Don't be like that, Jerry."

I wished he was standing so I could punch him the face. Instead, I turned and walked out.

WHEN I WAS TEN, I wanted a Gameboy real bad. It was November, nearly Thanksgiving, and Pa was out working the combine. It was late for harvest, but that happened sometimes. Ma was out doing grocery shopping with little Harriet. Chuck was at school. I was supposed to be in bed with the flu. I was sneaking around in the basement, looking for Christmas presents, when I found Pa's Dinosaur Diaries.

The dusty steps creaked under my bare feet. My thin cotton pajamas did little in fending off the cool air. My nose was plugged, my forehead warm, and I had been on and off the toilet most of the morning. I searched by the weak daylight slanting in from the high windows, afraid that if I turned on the overhead lights Pa would see them and know I was down here. The two freezers hummed. I searched the workbench area first, didn't find anything, then moved to Pa's reading corner. It was a nook created by three pine bookshelves, and they were packed with all his dinosaur books—hundreds of them, some shiny new, some with old library stickers on them. A metal desk sat in the center, a reading lamp with a movable arm clipped to one of the shelves.

The corner was too far away from the windows to see much, so

I risked turning on the lamp. Pa had expressly forbid us from being around his desk without him, so my heart was pounding hard. I searched the drawers, didn't find anything, and then on a whim decided to search behind the books.

I didn't find a Gameboy. But I did find a black book with a soft leather cover on the bottom right shelf, behind a four-volume Time Life set on dinosaurs. Curious, I pulled out the book. The leather was lightly pebbled. I thought it was a bible at first, but when I opened it, I saw lined pages filled with Pa's tiny, compact handwriting:

Third sun after full moon—Hunted brontosaurus today. Mate stayed to guard eggs. She will not leave the eggs. It rained hard and long.

Eight sun after full moon—More rain. Colder, and the sore from the fight with the Stegosaurus will not heal. Fed on a half-eaten Allosaurus carcass. The meat was rotting. It was not a good day, but I am strong and will survive.

The book went on for page after page like that until a third a way to the end, where the pages were blank. I was only brave enough to look at it for a few minutes before putting it back where I found it, and I was afraid for weeks that Pa would know I had touched it. He never said anything about it, though now and then he looked at me in a strange way that made me think he knew.

I never found the presents, but I did get a Gameboy that Christmas.

Ashley cried when I told her what happened with Chuck. The way she carried on, you'd think I'd died or something.

Three days later, another track appeared, this one behind the barn. Ma found it first and went into hysterics, then spent the next day- and-a-half locked in her room. Two days after that, we found another, this one by the house, and after that they showed up every day or so. Always the same T-Rex track. Always just one. I stopped trying to cover them up. I also stopped trying to convince myself it was just somebody's prank.

They were starting to make me afraid.

The other thing that showed up more often were Uncle Ed's letters, each one more desperate-sounding than the last. I didn't get to read all of them—Ma tore up plenty of them unopened—but the ones I did were comical in their reasoning. We should sell him the land because it was right. We should sell him the land because we were Americans and Americans would help each other out. We had to think of his family, especially his two sons (he didn't mention his daughter). They deserved it as their inheritance. Also included were pictures cut out from travel magazines, of tropical locales around the world. Hawaii. Tahiti. Puerto Vallarta. Scrawled on these pictures in black marker were comments like "Great this time of year!" or "I think you'd enjoy visiting this one!" The image of Uncle Ed sitting at his kitchen table and using a pair of scissors to neatly cut out the pictures made me laugh. Then it made me mad.

His price kept going up until it was nearly double what he first offered, far over market value. It was a lot money. Enough to put Ma in some type of home. Enough to put Harriet in a boarding school. Enough to at least give me a running start at college. But I never seriously considered encouraging Ma to sell it to him. That's when I realized that maybe I didn't really want to sell it, that it wouldn't matter if it was Uncle Ed or somebody else, and even though I sensed it was true, it was tough to swallow.

I hated farming. I hated every minute of it. I had always hated it, probably hated it as much as my brother hated it, and I could never see that changing.

I was also afraid of doing anything else.

Two weeks after returning from seeing Chuck, I drove over to see Ashley. We were closing in on August, and the date of her departure was ten days away. I wasn't looking forward to what I had to do. I could have waited until the last minute, but that wouldn't have been fair. She deserved to have her mind clear of Iowa cobwebs when she arrived in California.

"You don't have to do this," she pleaded.

The sun was low in the sky but not yet down. She lived in a double-wide trailer behind their store, a store which sat on the edge of one of the many two-lane highways that crisscrossed Iowa. We sat in the T-Bird in their gravel driveway, a giant oak shielding us from the sun. We were facing the trailer, and I saw the flicker of the television through the closed kitchen blinds. Behind us, an eighteen wheeler rumbled past, stirring up waves of dust.

"I think I do," I said. I was trying my best to keep from choking up. Later. Just not now. If I did, she'd break down and then it would be much worse.

She squeezed my hand. Her fingers were small and cold, not at all like her fingers usually were. "We could write. I could come visit during the holidays. In a couple of years—"

"No," I said.

"But why?"

"Because you don't need to be thinking about me way out here in Iowa when you've got all those things to do in California. It's not right."

"But I love you."

I had to keep looking through the mud-streaked windshield at her trailer. If I looked at her, I would lose all ability to speak.

"I love you, too," I said. "Always will, Ash. But my place is here. Yours is there. And nothing's going to change that."

She started crying then, leaning into my shoulder, and I put my arm around her. In some ways I was glad because I didn't think I'd be able to keep up my brave face much longer. I had told her I loved her, but I said it in the matter-of-fact way you'd tell your favorite aunt you loved her. It didn't sum up at all how I really felt. She had been with me for years, staying by me when she had every reason to leave. I had imagined putting a ring on her finger lots of times. She meant everything to me. I would be completely lost without her.

And I knew if I told her that, she'd never go.

After Pa's funeral, when all the relatives were talking in low voices in the living room, I stole away into the basement and looked behind the Time Life set for Pa's Dinosaur Diary. There was nothing there. I searched everywhere—behind all the books, in the desk, even in the workshop area—but it wasn't to be found. When I was about to give up, I saw a crumpled sheet of paper with my father's handwriting on it in the tin garbage can. I pulled it out, smoothing the paper on the desk. It was about a third-filled with the same strange diary entries:

Seventh sun after full moon—Food is scarce. Mate is not well. It is hard to both hunt and look after the hatchlings. But I am strong. I am strong enough for all of us.

Twelfth sun after full moon—There is a great storm brewing on the horizon. I sense its approach. I sense it may be the end of me. I want to run. I want to

The entry stopped like that, in mid-sentence. But there were a couple more lines below, in bold, blocky lettering:

I AM A TYRONOSAURUS REX, THE STRONGEST OF ALL THE DINOSAURS. I AM BRAVE. I AM POWERFUL. AND THERE IS NOTHING LIFE CAN DO TO ME THAT I CANNOT ENDURE.

When I read the final line, I buried my head in my arms and cried. I cried for the man I knew, and for the man I knew he wished to be. I cried because he had torn out the page from his diary and thrown it away, and I had no idea why.

I had seen his placid face in a walnut casket, I had put my arm around my crying mother, I had watched his coffin being lowered into the ground, but that was the first time I truly realized he was gone.

"Jerry?"

I was so astonished to hear my sister's voice in the barn that I dropped the horse brush in the hay. Our dun snorted and fidgeted. Harriet leaned over the gate, a skeleton in t-shirt and jeans, the baseball cap on her head turned backwards. The circles under her eyes were so big they looked like the eye-black football players wore to deflect the sun. She had hardly said a word to me since that night she told me about playing chess with Pa, and she certainly hadn't been out of the house.

"Hey," I said. "Something the matter?"

"No, not really. I just need to tell you something. I should have told you before. I just . . . I didn't feel like it."

I walked over to her. "What is it?"

She swallowed. "Well, it's Pa. It's . . . It happened before I talked to you. We were playing, and I don't know why I said it, but I told him I was mad at him. I told him I was mad at him for leaving us."

"You did?"

She nodded. Her eyes were tearing up. "I shouldn't have done it. He said he was sorry, and that he loved me, but he couldn't change it. He said he wished he could have been stronger for us. I didn't say anything, and then he didn't show up again. He hasn't showed up since. Jesus, Jerry. He must think I hate him. I just . . . I just thought you should know."

She turned and walked back toward the house.

A FEW DAYS after Ashley left for California, I woke in the middle of the night. I thought I heard something—a distant crackling, like fireworks over the hill. Moonlight streamed in from the window, so bright I could see the posters on my walls. The sheets were a tangled, sweaty mass wrapped around my legs. The curtains billowed in the breeze coming from the open window. I didn't hear anything, and then I realized how strange that was. The crickets were silent.

I was beginning to think I had dreamed the sound when it came again, far out in the fields, and this time it sent my pulse racing. I knew what it was. It was the sound of something crunching the cornstalks.

It came a third time. Then a fourth. Closer.

I slipped from bed, naked except for my boxers, and walked barefoot to the window. I looked out at the silvery fields, able to see all the way to the horizon. The crunch came again. This time I actually saw a gap appear in the stalks not too far out. There was nothing there to produce the gap, but it still had appeared.

I also saw something else. Ma stood at the edge of our drive, right where the fields began, her white robe glowing as if it had been painted with the moonlight. She stood still and silent, looking up at where I imagined the head of the T-Rex would be. Another crunch, another gap. Then the gaps were right by Ma, and still she didn't move.

She stood like that for a long time, then turned back toward the house. The sounds didn't come again.

THE STORM CLOUDS blew in the next day, thick and ominous. The tracks were everywhere now, and there was no denying something was happening. I just wished I knew what it was.

Ma gathered up me and Harriet after dinner and told us she had something to say. We sat on the moss green couch in the family room and she paced back and forth in front of us. She clutched a stack of her drawings in each hand, and she waved them at us when she was talking. She said a whole bunch of stuff that made no sense to me, stuff about the planets and the signs all being right, and then she laid the bombshell on us.

"I talked to your father," she said, and for a moment she seemed absolutely lucid. "I talked to him last night and he told me it's time for you to leave. You need to leave to be safe. So I want you to pack your bags and take the car."

"Ma!" I exclaimed.

"I'm not leaving you," Harriet said.

"Don't argue with me, little girl," Ma said. "It must be done." She patted both our cheeks. "I'm sorry I couldn't be a better mama for you both. I wanted to, you know. I wanted everything to be so perfect. I thought it *could* be perfect, if you wanted it bad enough. And then your brother Harry died . . ." She trailed off, and her eyes took on a far-off look.

"Ma," I said, "we're not leaving. You need us here."

Her face darkened. The sane woman who had made a brief appearance was again gone, and she screamed at us. "You need to listen to your mother!"

When neither of us offered a reply, she tossed her stack of drawings into the air and stormed out of the room.

"I can't be responsible! You should go tonight!"

Her drawings wafted down to the floor like snowflakes. I expected more crazy swirls of color, but when I saw what she had drawn, I froze.

Every single one was a Tyrannosaurus rex.

THEY CAME THE SAME NIGHT Ma told us to leave.

I lay in bed, listening to the distant rumble of thunder. The temperature had dropped, but it hadn't rained yet. The cool wind rustled my curtains, made goose bumps break out on my arms. I was thinking about getting up and closing the window when I heard a car or truck rumbling up our drive.

My breath lodged in my throat, I went to the window, and saw the gray van screech to a halt just inches from our porch. The license plate was obscured with mud. When I saw the two men in the front seats with pillowcases over their heads, big, jagged ovals cut out for the eyes, I froze. The clouds had smothered any moonlight or starlight, so the farm beyond the reach of our porch lights was a shapeless void.

They piled out of the van, a half dozen men. The pillowcases were various colors, everything from white to navy blue. It wasn't until I saw a flicker that I realized they were carrying torches. Soon all the torches were ablaze. Only one of them didn't have a torch, and the others watched silently as this man approached our house.

The creak of his foot on our porch finally snapped me back to my senses. My heart pounding, I rushed to Harriet's room and was about to bang on the door when it opened. She was dressed in shorts and a yellow tank-top, and by the alarmed look on her face I knew she had already seen what was outside.

"Come on," I said, running for Ma's room.

There were footsteps on the stairs. I heard thunder, and it was closer. I reached Ma's room, tried the knob, and found it locked. She never locked the door. I banged on it hard.

"Ma! We have to get out of here!"

The door didn't open.

"Ma!"

"Come on!" Harriet shouted behind me.

A small voice from within came back: "You kids go on. You're better off without me now."

"No!" I protested. "Ma, we're not leaving without you. You have to come."

Harriet screamed. I turned to see the man rounding the corner, his eyes bright white inside his dark pillowcase. By his size and shape, he could have been Uncle Ed, and I figured he was. I wished a lot of things in that moment. I wished I had bothered to move Pa's rifle up from the basement. I wished I had actually learned how to shoot a rifle. I wished I had worked harder to convince Ma to leave.

Hollering, I threw myself at the man and landed both my fists in his belly. He groaned and staggered back, but he didn't go down. He smelled like sweat and tobacco. I threw myself at him again and he grabbed my wrists and threw me against the wall. Harriet shrieked and launched herself at him, and he grabbed her and tossed her over his shoulder. With her pummeling his back, he turned and started back down the hall. I was on the carpet wheezing, and I grabbed at his ankle.

He kicked my hand away. "You best come with me if you know what's good for you," he said. He had dropped his voice, but I could still tell it was Uncle Ed.

"You bastard!" I said.

By the time I managed to stand, he was halfway down the stairs, Harriet screaming the whole way. I started after him, then thought about Ma still in her room, and stood there paralyzed.

"Come on, Ma! We have to go!"

I heard the downstairs door banging open. My sister cursed. I heard a slap, and then she was silent.

Not wanting to leave Ma, but not wanting to leave my sister with my asshole uncle, I stumbled down the stairs after him.

"Now!" I heard a man shout outside.

When I staggered onto the porch, I saw the men flinging their torches onto the house. I smelled gasoline. The man I assumed was Uncle Ed still had Harriet over his shoulder, but she was limp. I covered my head with my arms and leapt off the porch as the roof exploded in flames. At the same time, another peal of thunder rolled out over the farm.

I landed hard in the dirt. One of the men grabbed me and pinned me in his arms. I struggled, but he was much bigger than me, and I couldn't break his grip. The flames roared across the roof. All I could think about was Ma still inside.

"No!" I cried. "Ma! Ma!"

It started to drizzle. I wish I could say that the drizzle became a downpour, strong enough to put out the fire, but that's not what happened. That house was already so hot it was certain to burn to the ground, and there was little anyone could do to stop it. After tiring of struggling against my captor, I stood numbly and watched.

Then I heard another noise, a boom that was right upon us. I thought it was thunder at first, but it was too close and too loud. It came again, longer and deeper, and my captor loosened his grip. The sound was coming from the fields behind us.

It wasn't thunder. It was a roar.

All the men turned toward the fields and back-stepped toward the house. I wiped the water out of my eyes. I could only see the first few cornstalks, like bars in a gate. Everything beyond was murky darkness. Now there was another sound, and I recognized it immediately: it was the same sound from the night I saw Ma standing at the edge of the field, the sound of something heavy crunching down on the cornstalks. The men were now moving toward their van, none of them looking away from the approaching footsteps.

I saw Harriet had been left on the ground, unconscious, and I went to her and lifted her upright. She was as light as a broom.

"Wake up," I told her.

"Hmmh?" she said. Her eyelids fluttered.

"Come on, come on!"

The cornstalks next to us suddenly smashed to the ground, first one area, then another ten feet away. Harriet's eyes popped open. She jumped toward me, and I lost my balance and landed hard on my backside, her on top of me. Tracks—tracks I had gotten so used to seeing the past weeks—had appeared in the dirt. We looked up into the fine mist of rain. I saw nothing at first, but then the wind shifted, blowing smoke from the house right over us, and for a moment I saw the shape of the T-Rex's monstrous jaws in the shifting vapors.

The men must have seen it, too, because they ran for the van. Another track appeared, this one right next to us, and I felt the earth shake. The T-Rex roared, making my ears ring. I grabbed Harriet's head and pulled her down flat to the ground. Another track appeared up ahead, and then I felt the rush of air that must have been its tail passing over us. The tracks continued halfway to the house, then stopped.

The van squealed in reverse, doing a half circle, the tires already spinning in the other direction. I heard the T-Rex's booming steps, and this time they were moving toward the van. Again the thing passed through the smoke, and this time I saw its entire body. The huge, teeth-lined mouth. The puny arms. The massive, muscular legs. The legs appeared to move languidly, but because of the creature's size, it moved forward as fast as a galloping horse.

The dinosaur roared again.

The van was picking up speed, racing beyond the reach of our porch lights. The tracks appeared like bomb craters, each one coming faster. Another few seconds and the van would have gotten beyond the T-Rex's reach, but then there was a metallic boom and the van slid to the side like a croquet ball being struck by a mallet. The van rolled a dozen times before coming to a rest in the field, then burst into flames.

The house, totally consumed by the fire, was collapsing. The entire second floor was gone. I looked up and to my amazement saw Ma, her face and robe coated in soot, standing where her room would be. I ran toward the house, but couldn't get within three steps because the fierce heat pushed me back.

"Ma!"

The booms came again, the tracks now coming toward us, and my sister rushed into my arms. I thought that was it, the dinosaur was coming for us too, but the tracks veered at the last second toward the house. One footprint smashed through the porch, then another. The head appeared, wreathed in flames, stretching toward my mother. I was sure it was going to snap her up in its jaws, but instead it poised in front of her, and she climbed up onto its head.

Then she was lifted up and out of the fire. The thunderous steps came again, and the tracks moved off toward the cornfields. I watched as the dinosaur disappeared as it left the smoke, and then it seemed as if my mother rode an invisible magic carpet into the darkness. Soon the sounds of its footsteps receded, and with a final, distant roar, they were gone.

IF YOU READ the police report about what happened that night on the Dellanger farm, you'll see that it says that Ma burned up in the flames. No one ever found a body, but they claim that the gasoline-induced inferno consumed every last bit of her. My sister and I never contradicted them.

They also had a hard time piecing together exactly what caused the van to crash. Driver error is what it says in the report, although it seems hard to explain how driver error could cause the massive dent in the side of the van. But nobody seemed to want to work very hard to investigate, especially after it was obvious the men had deserved their deaths.

The fierce rainstorm that opened up that night also washed away a lot of things that might have raised questions, but there were still the unusual crushed areas in the cornfields. Nobody knew what to make of those. I told them I was learning how to make crop circles. That got them to laugh, and they never brought it up again. They seemed relieved to believe *something.*

I put the land on the market at a bargain basement price, and it only took a month to find a buyer—a farmer nearby who needed more food for his livestock. I also turned eighteen in the meantime, and the judge awarded me custody of Harriet. We are staying in a motel until the deal closes in a few days, a motel right off I-80, surrounded by oaks turning red and crimson.

The summer is gone. Fall is upon us. When the papers are signed, we'll hop in the T-Bird, everything we own packed into the back seat and trunk, and drive west until we reach the ocean. California is beckoning.

Even if things work out with Ashley, I have no illusions life will be easy. For some people, life is just hard. But whatever challenges lie ahead, I no longer fear them.

My father was a Tyrannosaurus rex, and he was strong in his own way. But I am only a man.

Yet I am brave.

And I am powerful.

And there is nothing life can do to me that I cannot endure.

Road Gamble

Whipping around sharp bends, tires squealing on wet asphalt, Simon pushed his little Miata close to eighty. The wall of pine trees on both sides, as well as the black sky above, created a dark tunnel into the hills. He was thinking about making it to the coast before midnight, early enough to squeeze in a few hands with the late night poker crowd at the casino, and he didn't see the motorcycle until he was almost on top of it. With no taillight, and with its rider clad in black, the bike emerged from the dreary gloom like a moth alighting on his windshield.

"Holy mother of—" he cried, stomping on his breaks.

The seat belt snapped taut against his chest. His car fishtailed, back tires screaming, front end coming inches from the bike's mud-caked license plate.

Up close, the Miata's headlights slashed through the rain and the dark, illuminating the man and his bike in vivid detail. The guy's glistening jacket bore a striking design: a white bear head in profile, glowing as if luminescent. It was the only thing on the rider that *wasn't* black; pants, boots, even the helmet melted with the stormy night, making the bear appear to hover over the road. Simon didn't know much about motorcycles, but the bike was definitely too sleek and compact to be a Harley. It looked like it belonged on a racing track, not a highway.

Heart pounding, Simon eased off the biker. He would have thought the commotion would startle the guy, maybe caused him to swerve, but the biker's only reaction was to turn his head halfway around, just far enough that Simon's headlights appeared on the helmet's mirrored faceplate like a pair of hot ember eyes. The guy looked for a moment, then turned back to the road.

And dropped his speed down to thirty.

Son of a gun. Simon could understand the guy being pissed—Simon *had* nearly plowed over him—but going half the speed limit, even in these conditions, seemed petty.

The squeaking wipers struggled to keep the windshield clear. Dashboard fans roared out a steady stream of warm air. There were few opportunities to pass on Highway 18, but Simon knew there was a passing lane in a few miles. He'd driven this road so many times, every pothole and mile marker was burned in his memory. He'd wait a few minutes, give the guy a chance to cool down. He really wanted to get to that poker game—he was already imagining the rush of tossing in his first ante—but he didn't want to get into some kind of stupid road game. In these conditions, one of them could end up dead in a ditch.

As his heart slowed, he felt a pang of remorse. What if he had died out here? Tomorrow—Saturday—was Jana's second birthday. He could just imagine the look on her face as she sat on their crappy lima bean couch in their mouse trap apartment—an apartment that should have been packed with children laughing and making noises with party favors, but instead would be empty and deathly quiet—as her mother explained why Daddy wasn't coming home.

She was so young . . . In a few years would she even remember him?

Guilt—it was the worst kind of feeling, a feeling Simon had come to dread because he knew it always lurked somewhere around the corner. The worst part, the absolute worst part was that Tracy would know, if he died on this stretch of road at this time of night (when he was supposed to be hanging out at Steve's watching horror flicks) that he had broken his word.

Promising to give up gambling forever was the only way he had been able to keep her from leaving him.

But what she didn't know couldn't hurt her. After all, he wasn't playing like last year when his losses forced them to file for bankruptcy. No, it was nothing like that. Just an occasional game here and there. For fun, really. Spare change he earned from his tips, money Tracy never saw. He'd never dip into his bank account again. He was in control now.

His radio, turned low, was losing its Rexton signal to static, and Simon clicked it off. When he did, he noticed his hand was shaking. Apparently the incident had gotten to him more than he thought it did. The biker went on puttering at thirty, the spray from his back tire misting in the beams from Simon's headlights. Not a single car passed from the other direction, but Simon knew the road was way too popular, even on nights like this, to chance passing with a double yellow.

Jana's birthday, he kept telling himself. Jana's birthday.

He honked his horn a few times, but the guy didn't react. A few minutes later, they crested a rise and rounded a bend, entering a brief downhill straight stretch. Ah, now here was the passing lane. The road opened up, the dotted white line appearing. Accelerating, Simon moved to the left. The biker stayed on the right and in a few seconds Simon was alongside him.

For just a moment, no more than a few seconds, Simon eased off the accelerator to look at the biker.

From the side, it was easier to get a good look. He was a big guy, not tall but broad, wide across the shoulders, thick in the middle. If he had a neck, Simon couldn't see it—his helmet sat right on his linebacker shoulders. His pants tucked snuggly into his boots, pulling tight around his bulging calves. His hands, covered with black leather gloves, were also huge. Clenching the handlebars, they made the bike seem undersized beneath him, like a toy.

Simon realized this guy didn't seem like a *guy* at all. He seemed more like the creature on the back of his jacket—a bear. He suddenly wished he could see the guy's face. Would he look like Grizzly Adams, hair all over the place? He chuckled at the thought.

As if sensing he was being mocked, the biker turned and looked. It was then that Simon realized he had made a terrible mistake, lingering like this; imagining the eyes staring at him from behind the face shield sent a chill up his spine. He did not know this man, had no idea where he was going or why, but he sensed that this was not somebody to mess with. This was not a man you stared at, not for five seconds, not even for one. He wasn't threatening in a Hell's Angel sort of way, all bravado and bullying. Most bikers acted tough because they didn't want to fight, hoping their image of toughness would be enough to scare you away. No, Simon got the feeling this guy didn't care about projecting an image of toughness.

He didn't need to act tough because he *was.*

As if he had just come face to face with a rattlesnake, Simon turned slowly toward the road, applying gentle pressure to the accelerator.

But as he accelerated, the biker also increased his speed. Forty-five miles an hour . . . Fifty . . . Fifty-five . . .

The end of the passing lane was coming up in a hurry. The guy stayed right there, across from his window. Simon didn't dare look, but he saw well enough with his peripheral vision that the guy was still looking at him.

A yellow sign warned of the end of the passing lane. Sixty . . . Sixty-five . . . Seventy . . . For Christ's sake, the guy would not back off. The dotted white line vanished, the two lanes merging into one. His heart racing, Simon punched the accelerator and his Miata jerked forward.

He hoped one last burst of speed would propel him past the biker, but the guy stayed neck and neck. Worse, the road brought them together like two canoes in a narrowing river, and soon the guy was so close to his passenger side window that Simon couldn't help but look. There, beyond the rain-streaked glass, lost in all that black leather, was the shiny faceplate still looking straight at him.

Cursing, Simon hit his brakes.

The biker sped past. Immediately the guy started to slow down—dropping, dropping some more, forcing Simon to keep tapping the brakes, until they were all the way back down to thirty again.

"I don't believe this," Simon said aloud.

He honked his horn a few more times. Again, the guy puttered along, not once turning to look back at his follower. There wasn't another passing lane for at least ten miles. At this pace, the poker games would be shutting down for the night by the time he got there.

Simon thought about taking his chances across the double yellow line, but as if in response to his thought, a pair of headlights emerged from the gloom and a van whipped past, rocking his car and spraying his windshield.

He laid on his horn, then gave the guy's back a double bird. Still nothing. Maybe the guy was deaf. He drummed his fingers on his steering wheel. He'd just have to bide his time. There was a place to pass in a few minutes, and if he had even a hint of open road, he'd go for it. Show this punk what real speed was all about.

But when he reached the area to pass, and started to make his move, the guy sped up again.

Totally unbelievable. The guy was determined to be an absolute prick. This went on for another ten minutes—slowing in the double yellows, speeding up in the passing areas—until finally Simon couldn't take it any more. He was going to pass and damn the consequences. The jerk was on a motorcycle, for Christ's sake. He would have to back off or he'd end up flying over his handlebars.

The nachos and cheese he had an hour earlier now came back to haunt him; his stomach churned and gurgled. He'd need a bathroom before too long. He was halfway to the coast now, in one of the darker stretches; the dense forest on both sides crowded the twisting road, the branches reaching overhead, creating a canopy. They passed a wooden sign indicating they were in the Van Duzen National forest. Simon knew that except for a rest stop and a campground, there wouldn't be any other sign of people for twenty miles.

At least the rain had lessened to a light drizzle, allowing him to turn down his wipers. He passed up a couple opportunities to pass until he hit the spot he wanted—another downhill slope with a passing lane. Then he bore down on the gas. His quick move got him alongside his companion, but as expected, the biker matched him.

Simon clamped down on the steering wheel. He felt his pulse in his hands. They streaked down the hill, the forest a blur on both sides. The extra speed increased the moisture spattering his windshield, making the glass blurry for seconds at a time, but Simon didn't want to take his hands off the wheel to speed up the wipers.

They barreled along, his speedometer passing over seventy, then eighty, then ninety . . .

As his engine screamed, Simon held his breath. The dotted white line vanished. The road narrowed. The punk *still* wasn't backing off, and there was no way Simon was letting off the juice now. He took a quick glance at the biker and, with a chill, saw the guy look over at the same time.

The extra lane disappeared, and then the two of them shared a lane, Simon partially over the double yellow. A bend in the road loomed ahead, a wall of trees beyond it.

Knowing his Miata cornered well, he kept his speed high and squealed around the bend. The biker stayed right with him, leaning into the curve, his shoulder nearly touching Simon's passenger side window.

That's when a pair of headlights appeared.

Simon had only a second to react. The gap between the lights made him think the vehicle was a semi or a motor home, and he jerked his wheel to the right. He knew the biker was there, but he had no other choice. As the truck—and it was indeed a semi truck—rumbled past, shaking his little car with its wall of wind, the Miata bumped the motorcycle.

The guy swerved onto the shoulder and beyond, kicking up a shower of mud. Simon's momentum drifted him toward the shoulder, and for a second he thought he was going to hit the guy again, but the biker suddenly dropped behind. By then they had rounded the corner and Simon had the Miata under control.

He gasped for breath, finally remembering to breathe. Heart pounding in his ears, he roared up a hill in the storm, nothing but open road in front of him. The surge of adrenaline lit every one of his senses on fire. He did it. He actually did it. Glancing in his rear view mirror, he saw only blurry darkness behind him. The guy was gone. He must have pulled off, shaken up by the whole thing. Simon had actually proven the cooler customer.

"Hot damn," he said.

The glass splintered instantly into a spider web of cracks, the sound as loud as a gunshot. Simon yelped and ducked to the right, car swerving. He glanced up just in time to see a fist strike the window—a black leather fist wearing gleaming brass knuckles.

This time the glass gave way in the center, shards landing on Simon's lap.

The wind roared in his ears. Wet air rushed into the car, smelling of pine and mud. Simon saw the outline of the biker outside the window, and seeing the shine of the leather through the broken glass suddenly made the guy more real—as if before he was merely a projection of Simon's tired mind, or a villain in a video game.

They neared the top of the hill. Leaning away from the window, Simon edged closer to the edge of the road, but the biker followed, punching the glass again. More glass went flying, and this time a piece struck him above his mouth.

Tasting blood on his lips, Simon hit the brakes, hoping his attacker would race by, but the guy slowed along with him. The fist came through the window again, and this time the burly hand struck him on the cheek. It was only a glancing blow, more leather than brass making contact, but it was still powerful enough to jerk his head to the right. Purple and red stars flashed in front of his eyes.

When his vision cleared, the Miata was halfway in the ditch.

As it plowed over the uneven ground, the car trembled and shook.

The side of his face throbbing, the skin around his left eye already swelling, Simon steered the car back onto the highway. The biker was there, but Simon wasn't going to get punched again. As they roared over the hill, the night a swirl of black and green around them, he let out a primal scream and swerved at the biker.

The guy was too fast. He moved even farther to the left. They banked around a gentle curve, and it was then that a white motor home emerged from the night like a whale surfacing from the depths of the ocean.

Just in time, Simon whipped the Miata back into his own lane. He cringed, expecting to hear a sickening crunch.

But there was no such sound.

After the motor home roared past, blaring its horn, there was the biker on the far left shoulder, keeping pace. He turned and looked at Simon.

Simon's stomach churned even worse—now he really needed a bathroom. As they hit another straight stretch, not a car in sight, the biker barreled across the lanes. Simon swerved back and forth, trying to keep his attacker at bay, but these feints didn't fool him. He turned along with Simon, and then deftly sidled up to him. Simon leaned away, expecting another blow, but this time the fist grabbed his steering wheel.

The brass knuckles, shiny with moisture, were still there. The leather glove was covered with hundreds of pin-sized holes. Simon had no idea what the guy was doing until the wheel moved to the right. Along this stretch, the pine trees grew awfully close to the road, and if he hit one of them at this speed . . .

Slamming on the brakes was the most obvious thing to do, and he almost did it, but then he had a flash of insight.

With his left hand, he grabbed the door handle and jerked the door open, putting his forearm behind it.

It worked better than he expected. The door struck the motorcycle's handlebars, sending them careening in the other direction. The biker obviously hadn't expected this move; he held onto the steering wheel a split second too long. His weight was going one way, his bike the other, and the bike began to tilt.

In the next instant the biker was gone. This time Simon *did* hear the sound of a wreck— a series of bangs and thuds. Swerving into the center of his lane, he glanced in his rearview mirror and saw, through the smear of black and gray, a flickering headlight in middle of the road, receding behind him. Then he rounded the corner and was alone with the rain and the highway.

In addition to his throbbing cheek, his whole body was trembling. Nobody could survive a crash like that. He had killed a man. He had actually killed. Dear, God . . . His life was over. Even if it was manslaughter, he'd go away for years. His wife . . . His daughter . . .

He tasted bile. He clamped his hand over his mouth, and only through force of will did he keep from throwing up in the car. He descended a slight hill and, with fortunate timing, saw the sign for the Van Duzen National Forest Campground—and then another, *Rest Area - 1 mile ahead.* He'd stupidly left his cell phone at home, so a pay phone was his best bet.

He could make it to the rest area.

The rain sliced into his car, dampening his left arm. The highway widened, a lane appearing in the center for a turnoff to the left, for the campground, and another lane on the right, to the rest area. Still shaking, he turned to the right, slowing gently, turning into the gap in the trees.

He'd never been to this particular rest stop. He'd passed it lots of times, even a few times when he had to take a leak, but by the time he reached it the pull of the casino had always carried him the last twenty miles. But this time he couldn't wait, and he was glad when he entered the pot-hole infested parking lot and saw no other cars. He didn't want anyone to see him in his present condition—or his smashed window. He still hadn't decided if he was going to go back and fess up to what he did.

His mind raced, trying to understand how it all had happened. He had just wanted to pass. He didn't even see what he had done wrong. Honked the horn a few times, maybe. Had that really been enough for the guy to want to kill him?

The rest stop was a lonely place, a few chipped picnic tables and a drab concrete box in a small clearing carved out of the forest; the pine trees, with their long, slender trunks and thick green branches high above, loomed a few dozen feet beyond a grassy area like a wall of spears. A single lamp shed its pale yellow light on the area. As he parked in front of the little building, the rain turned into a fierce downpour, and it sounded so much louder when he turned off his engine.

He killed a man.

Stomach clenching, he threw open the door and ran toward the building.

The frigid rain instantly soaked his hair, cutting through his thin cotton shirt like icy needles. The wind whispered through the trees, stirring up the paper plates and cups on the ground near the overflowing garbage can. The phone booth was on the far side, near the women's door, but he couldn't wait. Dodging the puddles in the sidewalk, he sprinted to the green door marked *Men*. When he grabbed the cold metal handle, the door opened (*thank God thank God)* and he sprinted inside.

The room was dank and cramped, smelling of piss and mold. A single amber light above the cracked mirror and the metal sink was the only thing keeping the darkness at bay. There were two urinals to the left of the sink, two green stalls immediately to the left of the urinals. Gritty tile floor, lots of small white squares streaked with mud. Shoebox-sized vents near the ceiling. Stumbling into the first stall, he took it all in with a glance.

He barely made it down to the bowl before the contents of his stomach surged out of his mouth. Again and again, he threw up, until there was nothing left but dry heaves and the horrible acid burn in his throat and his nose. He hugged the cold metal, his head bent into the bowl and all its foulness, sobbing now. The damp ground soaked through his pants and chilled his knees.

The restroom door swung open.

There was no creak, just the distinctive swoosh of the door and the increasing loudness of the rain. Simon froze. The stall door had shut behind him, but he knew whoever it was could see his knees. They would have seen his car. Might have seen the wreck. Maybe it was a policeman, already come to haul him away.

Simon didn't make a sound. The restroom door swung shut, muting the storm. Only a dripping faucet broke the silence. After a few seconds, he heard footsteps, water dripping on the tiles, the rustle of heavy clothing. He half expected his stall door to swing open, but instead he saw a glistening black boot appear on the ground, only inches from his knee. The mud-coated toe pointed in the direction of the urinal Simon knew was right next to the stall.

A black boot.

Simon's despair was quickly washed away by an all-consuming dread. His breath caught in his throat. It couldn't be . . . The man could never have survived. It had to be someone else. *It had to be.*

As Simon remained absolutely rigid, he heard a zipper, then the tinkle of fluid hitting the metal urinal.

He felt himself relax slightly. It was just some traveler, stopping to relieve himself of his coffee. Maybe he hadn't even noticed Simon. If Simon just waited, maybe he would go away.

But then Simon felt a splash of warm liquid hitting his knee, and he realized, with a shock, that the man was pissing on him. With a startled cry, he scooted away from the line of piss, which continued splashing against the tiles. His heart thundered in his ears. The piss dribbled to a stop, and then he heard the zipper. He saw the boot turn, two boots appearing, both facing his direction.

Simon pressed his back against the other side of the stall, his body shaking. The boots didn't move for the longest time. Simon waited for a gloved fist to smash through the stall, right in the middle of all the *Johnny+Suzie* and *For a Good Time Call* messages scratched on the green metal. But instead, the boots turned away. As Simon sat rigidly, waiting for his stall door to bang open, he heard the footsteps move away. The restroom door swung open.

Soon he heard nothing but the tinking faucet. Simon had no idea how long he knelt there, but it was a long time. Then, when he actually *wanted* to move, he found he couldn't. Would the biker be waiting outside? Or had it merely been mistake, pissing on him like that? Maybe it wasn't the biker. Maybe . . .

The roar of an engine out in the parking lot made him jump. He knew the sound. It *was* the biker. He heard the screech of tires, and then the sound of the engine moving away. He breathed a sigh. The guy was just toying with him one last time.

He was going away. It was over.

Shakily, Simon rose. He flushed the toilet, washed his mouth in the sink, then used damp paper towels to wipe off the piss on his pants. Breathing a sigh, he pushed through the restroom door and out into the rain. He didn't mind the water drenching him—he wished he could be submerged in it, like jumping into the ocean. He walked toward the phone booth, and as he neared it, he saw that the metal cord had actually been severed. Had the biker cut it? The rain suddenly felt colder, and he turned, taking a few cautious steps down the sidewalk toward his car.

Until that moment, he hadn't realized he was holding his breath. He took several long, shuddering gulps of air, then continued on to his car. Why would the biker cut the cord? Unless . . .

That's when he heard a roar from the trees.

He stopped. At first, he thought it was an animal, a mountain lion or a black bear, and he turned in the sound's direction. It was coming from somewhere in the forest beyond the asphalt. Then he caught a glint of metal, and he saw a black shadow emerge from the darkness. A wheel appeared. Chrome. And then he saw the biker rolling out of the trees, like an apparition of death itself.

The rain created tiny white explosions on the blacktop between them. The biker, front tire poised at the curb, gunned his engine. His headlamp was smashed. Simon was halfway between his car and the restroom, and he knew this was exactly what the biker had wanted.

He broke into a run, heading for his Miata.

The biker gunned his engine, his back tire spitting up grass and dirt as he barreled into the parking lot.

Simon was only a few steps away from his car. He was going to make it. Remembering he had left the door unlocked in his haste, he grabbed the door handle and pulled.

But the door *was* locked.

He didn't understand. As biker roared toward him, he fumbled for his key, but couldn't find it in either pocket. Then he remembered that he hadn't only left the door unlocked, he had left his key inside as well—and he realized, as he heard the sound of the biker's tires squealing, exactly who had it.

No . . .

Sensing he had no time to turn, he jumped toward the front of his car. The biker, his back end swinging around as he banked into the turn, smashed into the driver side door. Simon landed on the pavement, scraping his hands, but he was up instantly and running.

He headed for narrow line of trees separating the rest area from the highway. Through the darkness and the rain, he saw glimpses of the road, like a giant black serpent.

He would cross the road. Get to the campground on the other side. Find someone. It was his only chance.

He made it up over the sidewalk and onto the soggy grass, but then the roar was right behind him and something struck his shoulder. As he went sprawling, the biker thundered past, spinning around, his back tire carving a brown half-circle on the grass. Simon struggled to his feet, but a searing pain lanced through his right knee, and he collapsed onto the wet earth again.

He heard the engine die, the kickstand pop down; he raised his head to see the biker dismount. Simon rolled onto his back and scrambled backwards, the moisture soaking through the seat of his pants. Rain ran into his eyes, blurring his vision. The biker loomed over him like a black shadow. Gloves descended, grabbed his shirt, pulled him off the ground.

Blinking away the water in his eyes, he looked up at the faceplate inches from the end of his nose.

The black helmet now bore a jagged silver scratch on the right side. Simon tried to peer beyond the mirror, but he saw only his own face reflected back at him: his left eye purple and swollen, a line of blood dribbling from his bottom lip across his chin, his soaked hair plastered against his scalp. It was the face of a small and frightened man. It was the face of a man Simon didn't know.

"Please," he begged. "Please . . . I have a wife . . . a daughter."

The biker's grip on his shirt tightened. For the longest time, he held Simon there, the faceplate so close Simon's breath fogged the glass. He got whiffs of motor oil and leather. The rain lessened, a gust of wind shaking the trees, starting as a whisper and ending as a low moan.

Finally, the biker released him. He fell hard on his backside, and looked up, too scared to move. The biker looked down at him another moment, then reached into his pocket and tossed a pair of keys between Simon's legs.

As if he was in a dream, Simon watched the man turn and walk back to his bike, a bike Simon now noticed was scratched, the fuselage dented, one of the handle bars twisted. He watched as the man started the engine and, without so much as a glance in Simon's direction, drive away.

Exhausted, Simon lay his head on the grass, listening as the roar of the biker's engine moved beyond the rest area, out into the road, and then blended with the storm. He lay there for a long time, then finally rose, retrieved his keys, and made his way back to his car.

As if he was floating outside his body, he watched as he put the key in the door, climbed inside, started the engine, and drove his car toward the exit. He thought the moisture on his face was rain until he tasted the tears on his lips.

With his car idling at the entrance to the highway, the road stretching into darkness on both sides, he knew he had a choice.

To the right lay the casino, where a group of strangers waited around a green felt table, the dimly lit room hazy with smoke. In his mind's eye he saw an empty chair, a stack of chips in front of it, five cards face down. He saw himself sit, pick up the cards, and toss his ante into the pot. The pull was there. Even with his bloodied face and aching chest, he felt it. He wanted to go there. He wanted to join that table. There was still time. Nobody would care how he looked. *Nobody.*

But to the left, somewhere beyond the shadowy hill, he saw something else: his daughter's dark room, the streetlamp in the parking lot breaking through the gaps in the blinds. It was as if he was standing there in the doorway, his clothes still dripping. The room smelled so much different than the casino—no smoke, but instead the faint stench from her soiled diapers, an odor her diaper pail couldn't quite contain. It didn't smell bad to him, though. It smelled wonderful. He saw himself move quietly into the room, navigating around dolls and blocks and board books littering the floor. He saw himself ease down in the glider across from her bed, cringing when it squeaked. He saw his trembling hand reach for her sleeping form, his fingers inches from her hair.

He closed his eyes. He saw her so much more vividly this way. If he concentrated, he could almost feel his fingers brushing against her hair. Soft, like the finest silk. If he thought about how it felt, if he didn't allow himself to think about anything else, not even for a second, the feeling could save him. He knew it could. It had power. All he had to do was surrender himself to it. All he had to do was turn his hands to the left.

It should be so simple.

It should be so easy.

And yet, as he opened his eyes, and with a last convulsive shudder forced the wheel to the left, he knew it was the both the hardest and the greatest thing he had ever done.

A Dark Planetarium

WHEN THEY ARRIVED at Portland's new planetarium, they found the clerk in the ticket booth affixing a hastily-written sign to the glass window. The storm had worked itself into a rage by this time, and a cold rain mixed with sleet crackled against their black umbrella. The gray, mottled skies had brought on an early darkness, and Jack could not read the window's sign until he was nearly up to the booth. *No shows today. Equipment malfunction.*

The clerk, a boy with a fuzz mustache and bleached blond hair, put the last piece of clear tape on the sign, then glanced at Jack. He frowned and flicked off the light in the booth. This replaced the boy's face with Jack's own reflection—a pale, gaunt face that did not match up with the image he had of himself. There was a time not long ago that he was a healthy, rosy-cheeked man, not this wasted thing lost in the folds of his trench coat.

Next to him, bundled in his green parka, Travis held tightly to Jack's hand. Wherever they went these days, they always held hands. His son's balance was one of the first things to go.

Inside the booth, a vertical strip of light appeared in the darkness. The clerk was leaving through a back door.

"Wait," Jack said.

There was a pause, then a voice came back: "We're closed. Sorry."

"But . . . hold on a minute, will you? Can we talk about this?" The clerk's face appeared in the window. He was so incredibly young, Jack thought. He was trying to think of what to say when Travis squeezed his hand.

"Daddy?"

Travis looked up at him with vacant, unseeing eyes. His sight was mostly gone now—only a vague awareness of light and dark remained.

"Just a minute, son."

"What's wrong, Daddy?"

"Nothing. It's all right."

"Are we going to see the stars?"

"Yes, yes." Jack looked at the clerk, whose bland expression had not changed. "We drove over four hours to get here. Isn't there something we can do?"

"I'm sorry, sir," the clerk said. "The equipment is broken. It should be working tomorrow."

"We won't be here tomorrow."

"I'm sorry, sir."

Jack felt his anger rise at the nonchalance in the clerk's tone, but he suppressed it. There was no time for anger these days. He had long since proven that anger was only a hindrance to making their way down the list. They had seen the cobalt blue waters of Crater Lake. They had flown a box-kite on the Oregon coast. They had done so much in the last few weeks, but there was still much to do. The planetarium was one more thing, and he could not let his own anger prevent him from making the clerk understand how important it was they do this.

He held up a finger for the clerk to wait, then took his son around the booth to the cast-iron bench under the overhanging roof. He seated Travis on the bench and handed him the umbrella.

"I'll be right back," he said.

"My head hurts, Daddy."

"Is it really bad? Do you want to lie down?"

"No, I want to see the stars. I want to see Saturn and Jupiter."

"Well, that's what we'll do then."

Jack returned to the ticket window, blinking away the rain that ran down his forehead into his eyes. The clerk, wearing a bored expression, had his arm on the counter and rested his head against his fist.

"What's the ticket price?" Jack asked.

The clerk sighed. "I told you, the equipment—"

"I'll pay you the ticket price and give you twenty bucks. How's that?"

This made the clerk pause. He pursed his lips, then shook his head. "I could lose my job, sir. Look, the stuff is broken. Seriously."

"That's all right," Jack said. "We want to go in anyway."

"But why?"

Jack swallowed. He hated how the events of his life had conspired to bring him to this point, when he had to share the intimate details of his own pain with this stupid kid who had probably never suffered, who had never known loss or pain, who could not possibly understand why it was so important that Jack take his son inside.

"What is your name?" he asked the clerk.

"Robert," the kid said, sighing. "You want to know the name of my supervisor, I guess?"

Jack shook his head. "Robert, my son has an inoperable brain tumor. This is one of the things I want him to do before he dies."

He wondered at first if the clerk would think it was a bluff, but either the thought had never crossed the kid's mind or there was no denying the conviction in Jack's voice. The boredom was gone. In its place was something Jack hated even more: pity.

"Oh, I thought—I didn't—I'm sorry, sir," the kid stammered.

"It's all right. Can we come in?"

"Oh . . . well, it's not working. Like I said—"

"My son is blind now," Jack said. "He wouldn't be able to see it anyway."

Jack saw the question forming on the kid's lips: *Then why?* But the kid didn't ask. He just nodded and pointed to the glass doors next to the booth. Jack went back to the bench.

"Are we going inside?" Travis asked.

"Yes," Jack said. "They were closed, but they are going to make an exception for us."

The clerk rattled open the deadbolt and opened the glass doors. Jack took his son's hand and led him inside. The entry room had a high ceiling, and the room was nearly as cool as outside.

"Sorry about the temp," the clerk said, locking the doors behind them. "They turn down the heat when we're closed."

"That's all right."

Wet tennis shoes squeaked across the tiled floor. Jack had not told the clerk, but he had another, stronger reason for wanting to come inside. He had not yet told his son he was going to die. He was waiting for the right time. He did not how to break it to Travis, especially since Jack was an atheist who believed there was nothing waiting for them after death, but he knew he could only go on for so long pretending the headaches and the blindness would go away. And he refused to lie. He would *not* give the boy false hope.

But how could he explain what the word oblivion meant?

Walnut paneling decorated the far wall, and the kid led them to a double door that was wide open. In the dark, circular theater within, Jack saw rows of empty, felt-backed chairs. The kid stopped at the door.

"I'd like to let you stay awhile," he said. "But we're supposed to be closed. My girlfriend, she's waiting for me outside."

Jack smiled. "We won't stay long," he said.

The kid nodded. "You want the door closed?"

"If you wouldn't mind."

"Sure, I'll wait until you get to your seat."

Jack led Travis down the carpeted isle, taking a pair of seats somewhere in the middle. They had no sooner sat down when the kid shut the door, sealing them in darkness. Jack was sure that usually there were at least lights along the aisle, but the clerk had left them off. The darkness was so complete that Jack could not see his hand in front of his face, nor his son sitting next to him. High above them, he heard rain tapping on the roof.

"I'm scared, Daddy."

Jack squeezed his son's small fingers. He did not know if he could go through with this. It would be much easier to talk about the stars and the planets. He could talk about Saturn's rings. He could talk about Jupiter's moons. These were facts—knowable, comforting, and easy. He could talk about these things and then they could go home.

"It's all right," he said. "I'm here with you."

"Is it starting?"

"Yes, it's starting now."

The boy squirmed in his seat, his pants rustling against the vinyl. "I can't see it, Daddy."

"I know. "

"What do you see, Daddy? What's the first thing you see?"

Jack peered up into the darkness. If he strained, he could almost make out the stars. He believed he could see them. It had been a long time since his college astronomy, but he thought he could make out some of the constellations. There was Cassiopeia. On the left was Andromeda. Down below, Sagittarius. He remembered some stories about the constellations. He could talk about these stories. It would be something to do. It would pass the time.

"The first thing we see," he said, "is heaven."

The Liberators

I HEARD THE REPORT of a cannon a half second before the boulder on the ridge above us exploded.

Pebbles pinged off my helmet. The ventilator fans whirred behind my ears, and a bead of sweat trickled down my check. The suits did a good job of filtering the air, but the inside of my helmet still smelled slightly metallic.

It was the dead of night, but my Visosuit enhanced the image, giving the rocky gully an amber tint. The Dulnari had lousy night vision, so we always fought after sunset. I quickly counted ten black, sleek-domed helmets in the gully. Each helmet was marked with a different number, and Rina's number 22 was on the far end. We broke up two weeks earlier, but I still liked having her close during combat.

"Major Steed," my brother's voice crackled over the all-suit frequency, "report."

Damon sounded calm as a man could be. I watched Rina for a reaction, but she didn't move. I knew she had been spending her time lately with that egghead, Lieutenant Dyle, but I still wondered if she and Damon would hook up now that I was out of the picture.

"Got a group of two hundred Dulnari pinned in a mountain bunker, Colonel," I said to him. "The rest of the target planet has been contained."

I stopped thinking of the planets as having names long ago. After a while, they all blurred together.

"Good . . . We need to finish this planet up and move on to the next one. Get it done quickly."

"Yes, sir."

He cut the transmission.

I suddenly felt tired. There was always another target. Such was the way of life in the elite LS-37, a Liberation Squad who had liberated more planets from the tyrannical rule of the Dulnari than anyone else. We were legendary in the Unity Defense, our slogan whispered among lesser soldiers like a hallowed prayer. *LS-37, Angels Protected by the Glory of Heaven.*

I peered over the edge of the gully. The mountain sloped up gently until it reached the rectangular peak. An opening big enough for their cannons circled the peak; there were two or three cannons on each side. We could fly up there in under three seconds.

The problem was that we'd be easy targets. What we needed was a distraction.

Our suits were controlled by the electrical impulses in our brains. I *thought* the all-suit frequency on, and it was. "Lieutenant Dyle," I said, "take Delta Group and do a flyby over the mountain, dropping flash grenades. The rest of us will storm the bunker. Hold for my command."

There was a brief pause, and then his reply came back.

"Yes, sir," he said.

"All other teams, await my command," I said.

Before I even finished the sentence, Rina was scooting in my direction. She was a small woman, but inside the bulky black Visosuit you would never know it.

Our suits were mini spacecraft in their own right. The slim packs on our backs were loaded with various bombs and missiles, and the fingers of our gloves were equipped with lasers. The metaplak material could withstand a direct hit from almost any handheld weapon.

Since the Defense had equipped us with the suits, our battles lately had been decisively won. We moved in fast, destroyed the Dulnari's local military, and left just as quickly. A recovery team followed within a day, helping the planet rebuild.

When Rina was close, I could see through the tinted faceplate to her face—or not really her face, but a re-creation of her face on the external screen. She was Asian-Latino by heritage. She had narrow, slanted eyes, and her skin was the color of coffee with cream. The dust in the air made it hard to read her expression.

"Sir," she said, and I could tell she was fighting to keep her voice calm. "Sir, could I suggest that we all attack as one? There's no need to put Delta Group in danger."

I wondered how close she and Dyle had truly become. "We need a distraction, Private," I replied.

"But, sir, if we *all* attack—"

"End of discussion," I said curtly.

She glared at me through the dust, then scooted back to the end of the line. The rest of the faceplates were turned toward me. I knew my history with Rina was no secret.

I switched to the all-suit frequency. "Delta Group, attack now!" My own suit had something my soldiers' suits didn't—a small monitor, mounted inside my helmet just below my faceplate, that allowed me to see what any of my soldiers saw. I thought the command *Screen 40* and up came Lieutenant Dyle's view.

Dyle was directly over the mountain. The enemy's cannons fired, one after another in rapid succession, and the ground beneath us trembled.

I turned on the all-suit frequency. "All other groups, attack now!"

We took to the air just as white flashes began to spot the mountain. There were five teams, each with ten drop soldiers, so the sky was filled with fifty of us. I felt the antigrav thrusters trembling beneath my feet.

We descended on their bunker like a swarm of black hornets. All around us were flashes of white light. I followed my men through the opening, blasting the Dulnari standing there with my finger lasers.

We stepped over the bodies we just brought down. They were humanoid, much like us: similar height, two arms and two legs, breathing air and expelling carbon dioxide. One of the most amazing discoveries since contact was made with other species was that these facts held for most of us.

But the Dulnari had a more pronounced, wolf-like nose, and their sense of smell was keener. Their leathery skin was dark gray except for the skin around their yellow eyes, which was a luminescent blue. Their heads were smaller, and individually, they were not as smart. But they had more specialization in intelligence; when they acted in concert, their total intelligence exceeded ours.

The big difference, though, was that the Dulnari were ruthlessly ambitious in a way we never were. Every sentient species we encountered had the *option* of joining the Unity Worlds. The Dulnari took them all by force.

Until we decided to stop them.

A dimly-lit tunnel circled the bunker. We took out each cannon-room one at a time. It all seemed to be going well until Lieutenant Dyle shouted out over the radio.

"Hit! . . . Going down!"

Rina stared at me. Grimacing, I changed to Dyle's screen, and saw the image of the ground rushing up at him. My screen went to static, then the image returned. Now he was looking at the sky.

"Must do this . . . " he groaned.

Then the worst possible thing happened.

He removed his helmet.

I knew this because I was suddenly seeing *his* face, bloodied and bruised, on my screen. His blond hair was matted against his scalp. The helmet must have been down on the ground next to him.

"Lieutenant Dyle!" I cried.

It was no use. Without his helmet, communication was impossible. As every drop soldier knew, the one thing that you could not do—that you were strictly *forbidden* to do—was to remove your helmet. Even if a planet had a breathable atmosphere, the helmet gave a soldier full access to the Visosuit's abilities, allowed him to remain in contact with other soldiers, and permitted his superiors to use his visuals for tactical decisions.

I was deciding what to do when my brother bellowed over the frequency.

"Just what the hell is going on down there, Major?"

"Sir," I replied, "Lieutenant Dyle's helmet—"

"I can see what happened. What I want to know is why."

"I don't know. Perhaps —"

"The Med will be there in less than two minutes," he said. "Let it get him out of there. Subdue the bunker."

"Sir, don't you think we should provide cover for the Med?"

"No time. The Dulnari are fleeing the bunker as we speak. Concentrate your troops on stopping them."

He clicked off. The rest of the troops had moved ahead, and it was just me and Rina lagging behind.

"Let's go," I said, stepping past her.

She didn't move.

"Rina? You heard the orders."

"Kaden needs us," she said.

"The Med—"

"I'm going."

She ran back into the last cannon-room. I followed, yelling her name, but she didn't stop. She took to the air, rocketing through the opening.

If she died out there, I would hate myself forever. Knowing I was risking a court-martial, I followed her through the opening.

Her foot thrusters were a yellow spot ahead. A cannon boomed. A second later, the projectile glanced off my arm. It didn't puncture my suit, but it sent me crashing into the rocks.

I lay there on the ground, gasping until I got my wind back.

When I took to the air again, I came upon Rina almost immediately. She was in the gully where we were before, exchanging fire with some Dulnari up the slope. Between them was Lieutenant Dyle. His blond hair among all that gray rock stood out like a flame.

He was running toward Rina.

"Major Steed!" my brother shouted inside my helmet. "What the hell are you doing?"

Before I could do anything, a Dulnari got Dyle in the leg. He crumpled to the dirt. One shot could take him out.

Rina must have known this, because she took to the air again. Her blue lasers sent rock and dirt flying.

"Rina!" I cried. I forgot to turn on the radio, so it was only me that heard it.

I swooped down, firing wildly at the enemy. We should have died. But whether it was due to luck or our crazy behavior, we managed to take out all the Dulnari in the area.

We were circling back to Dyle when the Med's egg-shaped pod whooshed out of the sky. The shimmering surface of the pod mimicked the landscape behind it, so it was difficult to see unless you knew it was there.

Rina and I pulled up, watching as the base of the pod popped open and a grasping arm descended. It was only on the ground a second, and then up it went, Lieutenant Dyle in its grasp.

When the pod was gone, I noticed that the cannons were quiet. The battle was over.

After returning to the *Stag*, I showered, squeezed in a quick meal, and reported to my brother's quarters.

Our ship was small, with narrow halls and low ceilings. When we were on our way to another target, as we were then, you could feel the metal gangplanks trembling beneath your rubber soles.

Temperatures varied throughout the *Stag* due to the ship's poor ventilation system. Standing in front of my brother's door, I felt cold, and shivered.

I punched the intercom. "Major Steed here," I said.

"Enter," he said.

He was sitting behind his mahogany writing desk, typing into his computer. The room was dark except for the yellow glow from his tiny desk lamp.

Though he was a year older than me, many people mistakenly thought we were twins. We both had long, thin faces, auburn hair, and big noses that looked as if they had been carved out of granite.

"Go ahead," he said, continuing to look at his monitor.

I told him that I was trying to protect one of my troops who had made a bad decision, and that I thought my troops in the bunker had everything under control. When I was done, he nodded but still didn't look at me.

"I should have you court-martialed for what you did today," he said.

He said it the way most men would ask for butter for their toast. It was rare these days to get a rise out of him, although it hadn't always been that way.

When we joined the Defense two years earlier, his hatred of the Dulnari ran so deep that he spoke of little else. He had learned it from our father, who had been in the Defense his entire life. Damon had waited a year so he and I could go in together. I thought we were inseparable, the Unstoppable Steeds as we called ourselves. Then, at training camp, we had the misfortune to fall in love with the same woman.

Rina Pullman lost both parents and three brothers to the war. Damon courted her relentlessly, as he did everything relentlessly, but she told me later he was too intense. With me, she said she could be at ease, and that my relentless optimism that we would win the war made her believe, too.

After Damon lost Rina, I tried to make amends, but then we got word our father's ship was destroyed. I tried to be there for him, but he ignored me and threw himself into his studies. It paid off. He was tapped for command of a drop ship.

I did well, too, making Major. Rina was never one to study, so she ended up a drop soldier. After our ship was destroyed, we ended up reassigned to the *Stag* under Damon's command. We had been there six months.

And he hadn't said one word more than necessary to me the entire time.

"Could I say a few things in my defense, sir?" I asked.

He looked at me. His flinty eyes were completely unreadable. "I'm *not* going to court-martial you," he said. "I merely said I *should*. You disobeyed a direct order from your commanding officer. The violation must still be noted in your file."

I gritted my teeth. Any such note in my file would make it hard to get promoted.

"I understand, sir." And then, after a pause, I added, "And Rina?"

There was a flicker of anger in his eyes, before it was replaced by his usual stone-cold gaze. "Private Pullman is not your concern." He must have sensed he was in the wrong, because he added, "Since she has been a valued soldier, I will assume this is a momentary lapse in judgment. Due to the circumstances with Lieutenant Dyle, I decided not to note this in her log."

I realized something had happened. "Circumstances with Lieutenant Dyle?"

"That was the other matter I needed to speak to you about," he said. "A covert nex-link was discovered in Lieutenant Dyle's quarters. It appears he was in contact with the Resistance."

I was stunned. I never liked Dyle because he was always debating the political intricacies of the war, how who was right all depended on your point of view, or how the interstellar corporations really controlled everything. It seemed phony. The Dulnari were the enemy, and that's all any soldier needed to know. But despite my dislike for him, I never thought of him as a Resistance sympathizer.

The Resistance was made up of soldiers who had defected to form a terrorist movement opposed to the Defense. They had a few ships, a few thousand soldiers, and a lot of hidden operatives. As far as the Defense was concerned, anyone caught aiding the Resistance was a traitor.

And in the Defense, there was only one way to deal with traitors.

"PRIVATE KADEN DYLE, you are hereby found guilty of collaborating with known terrorists, a treasonous offense, and by Unity Defense regulations are herby sentenced to immediate execution."

The Med, its deep voice resonating throughout the mess hall, put down the paper and looked at the blond man bound and gagged in front of him. In truth, the Med had no need to read the paper, because it was a robot with perfect memory and real-time access to the Unity grid. But the Med was always trying to appear more human so people would be more likely to trust it.

Not that it ever worked. It was hard to think of a seven-foot tall, silver-skinned, hairless machine as trustworthy, even if it looked vaguely human. If it only acted as a medical robot, that would be one thing, but it's dual role as disciplinarian didn't help. Most soldiers derisively referred to them as *plugs* because of their occasional need to plug into a power source.

Dyle's face was dotted with perspiration. Such a baby face. I had forgotten that he was barely eighteen—and then I had to remind myself that I was only twenty.

"Private Dyle," the Med went on, "you are not permitted to speak, for fear that your lies will contaminate your more loyal shipmates. But if you would like to show that you regret your treason, you may now salute your commanding officers."

The room still smelled like the awful meatloaf we had for dinner. Nearly all seventy-five crew members were present. The lights everywhere but at the front had been dimmed, so the crew members were just shadowy heads to me. But I could see Rina. She was near the front, and her brown cheeks were glistening.

There had been five executions for treason in the last four months, and men much older than Kyle had broken down and sobbed. To his credit, he did no such thing.

He didn't salute me or my brother either.

Instead, he turned to his shipmates and saluted *them*.

There was a moment of stunned silence, then two troopers quickly bound his hands. The Med stepped forward, its feet clanging against the metal floor. It raised its right hand so it was level with Dyle's shoulder.

"Permission to carry out the execution, Colonel Steed," the Med said.

"Permission granted," my brother said. Hell, not even a pause. The man showed fewer emotions than the Med.

A hypodermic needle jutted out of the Med's index finger and penetrated Dyle's skin. He let out a muffled cry. His eyelids closed and his head slumped to his chest.

The Med put a slender finger on Kaden's neck.

"Well?" my brother said.

"Private Kaden Dyle determined to be dead, sir," the Med said.

"Very well. Take him to the morgue."

With that, my brother dismissed us. The soldiers, subdued, shuffled out, and I went with them. Rina was keeping to her self, walking slower than the others.

I saw her turn into the fitness room, and I ducked in after her, feeling my body sag. Normal ship gravity was one-half Earth's, but the fitness room was three times that. We were the only people inside. Rina was already at the punching bag in the corner, and she smacked it with a good roundhouse.

"Nice one," I said. I didn't mean for it to sound patronizing.

She glared at me. Her hair was as black as obsidian, even blacker than the uniform which hugged the curves of her petite figure. When I first saw her in training camp, she took my breath away.

It was still hard for me to understand why we broke up. In the beginning, we were all about having fun, playing virtual hockey, watching holovids, sharing a pizza, and that was fine by her. But once we were on our drop ship, she began to read—history, philosophy, anything she could get her hands on. When she broke up with me, she said she wanted somebody who would challenge her to think deeper, and she knew I never would.

"What do you want?" she demanded.

"Hey, easy, Pair-o-Deuces, I just thought you might want to talk."

It was an old nickname, and it usually got me a smile. No such luck this time. She laid into the bag with her left. "About what?"

"About Kaden. I knew you were becoming friends."

She snorted. "We weren't sleeping together, if that's what you're worried about."

"No, I wasn't . . . " I began, feeling my anger flaring. So she wasn't in the mood for reconciliation. Fine. "Look, I just wanted to say I'm sorry. I understand why you went to help him on the planet. Not too long ago, you might have done the same for me."

I headed briskly for the door. She pounded the bag with a series of vicious punches, but when I was about to open the door, stopped.

"Vince," she said.

I looked at her. Her forehead had already beaded with sweat.

"Yeah?"

"Do you even know what his crime was?"

"He was caught sending covert transmissions to the Resistance."

"Bullshit." She gave the bag one last punch, then crossed the room. Her fist was still clenched, and I tensed, thinking she was going after my head. It wouldn't have been the first time. "Bullshit," she said again. "Even if he *was* helping the Resistance, that's not why they killed him."

I took a deep breath. It wouldn't help if we both got angry. "You know, I *am* your commanding officer. I should report such things."

"Report me, then," she shot back. "You want to see me up at the front of that room? I'll tell you why they took out Kaden. It's because he found out something they didn't want him to know."

"That's nuts."

"I'm telling you, the man was not a spy. I've been in his quarters and I would have seen the nex-link equipment. He said he wasn't sure we should trust the Unity Defense, but that's as far as it went."

I felt a pang of jealousy. She said she wasn't sleeping with him, and yet she was in his room? I suppressed the feeling. "And what did he find out?"

"Something they don't want us to know."

"Like what?"

"I'll let you know when I find out."

"Rina, I'm going to pretend I didn't hear that. The Med probably found something you missed, that's all."

She shook her head. "You are so goddamn naive," she said. And then, on her way out, she muttered under her breath the most painful thing she had ever said to me. "I can't believe I wasted two years on you. I should have slept with your brother."

I was preparing to snap something at her about the value of loyalty, but the words died on my lips.

WE COASTED into the atmosphere under the cover of night, coming down over one of the major oceans to avoid detection. My Visosuit enhanced and brightened the emerald waters beneath me. There was no land in sight. A flock of large, lizard-like birds were moving off to the north.

My group flew on in silence, no need to speak because we had done this dozens of times before. Rina was with me. We hadn't spoken since the exercise room five days earlier.

By now, some teams had reached their targets, and I watched their ensuing battles on the monitor in my helmet. The Dulnari seemed particularly weak. One team was locked in combat with some ground troops, easily annihilating them. Another met hardly any resistance at all as they destroyed a whole fleet of sea vessels.

My team took out some pitiful attack pods with long-range missiles, then descended on the military base. Blue plasma bolts buzzed past, fired from the turrets below.

"Go to ground," I said.

As my boots hit the dirt, my suit reverberated from the impact. Dulnari soldiers, armed only with shoulder-slung rifles, streamed out of the single-story buildings. We mowed them down. There were thousands of Dulnari, though, and my team got separated, each of us dodging behind a different building. Still, I was confident we would have the planet contained in no time.

That's when I got the distress call from Rina.

"Vince," she said, "I need your help."

The tone of her voice made me freeze. I glanced down at her screen and saw something that didn't make sense. I was looking at her own face.

Then I realized: her helmet was off.

She appeared to be okay. She was looking straight at me, her black hair matted against her forehead. My suit's computer showed her only a hundred meters away, inside one of the largest buildings.

The Dulnari had the building surrounded, but I smashed through one of the windows. I ran down the hall, blasting dozens of Dulnari. I almost ran past her. She was hiding in a storage closet.

"In here," she said, yanking me inside.

She closed the door. It was a tight squeeze, our backs up against rows of shelving. There was one window on the far wall. Rina's exposed head looked puny, dwarfed by the bulky suit. There was a long, red gash along her forehead.

"You're hurt," I said.

She put a finger to her lips and scooted over to the window, the breastplates of our suits clinking against one another.

I saw then that her helmet sat on the ground, apparently undamaged. "Did you take it off?"

Explosions rocked the shelves, scattering dust over us, and dropping a few blankets on the floor.

"Rina," I said.

She looked at me. "I've figured it out, Vince. I figured out why they killed Kaden."

"Rina, we've got to get out of here."

"Come here. I want you to look out the window."

I looked outside. I saw two of ours crouched behind a burning, eight-wheeled transport. A number of the gray-skinned Dulnari littered the ground, but none of my soldiers. So far.

We shouldn't have been watching. We should have been out there.

"Rina . . ."

"Take off your helmet off," she said.

"What on Earth for?"

"It's the only way you will believe me."

"Believe what?"

I heard the guttural Dulnari voices out in the hall. I reached down and picked up her helmet. "Put it on."

She shook her head firmly. "No."

"Put it on!"

"No, listen to me. You're not seeing the truth. We're not fighting the Dulnari."

"What?"

She took my gloved hands in her own. "It's all a lie," she said. "A big lie, Vince. There's just the local military out there. Natives. The Dulnari must have left this planet long ago. Our suits, we thought they were so wonderful. They're just making us see what they want us to see, hear what they want us to hear. That's why they don't want us to take them off. We're not liberating. We're conquering."

I stared at her, trying to comprehend. Inside my helmet, I could flick from one screen to another of all the battles currently happening. My troops. My friends. Fighting for what they thought was right. She was saying it was all a lie?

"Take off your helmet," she said. "Vince, you can't just follow orders. You've got to think for yourself, too."

I was opening my mouth to speak when my brother's voice boomed inside my helmet.

"Major, what the hell is going on?" he said. "Is Private Pullman's helmet damaged?"

Rina was about to say something and I held up my finger.

"Sir . . ." I said, wondering how much to say. "Sir, I'm not sure. It may have malfunctioned, sir."

"Well, get it back on! Your men need you!"

"Yes, sir." I looked at Rina. "Yes, sir, we'll be re-engaging momentarily."

I handed her the helmet. The voices out in the hall were getting louder. Rina hesitated, then put the helmet back on her head.

"I won't shoot anyone," she said.

She looked dead serious. But when we left the supply closet, and the Dulnari were there at the end of the hall, she was faster at shooting them down than I was.

When I looked at her, she frowned.

"Training," she said, sounding disgusted.

THE BATTLE ended quickly. Rina fought, too, but I could see that her heart wasn't in it. When we returned to the ship, I ordered her to see the Med to get the gash on her forehead treated.

"Vince," she said. "Don't make me. The plug'll throw me in the brig . . . or worse. Maybe brainwash me."

"Don't be ridiculous," I said.

She did as I asked, but there was a sullen, resigned look about her. I took a hot shower, letting the warmth seep into my aching muscles, then put on a clean uniform and went to see her. Damon would be expecting a debriefing. I needed to know what to tell him.

I still couldn't believe what she said was true. It had to be some kind of hallucination.

She wasn't in her quarters, so I assumed she was still in the medical facility. When I got there, the Med was zipping up a black body bag. A single lamp shined its garish white light over the bag. No one else was in the room.

A cold feeling of terror swept over me.

We had taken no fatalities.

"Where's Rina?" I asked.

Its silver head swiveled to face me. The light from the lamp gleamed on its metal scalp. Its solid black eyes narrowed. These were sentient beings, but they were not like us. No one I knew had ever become friends with a Med.

"I'm afraid that Private Pulman's wound was fatal," it said.

"What?"

"Apparently the atmosphere—"

I pushed past the Med and unzipped the bag. Rina's pale face, eyelids closed, lay before me. I touched her skin and found it cold.

"I'm sorry, Major," the Med said. "I did all I could."

I couldn't believe what I was seeing.

"It was only a cut!"

"As I was saying, sir, apparently the atmosphere of Verexia contained an air-born virus which penetrated her bloodstream through her wound. It brought about immediate heart failure. It's why it is vitally important our drop soldiers wear their helmets."

Only an hour ago she had been fine. I glared at the Med, wondering what it would take to rip the thing's head off. That it was a full foot taller than me, and probably stronger by five times, didn't concern me.

"You goddamn plug," I said, "you killed her."

The Med was unfazed by my outburst. "Sir, I understand you are upset. However —"

"You killed her because of what she found out."

"I don't know what you mean."

My mind still had a hard time grasping that what Rina said was true, but she must have been on to something. A wave of nausea passed over me. My lovely Rina was dead. My Pair-o-Deuces. All because I didn't believe her.

"You saw what she saw," I said. "And what I saw. You know what she was saying."

"Sir, the transmissions from your Visosuits were garbled. When I went back to review the recordings, I found there was no way to know why she lost her helmet. I was assuming you could enlighten us."

The Med spoke with a chilling tone. I knew it was lying. It made sense. Of course the Med would be the Unity Defense's lapdog, making sure everything went the way they wanted. The pieces were all starting to fall in place.

"I'm going to see Colonel Steed," I said, backing to the door.

"He already knows," the Med said on my way out.

Of course the Med would have informed the command officer if there was a death on the ship. How my brother would respond to the death of a woman he had once been infatuated with I didn't know. What I also didn't know was how much he knew about the truth—a truth I was still trying to wrap my mind around.

We aren't liberating, she said. *We're conquering.*

When I reached his quarters, I barged inside. He was at his desk. The computer screen, however, was off.

"Damon," I said.

He turned and looked at me. His eyes were red, his hair disheveled.

"Isn't it standard protocol," he began, "to knock before entering an officer's room?"

"The plug killed her," I said.

"What?"

"It killed her! It didn't like what she found out so it killed her!"

He sighed. "I know it's hard for you to accept, but she's gone. You need to accept that and get on with your duties." He turned back to his blank monitor, as if it held something of vital importance.

I expected rage. I expected sorrow. But his voice had been devoid of emotion.

"How can you be so callous?"

"I'm dealing with this in the only way I can," he said

"You know, don't you? You know the truth about the Dulnari."

"What are you talking about?"

"The Dulnari! We've already won the war. Our suits—our suits make us see Dulnari, but it's just the local life forms and whatever military they have. We're not liberating, we're conquering. It's the truth and you know it."

"That's nonsense. Where did you get that idea?"

"Like you don't already know. You saw the conversation Rina and I had. You know why she took off her helmet."

He got to his feet, looking puzzled. "No, I didn't. I only saw a few seconds. The Med informed me the transmission was garbled."

"That's another lie."

"Major," he said, holding up a finger, "I'd watch what I was saying if I were you."

"Don't you think it's odd the Dulnari had extended their empire so far? That they have so many planets under their control?"

"Major—"

"The terrorists are right. What we're doing is wrong."

"Major! Your statements are bordering on treason. If you don't—"

"Damon, you know Rina. She wouldn't make this up. I'm not totally sure myself, but don't you think we need to find out before we kill anyone else?" I swallowed, pausing before delivering the line I knew would get through to him. "What do you think Dad would say if he knew we were killing innocent people?"

The punch to my cheek was swift. He hit me so hard I fell over backwards, landing on the floor. The blow brought tears to my eyes. I lay there, stunned, looking up at him.

"Don't you *ever* talk about our father that way!" he shouted. "He served with distinction!"

It was the first time in as long as I could remember that he had used my first name. I could make him angry. And if I could make him angry, I might be able to make him see beyond his uniform.

"Damon, *he* was right," I said, massaging my cheek. "Back then, he was still fighting Dulnari. But now—"

"Not another word," he said.

"But—"

"*Not another word*! I swear, Vince, you may be my brother, but if say one more treasonous word, I'm going to turn you over to the Med." He stood there, breathing hard through his nostrils, as if waiting for me to challenge him. "You have two choices," he went on. "You can continue to piss on what we're doing, or you can get off your ass and get on with your duties. Which is it going to be?"

There were a hundred things to say leaping through my mind. But instead of saying any of them, I got off the floor and headed to the door. There was no reasoning with him.

I would have to find another way.

I DIDN'T SLEEP that night. Instead, I tossed in my bunk, Rina's words echoing through my brain.

Vince, you can't just follow orders. You've got to think for yourself, too.

She was right. Who knew how many innocent people had died because of me—the last being the woman I loved? I could have resigned immediately from the Unity Defense. Service wasn't mandatory. But I couldn't let any more innocent people die, and I couldn't let my brother take part in it either.

WE HAD CHASED the enemy into a canyon, and now we were up on the ledge, looking down at them huddling behind the boulders below. The vegetation was sparse and withered-looking. It was dark, but of course our suits made it seem brighter.

I realized there were hundreds of planets where wars were being fought by Liberation Squads right now. We were only one of them.

Hundreds of planets.

Hundreds of lies.

There were thirteen Dulnari—or what I knew *weren't* Dulnari, but what my suit showed me were. Now and then, one popped up from behind a boulder and fired at us with a pitiful projectile gun. They couldn't even leave a scratch on our suits. Absurd, I thought, that anyone could think the Dulnari could have sunk to fighting with such meager weapons.

I had arranged the drop so that we did a major offensive first, keeping all my soldiers together, telling them not to kill until we had them surrounded. My soldiers were on their stomachs, lined up on the edge. I looked up at the three moons, two of them full. The Visosuit made the moons seem like pale yellow disks, but I hoped they would provide the light I needed.

"Sir?" one of the men said. "Sir, should we fire?"

Who was it? Number 17. I couldn't remember the name.

"Hold your fire, Private," I said.

"But, sir—"

"That's an order."

The enemy continued to fire. Now and then, their shots grazed the canyon's edge. After a moment, my brother's voice boomed inside my helmet.

"Major Steed, what the hell is going on?" he said.

"Absolutely nothing, sir," I said.

"I can see that. Finish the enemy and so we can get out of here."

"Negative, sir."

"What?"

"I can't follow that order, sir."

"Major, if you don't—"

"I'm perfectly aware of what I'm doing. Steed out."

Procedure required him to do one thing. If the Major in the field couldn't carry out a drop, then it was up to the Colonel to take over. It also meant the Med would accompany him, because it was assumed the Major would be injured.

My soldiers continued to look at me, hungry for me to give the order to attack. It wasn't long before we saw the pod streak out of the sky. Breaking thrusts fired and the pod landed a few dozen feet away on eight spidery legs. When the bottom hatch popped open, two figures emerged—my brother, wearing a Visosuit, and the Med, needing none of its own.

"You better have a goddamn good reason for this," he said over the suit-to-suits. As they approached, I could see that the Med was carrying a laser rifle.

Before they got too close, I did what I had been waiting to do. The planet had a breathable atmosphere.

I reached up and popped off my helmet.

Both Damon and the Med pulled up short. I let the helmet fall to the ground. The air was cool and thin. The moonlight was bright enough: not only could I see the astonished faces of my brother and my soldiers inside their black helmets, but I could also see what was down in the canyon.

The faces and bodies of our enemies were covered with shiny black fur. They were much shorter than us, the size of our children, with four arms instead of two. Even at a glance, it was apparent they weren't Dulnari.

Rina had been right.

"What the hell are you doing?" Damon cried.

The Med was walking forward. "This is a clear violation of protocol," it said, its shoulder rifle pointed at me. "Major Steed must be taken into custody at once."

"Don't come any closer," I said, and the tone of my voice was enough to make the Med hesitate. "Damon, take off your helmet. You've got to see what I see to make up your own mind."

He didn't answer.

"Damon . . ." I said. "Damon, it's all lies. We're killing innocent people. We're not—"

"Stop!" the Med cried. Curiously, the enemy had stopped firing, as if they knew something was happening. The Med started forward again. "Major Steed is uttering treasonous lies."

One pull of the trigger and I would be dead. The suits were strong, but I had chosen to take off my helmet, and the Med had it pointed right at my face. If I even made a movement of bringing up my finger lasers, I knew the Med would gun me down.

"Damon!" I shouted. "Take your helmet off! It's the only way you'll know! "

The Med turned and looked back at my brother. I waited for him to do something.

"Take him into custody," he said.

"Yes, sir," the Med replied.

My heart sank. So this is what I meant to him, I thought. I couldn't even get him to take the helmet off.

Rina died for nothing, and so would I.

But then, as the Med headed for me, I heard a blast. I jerked, thinking it was me that was hit, but then the Med went down. Even in the dim light, I could see the charred hole in its back. I looked up and saw my brother lowering his hand. The soldiers stood motionless, as if afraid to move.

"I had to get it to turn around," he said.

And then, without another word, he reached for his helmet.

THE LIST OF DEAD grows everyday. My father died protecting us. Rina died because she didn't want to live with a lie. My brother and I, we're still fighting, but it's no longer a certainty we'll win this war. We've joined the Resistance. When the soldiers of the LS-37 took off their helmets and saw what we saw, all of them joined us.

When we were on our way, Damon turned to me and asked, "Do you think Dad would approve?"

"If he knew what we know," I said.

Our father died fighting for something noble—liberating those who suffered under the tyranny of the Dulnari. There was no way I could know what he would do, but I *believe* he would not fight an unjust war. A war with no true enemy, only victims.

I believe that, knowing the truth, he would do as we have done.

I believe that he would throw off his helmet and fight—in daylight, in darkness—with his eyes open.

Tommy Top Hat

I DEBATED FOR A LONG TIME how to tell this story, or whether anybody would believe me if I did. It's obvious it will be read as fiction, even though it shouldn't be. And how do I tell a story whose ending is the beginning? Where do I start? I ultimately decided I *had* to tell it, because Tommy would want it told, because Tommy might think it would make a difference, and then it was obvious where I should start. I should start with Tommy.

I met him in Central Park on September 21, 2024, the same day I got canned from my job as a motorman for the Metropolitan Transportation Authority. The oaks and maples—the ones that hadn't burned during the April riots—were just starting to turn scarlet and gold. The weather the last few weeks had cooled, but that Saturday was the summer's last hurrah, balmy and bright, and kids in swimsuits were splashing around in the Giuliani Fountain. Tommy, a six foot four Native American with a wiry build and long, raven-black hair, was wading in the fountain with the kids.

Usually I wouldn't have given this scene a second look—you see a lot of strange things living in New York for ten years—if not for his clothes: he was dressed in a shiny black tuxedo and top hat.

I sat down on a metal bench at the edge of the concrete, placing my sweat-stained uniform jacket next to me. The smell of buttered popcorn from the boxy, robotic vendor across the way made my stomach grumble; it was nearly time for dinner, but I was too depressed to even think about eating.

My prospects of getting another job weren't good. I was fifty-two years old, bald except for fringes of silver hair, and the early onset of arthritis made my hands hurt most days. Who would hire me? On top of this, the unemployment rate was twenty percent, and the country was in the worst economic slump since the Great Depression. The situation with China over the inability to forge a new trade agreement had deteriorated badly in the past few weeks, and RadicalX, the underground dissident movement, wasn't helping by demanding (through anonymous letters posted on the Net) that new labor laws be put into place in both countries before any agreements were signed.

Smiling broadly, Tommy stepped out of the fountain, his pants soaked to the knees. As he loped away, his black loafers squished on the concrete, leaving wet footprints that quickly faded. I found him strangely compelling, but even then, I wouldn't have talked to him if not for one last thing: before he was out of sight, he stopped in front of two suspender-clad geezers sitting on a green park bench. I had seen these guys before. They sat in the same place day after day, wearing the same white t-shirts and plaid pants, and never once had I seen them smile.

Tommy took off his cap and did a little bow. The clothes suddenly made sense: he was a street performer.

The geezers' scowls deepened, and I thought, uh-oh, this guy's asking for trouble. But as Tommy did a routine—nothing fancy, just a disappearing feather trick—their scowls disappeared. By the time he finished with another bow, the geezers were grinning like little boys at the circus.

Even more incredible, one of the geezers reached for his wallet and pulled out a wrinkled ten-dollar bill.

Tommy, however, had already loped away.

That was what made me react.

Because long ago, back when I still lived in Oregon, before my wife and I divorced, before the kidnapping of our baby girl in a Portland mall, before the discovery of her wasted body in the woods near Mount Hood and the eventual capture, trial, and execution of her killer—in fact, much further back, thirty years almost, when I was still in college, I was something of a part-time street performer myself.

And to see another street performer walk away from a ten-dollar bill was unbearable.

I threw my uniform over my shoulder and jogged up to him. "Hey, man," I said. "Hold up."

He stopped and looked at me. I didn't know enough about Native Americans to guess whether he was Sioux, Cherokee, or something else altogether, but there was no mistaking his heritage. I couldn't say exactly *what* it was, but it had something to do with the wide mouth and thin lips, the reddish tint to the skin, and the coal-black hue of his hair.

Even when he wasn't smiling, he seemed to be, his eyes twinkling like shiny opals.

"Hello," he said.

"Yeah, hey," I said. "You didn't see that one of those guys wanted to give you money?"

We weren't far from hubbub of traffic, and the rumble of engines and the blare of car horns carried over the trees. The smell of freshly cut grass made my eyes water; my allergies had gotten worse over the years.

Finally, he smiled. "I don't need money. My name's Tommy. What's your name?"

He hadn't said much, but it was already enough to know that Tommy wasn't quite right in the head. He could have been anywhere from thirty to forty, it was hard to tell, but he spoke like a five year-old.

"Hey, Tommy," I said, smiling back at him. "Name's Kevin. Kevin Husby." I glanced around, wondering if there was somebody looking for him. "You here with somebody, Tommy?"

"No."

"Live close by, then?"

"No."

"Well, how'd you get here?"

He didn't answer. I figured he was just being coy, and that he would tell me if it suited him.

"You been doing street performing long?" I asked.

"I'm here to make people forget," he said.

"Well . . . yeah, I guess that's what all good street performers want to do. Make people forget about their little troubles and just enjoy being entertained."

He laughed. It was a strange laugh, like a cross between a hiccup and a giggle. "I'm here to change things," he said.

Now he wasn't making any sense. I was worn out from the events of the day, but I wasn't going to leave until I got at least one thing straightened out.

"Look," I said, "I used to do some street performing back in college. Just little stuff, card tricks, walnut shells, but it helped pay the bills. One thing I never did was walk away from a payout."

"What's a payout?"

I chuckled. "You know, the money." "But I don't need money."

"Doesn't matter. It's a crime to leave it. Here's what you do. When you're done, bow, hold out your hat, and say, 'Thank you for your kindness. Any small donation would be appreciated.'"

His permanent smile finally melted.

"Any small . . ." he began, trailing off.

The words were hard for him, but I refused to quit until he repeated the statement back to me. Still not satisfied he would do it, I asked him to perform for a woman and a little girl, both blond, I spotted having a picnic in the lush grass under a hickory tree. Dutifully, he marched over to them. They looked apprehensive as he approached, but the first thing he did, a cartwheel, got them both to laugh. His hat stayed on, a neat trick. He pulled a pair of roses out of his sleeves, handing one to each of them. Last, Tommy removed his hat and rolled it from the tip of one outstretched hand, across his shoulders, and right up to the other outstretched hand.

His audience clapped wildly. Tommy bowed. I waited for him to do as I asked, but instead, he turned and walked toward me.

No way I was letting him walk away from this one, especially when the woman was digging into her purse. I ran toward him, snatching his hat right off his head

"My dear ladies," I said, holding out the hat to them. "My partner would appreciate any small donation you could spare in appreciation for his little performance."

The little girl was still clapping. The woman, whose face practically glowed, tossed a twenty dollar bill in the cap.

"He's wonderful," she said. "Absolutely *wonderful.*"

I nodded to her, winked at the girl, and walked back to Tommy. The woman's reaction seemed odd. Tommy had talent, no doubt, but he wasn't *that* good.

"See how easy it is?" I said, handing him his hat.

He grimaced down at the twenty-dollar bill as if it was coated with acid.

"But I don't *need* any money," he said.

"Yeah, but they really want you to have it."

"But I don't—"

"Okay," I said, holding up a hand. "But what if I told you it makes people really, really happy to give it to you? Would that change your mind?"

His eyebrows furrowed and he pursed his lips. He picked up the bill, examined it, then looked at me suddenly. "Will it help people forget?"

"Sure," I said. "Yeah. Giving money helps people forget their troubles so they can . . . can . . . more easily remember the fun of watching you."

Tommy didn't seem entirely convinced, but he stuffed the bill into his jacket pocket.

* * * * *

SINCE I DIDN'T have anything planned that evening except a couple of microbrews and reruns of *The New Jeopardy*, the best way I knew to forget my troubles, I decided to stick with Tommy for a while. After watching him perform for a dozen groups, I became even more amazed at his ability to get people to offer up the cash. In just under two hours, he had pocketed over five hundred dollars.

Five hundred dollars . . . After taxes, that was nearly a week's pay.

Hell, even some of the vagrants, which were sprouting up all over the city these days, chipped in with a quarter or two. Half the time, Tommy forgot to collect, but I was always there to bail him out. The larger the crowd, the bigger the payday. His act seemed the typical stuff you get from any cut-rate magician, but you couldn't argue with his results.

It was only when the sky started to go pink that I realized how late it was getting. We were sitting on a park bench back at the Giuliani fountain. The kids were gone, as was most everyone else. After counting the bills, I handed him the wad of cash.

"Got to be going, pal," I said.

Frowning, he stuffed the money in his pocket. "Where?"

"Well, home, of course."

"Can I come?"

"Can you . . . you're serious?"

He nodded vigorously. I had thought he was toying with me earlier when he didn't tell me where he lived, but now I was beginning to wonder.

"You don't have a place to go?" I asked.

"No."

"Well, where were you before you came here?"

He stared at me. It was like looking at a mannequin. I would have asked him if he lived on the streets, but considering the newness of his tuxedo, it seemed unlikely. Perhaps he had wandered away from some sort of group home and was just confused. Maybe they were having a costume party.

It wouldn't have been right to leave him there in the park, especially with it getting dark.

"All right," I said, "you can stay with me until we figure out how to get you home."

His smile was the biggest one yet.

I HAD NOT DREAMED the mall-dream in months, but I dreamed it again that night. For the first time, the dream was different.

It started the same: I stood in front of a shelf filled with green and white shaving cream bottles, beneath me a blue tile floor. Above, hygiene products extended upwards, shelf upon shelf of toothpaste, q-tips, and tampons, hundreds, maybe thousands of shelves extending ever upwards, finally disappearing into the glare of fluorescent lights.

Then, as always, the terror seized me. I knew where I was—back in the Rite-Aid in Portland, Oregon's Clackamas Town Center. I knew what was happening—outside, somebody was stealing Tamara.

In real life, I wouldn't know about her kidnapping until Liz, pink-faced and breathless, found me twenty minutes after it happened. But here in the dream, I had a chance to save my baby.

I ran. There was no one else in the store. Just then, I heard a faint cry—Tamara. I needed to find an exit, but as I rounded the corner, I entered an isle identical to the first. No matter which way I turned, every isle was the same. The crying got louder.

I made an attempt to climb the shelves, the metal bowing against my weight. Four shelves . . . Ten . . . Twenty. I climbed so high the floor was like a thread below, but there was no end to the shelves.

The crying was gone.

"Tamara!" I cried, and jumped.

As I fell, everything became a blur—the shampoo, the fingernail polish, the hand lotion swirling yellow and pink and blue. This was usually when I woke, but not this time. I heard a flutter, and I turned to see giant raven, at least as large as me, plummeting with its wings tucked against its sides.

The raven opened its beak.

"The little angel is here to change things," it said. "The little angel will show us the way."

And then everything disappeared in a blinding flash of white light.

SOMEONE WAS shaking me. I opened my eyes to darkness, warm air blowing against my cheek from the whirring fan on the dresser. My t-shirt was soaked; I tasted sweat on my lips. It took a moment for my eyes to adjust to the green light cast from the neon sign shining through the cracks in the blinds. A human shape stood over me, dark except for in silhouette, and then I saw the long hair.

"Liz?" I said.

"No," Tommy said.

Then the events of the evening came back to me. Bringing Tommy home to my little flat in Queens. Calling the cops and finding they had no record of a missing person matching Tommy's description. Offering Tommy a microwave dinner and having him tell me he doesn't eat. Telling him he can sleep on my ratty, lime-green couch and him saying he doesn't sleep, either. And me, reading the want-ads until my eyes went bleary, wondering just what the hell I was going to do to pay the rent.

Blinking away the sleep in my eyes, I sat up on my elbows. "What is it?" I said.

"You were yelling," Tommy said.

"I was?"

"Yes. It hurt my ears."

"Sorry."

"S'okay . . . Kevin?"

"Yes, Tommy?"

"I need to make more people forget. Lots and lots of people."

I had realized by now that *making people forget* was his way of describing his performances. I was about to tell him I'd be happy to help after I got off work when I remembered that I wouldn't be going to work—which, in turn, made me realize that I was overlooking an employment opportunity right in front of me.

"Tommy," I said, "if I help you, can I manage the money for us?"

"Okay. I want you to help me, Kevin."

Just like that, I became Tommy's manager.

THE NEXT DAY, after grabbing a quick plate of eggs and pancakes at the diner on the corner, Tommy and I headed back to Central Park. Tommy didn't eat a thing, just sat there with a goofy grin on his face and watched me shovel it down. No food, no sleep—it was really beginning to bug me, but he looked as fresh and alert as the day before.

The temperature had dropped during the night, and a swell of dark clouds had moved in off the Hudson. I brought my rain slicker to be safe, and was glad I did, because it was drizzling before noon. I brought an extra for Tommy, but he refused to wear it.

Even with the rain, we still managed to haul in over a thousand dollars by the end of the day—all with nothing more than a few penny-ante tricks any kid could learn from a few hours with a magic book. Coins behind the ears. Red scarves transformed into fake roses. Making people's wristwatches and earrings appear in his hat.

By the end of the week, we had raked in over five thousand dollars. Two things became obvious. First, if I stuck with Tommy, I was going to become very rich; and second, Tommy was not a normal human being. He may not have been a human being at all. Despite my plea for him to eat something, or at least have some water, he never once did. He didn't go to the bathroom, he didn't change his clothes, and after a while I noticed that he didn't even *blink*. Through it all, he looked the same—cheerful, vibrant, and ready to please. Even his tuxedo, despite sun, rain, and constant use, continued to look brand new.

The last day of that first week, I found myself awake at three in the morning, and I went to find Tommy. He was sitting in the dark on the sofa, staring blankly at the opposite wall, his top hat on his lap. It was the way he passed every night. Only the dim light over the stove lit my way. When my footsteps made the floor creak, he looked at me.

"Kevin," he said.

"Don't get up," I said. "I need to know something. Maybe you can't tell me, but I need to ask . . . Are you . . . Tommy, are you some kind of angel?"

He shifted on the couch. I couldn't see his face in the darkness.

"I'm here to change things," he said.

"What things?"

"Just things."

"Dammit, Tommy, I need to know."

"Know what?"

"Know *what? Aargh*!" I threw up my hands and paced away, then whirled around. "I need to know what you are. What are you doing here? Where did you come from?"

Tommy was silent for a moment. "I'm here to make people forget," he said.

"But what does that mean?"

He didn't answer. Groaning, I stomped back to my room, slumping onto my bed. My hands were shaking. Truth was, I was scared—and it wasn't just Tommy. There was something else, something I couldn't explain, an itch at the edge of my mind that I couldn't scratch.

Part of me wanted to throw him out of the street, and the other part wanted to help him. I had long dreamed about heading back to the west coast, finding a cozy town on the beach and starting a little business—a kite shop, maybe, or a bookstore. After my daughter's death, I lost my drive to do just about anything, but here was an opportunity falling in my lap. It would be crazy to pass it up. Maybe Tommy could come with me. Maybe he would like that.

I was still trying to decide what to do when Tommy appeared in the doorway, his head now sporting his top hat.

"We need to leave tomorrow," he said. "We need to leave the city and go to other places."

I didn't even bother asking why. I just nodded, and realized, at that moment, I would go with him wherever he needed to go.

I HAD LIVED a quiet, gray existence for ten years, without friends of any kind, and so I didn't give leaving New York a second thought. In the span of a day, I sold all my stuff to a pawn shop at bargain basement prices (so long as they would take everything), gave my notice on the apartment, and bought a dinged-up '99 Ford Thunderbird with an interior that smelled of cigarettes. It drove like a luxury ocean liner and had the space in the cab to match, plus it was one of the gas-only models that was an environmentalist's nightmare. But it would do.

By six o'clock that evening, Tommy and I were heading west over the Hudson River, a couple of stuffed suitcases all I had to show for my decade in New York—that and the eight thousand dollars hidden in the spare tire, five of which I made in the last week. My goal was to make a hundred grand. That would be enough to get us started in business, I figured.

We left the city at the right time. As we headed out on I-280, I heard on the radio that a new wave of protests broke out that day, the biggest one happening in New York. A non-violent march down Fifth Avenue got ugly: bricks through windows, pipe bombs in mail boxes, and another set of fires in Central Park. RadicalX sent emails to all the media outlets that they claimed no responsibility for the violence, but everyone knew they were often the instigators in such situations.

Maybe because of these events, people seemed even happier to see us. Over the next two weeks, we made a grand in Cleveland, drifted down to Indianapolis and on to Springfield, Illinois. The skies stayed sunny. Tommy performed in shopping malls, university campuses, national parks, and even rest stops. While the riots spread from New York to many other cities, and the National Guard was brought in to quell the disturbances, the money in the trunk grew exponentially. By the time we rolled into Chicago, we had fifty thousand dollars.

That was also when I noticed a change in Tommy. When we

stepped out of the car on the south shores of Lake Michigan, intent on making a few quick bucks from the people strolling through Burnham Park, Tommy tilted back on his heels and then steadied himself with a hand on the roof. The strong wind off the lake blew off his hat, but he made no attempt to retrieve it.

I chased down his hat. When I returned to the car, he was still leaning against the roof, his eyes closed. His face also looked slightly gray, as if the color had drained out of his cheeks.

"You okay, man?" I asked.

"Dizzy," he said.

I still figured it had something to do with his not eating a blasted thing, but I didn't say it. I knew he would just tell me he wasn't hungry.

"Why don't we take a break?" I said. "Skip this one. Maybe go watch some television, huh? "

He shook his head and leaned away from the car. "I want to make people forget."

"But Tommy, maybe some rest—"

"No," he said, taking the hat from me.

He placed it squarely on his head—how it stayed on in the wind, I couldn't say—and headed down to the sidewalks along the lake. A few minutes later, while performing some hat tricks for some girl scouts, he seemed back to his old energetic self. Still, as soon as the sun started to slip behind the jagged horizon, I told him we should go find a hotel. He had just finished his act and the crowd was dispersing.

"But I want to make more people forget," Tommy said.

"And you should," a man said.

I turned and laid eyes on a short, round-faced fellow in a tan blazer. He sported a white handlebar mustache and thick white eyebrows, but otherwise, his deeply tanned head was bald.

"Tommy," I said, "I think the man wants to make a donation."

Eyes twinkling, the man chuckled and stuck out his hand to Tommy. "Not a donation," he said. "An offer. Name's Harold Ripton, son. And you are . . . ?"

Tommy smiled and pumped Ripton's hand. "My name's Tommy."

"Yes, I gathered that, but your last name?"

"Just Tommy," Tommy said.

I figured Tommy would say that. I had been trying to get a last name out of him since I met him to no avail.

Ripton scratched his chin. "Hmm. That won't work. You need some kind of unique moniker. How about Tommy Top Hat?" He made a sweeping flourish with his hand. "Ladies and gentlemen, I give you *The Amazing Tommy Top Hat!*"

Tommy clapped his hands and laughed.

"Where is this going?" I asked. "I'm his manager by the way. Kevin Husby."

Ripton looked at me. "Ah, I see. Well, your friend here is absolutely terrific, and believe me when I tell you, I've seen a lot of acts. I'm the manager for Michael Van Michaels, and I'm looking for an opening act for a show he's doing in Vegas in a week. The fire breather we were going to use came down with the measles. Can you believe that? The measles, in this day and age."

I blinked in disbelief. Michael Van Michaels was the world's most renowned stage magician, performing to packed theatres wherever he went. This guy thought Tommy should open for him?

"I'm sorry," I said. "Are you saying . . . ?"

"God, I'm glad I came down to the lakefront," Ripton said. "Was in town visiting my mother and thought it would be a good night for a stroll. So what do you say? You interested? Pay you twenty-five grand, and if we like you, we'll contract with you for other shows. Did I mention it will be broadcast live?"

It seemed too good to be true. "You've seen Tommy for, what, ten minutes, and you're saying you want him to open for Michael Van Michaels?"

Ripton wore the same dreamy-eyed expression that just about everyone wore after seeing Tommy perform.

"I don't need to see any more," Ripton said. "I can write up a contract back at my car. All you have to do is sign."

I shook my head. It must have been a scam.

"I don't think so," I said. "Come on, Tommy."

I took a few steps, but Tommy didn't move.

"Will lots of people see us?" he asked.

"Tommy—" I began.

"Oh yes," Ripton said. "Millions, and not just here in the States. This is being promoted heavily all over the world. Michaels has built up quite a following, you know."

"Okay," Tommy said. "I want to do it."

I pulled him aside and argued with him, telling him there was no way it could be legit, but Tommy wouldn't budge. In the end, we ended up signing on the hood of Ripton's Cadillac rental, and I had to admit that the contract looked real enough.

No matter how I tried to convince myself, though, I didn't have a good feeling about it.

THAT NIGHT, I dreamed the mall-dream again.

"The little angel is here to change things," the raven said. "The little angle will show us the way."

This time, before the white light enveloped everything, the raven burst into flames.

THE NEXT MORNING we were back on the blacktop, cruising down I-55 to St. Louis. There was no reason, I thought, not to make some money on our way to Nevada. A mall in Kansas City . . . the capitol in Topeka . . . a park in Burlington . . . We made money everywhere, but it was getting harder to find safe places to go. There were protests breaking out all over, and not just in the big cities. I listened to the radio intently, trying to avoid any hot spots, but the country was coming apart at the seams. When Tommy was performing in downtown Denver, a riot even started right around us.

"Jobs for Americans!"

"A new minimum wage!"

"Take back the country from the rich!"

I didn't think things could get any worse, but then, as we were finally heading down I-15 into the desert wasteland outside of Vegas, it did. We heard on the news that RadicalX, in an elaborately planned operation, had taken over a missile silo in Alaska. They were demanding new trade agreements be signed with all countries or they were going to fire at China. A debilitating computer virus had paralyzed much of the U.S.'s military infrastructure, and to make matters worse, the nuclear missile was one of the new ones, outfitted with lasers capable of destroying anything that tried to stop it. Despite this, China, believing it was all an elaborate ruse to give the U.S. an excuse to attack them, said they would launch their whole arsenal at us if provoked.

On top of this, Tommy had started to look ill again, his face ashy, his lips dry and cracked. This was nuts. There was no need to go to Vegas. We had eighty grand now, more than enough to get a fresh start.

At the city limits, I pulled the car over to the side of the road, cars buzzing by doing eighty.

"We don't have to do the show," I said. "We can just head up Highway 95 until we get to Oregon. Wait until all this craziness ends. We could—"

"No," Tommy said, his voice now hoarse. "No, we need to go make lots of people forget."

"Why?"

"I need to change things."

"What things? What are you changing, Tommy? Is something bad going to happen? Is it this missile thing in Alaska? What can you possibly do to change that?"

He didn't answer, and I gave up arguing. I was hoping the show would be canceled because of the crisis, but when we got to the Golden Tower and met Harold Ripton by the fountain in the decadent lobby, he clapped us both on the back and said he would show us to the green room.

"The show's still going on?" I asked.

"Of course!" Ripton said. "It's possible we might get preempted, but it will all blow over, I'm sure—and think of all the people watching! Everyone wants a distraction right now."

Before I could argue, we were ushered down a plush purple hallway, back through a narrow concrete hall, and into a rose-smelling room full of fuzzy white sofas and mirrors. Michael Van Michaels, a suave, bronze-skinned man in a white, skin-tight suit, nodded at us, said not a word, and headed out with Ripton.

Tommy slumped onto one of the couches. He was so white now I would have thought him a corpse if not for his piercing eyes.

"We could go right now," I said to him. "We don't have to do this. Really."

Tommy shook his head. We sat in silence for a half hour, and then, for the first time since I had known him, Tommy closed his eyes. I thought he might be dying. I slapped his hand and he didn't budge. I shook him, saying his name over and over, but he remained still. I was about to run for help when a lady dressed in peacock feathers and little else burst into the room and shouted, "Curtain!"

It was as if she had plugged Tommy into an outlet; his eyes flickered open and he bolted to his feet. He walked quickly through the narrow hall, past a pacing Michael Van Michaels, and straight out into the bright lights of the stage. A gravelly-voiced announcer cried, "The Amazing Tommy Top Hat!" Thousands of people had packed the theatre; the murmur died as soon as Tommy came into view. Four different cameras pointed at him. I hid behind the purple curtain and watched him launch into his act.

I expected the same shtick he had been doing for weeks, but this time he just opened his arms.

And did nothing.

He stood like that for maybe twenty seconds. Some hissing broke out, and then some boos. I was about to go grab Tommy, thinking it was going to get ugly in a few seconds, when someone screamed from one of the back rows.

"The crazies fired a missile at China, and they just fired back! There's one coming right for us!"

Pandemonium broke out; screams, people crashing over one another, and amidst it all, Tommy slumped to the floor. I weaved my way through the fleeing stagehands and bent down to him. He looked at me through partially open eyelids, his cheeks bone-white. While the people fled in terror, I sat there on my knees and cradled his head in my lap.

"Is this what you were here to change?" I asked him.

He nodded.

"I'm sorry," I said.

He shook his head. "No. No, Kevin. I changed things. I made enough people forget and now things will be different."

His eyes closed. Thirty minutes later, when the missile hit, and my life disappeared in a blinding flash of white light, I was still holding him.

I DON'T KNOW how this story ends, but I can tell you how it begins.

One moment you're facing oblivion, and the next moment you're standing in front of a shelf full of shaving cream and plastic razors, someone announcing over the intercom that toilet paper is on sale.

The first thought that crossed my mind was that I was in hell, doomed to repeat the same awful dream that had plagued me the last twenty years. But there was a crispness to the world around me that wasn't there in my dream—the shelves had dust on them, the blue tile floor had scuff marks, the air smelled sterile—which made me realize it wasn't a dream. And it wasn't hell.

It was a second chance.

I bolted out of the store into the bright sunlight, and saw the greasy-haired man in the green nylon jacket pushing our stroller across the black asphalt. I screamed. He froze for a second, then left the stroller and bolted for his emerald Ford Van, a van I recognized from the pictures I had seen at the trial. I pursued for a few steps, then let him go. I knew how to find him.

I returned to the stroller. Tamara looked up at me with her sparkling hazel eyes, and I seized her up in my arms, pressing my lips against her black hair. There were tears streaming down my cheeks. She was so warm, so real. Liz was there a few seconds later, and she was crying, too.

"Oh God, I'm sorry," she said, hugging us both. "I turned away just for a minute . . . and I almost lost her. I almost lost our little angel."

Shatterboy

The day her husband of thirty-six years filed for divorce, Rebecca Wilson found the glass boy at the recycling transfer station on the corner of 25th and Jefferson.

He was there at the back of the bin marked GLASS ONLY, his translucent body swathed in saran wrap and couched in a bed of foil. A ring of root beer bottles surrounded him like perfectly-shaped stalagmites. If it hadn't been for the pen light in her mouth, casting a narrow beam on ten agate-like toes, she surely would have missed him. Later, she would thank her lucky stars she had the presence of mind—after getting off the phone with her husband's lawyer—to grab her purse on her way out the door. Her cheeks puffy and stinging, and dressed only in the green terrycloth robe, she had driven aimlessly for hours. The clinking from the back seat made her remember—oh, yes, need to drop off the recycling, need to get that done right now—and she had driven straight to the transfer station.

Now, standing there with her slippers steeped in a puddle of gasoline, a wet breeze on her legs, she pushed her paper sack of bottles aside. Her first thought, with what little she could see, was that it was some kind of collectible doll. Braving the scent of stale beer and the stickiness of pop bottles, she leaned against the wood panel and reached for the glass toes.

They moved.

It wasn't much, just a wiggle, but it was so unexpected that she lurched back. She shined her pen light deeper into the bin. The feet, and the legs to which they were attached, were definitely moving. She saw glass arms rise above the root beer bottles and glass fingers grasp at the air.

It giggled. It was a giggle as real as any baby giggle. It was so real her apprehension slipped away, and she lunged into the bin and pulled out the lump of foil. It felt no heavier than the foil itself. Shining her light on it, she saw that was indeed a boy made entirely of glass—a boy that cooed when she touched her forefinger to his smooth, cool belly.

His body was as clear as an empty fishbowl. She saw the bulges her fingers made in the foil beneath. He reached for her, arms swinging up like those of a marionette, and when his fingers came together they clinked like champagne glasses coming together in a toast.

She took him home.

Fifty-four, childless, and so lonely in her condominium the last eight months she had long conversations with her great-grandmother's teak clock, Mrs. Rebecca Wilson took the appearance of the glass boy as a gift for the many years she suffered with Don, her husband. The night Don moved out, he frankly admitted he cared more about Arnold Palmer and Tiger Woods and every golfer in between than he had ever cared about her. Still, if it hadn't been for his insistence on drinking beer out of glass instead of aluminum, she never would have found the glass boy. In a way, Don had given her this child.

She retrieved the oversized crib from the attic she had inherited from her mother, dusted off the thin mattress, and placed the boy inside. That first night she did not sleep, instead sitting wrapped in a wool shawl in her rocker, watching how the orange nightlight made his skin glow.

In the morning, he had grown, and he was as tall as a two-year old.

He walked. His knees did not bend so he walked about as if on stilts. He loved to stand in the sunlight and watch the motes of dust float through his own body. His murmuring and babbling shaped into words.

"Mom!" he said, pointing at her.

The third day, he was as big as a four-year old, and they played hide and seek. The boy always won because she could look right past him and not see him standing there in front of the lavender curtains.

The day after that, he learned that instead of lurching through the house, he could glide over the carpet and the vinyl like an Olympian figure skater, and was so beautiful when he did that it left her speechless.

On the fifth day, the boy came to understand that other children his age did not stay home all day, but instead went to school.

"Why can't I go to school, Mom?" he asked.

"Oh, my sweet boy," Rebecca said, hugging him gently. "Oh, I would let you go, I would—but you see, you are made of glass. "

To anyone else, the boy's face would have been impossible to read, but Rebecca was attuned to the subtle changes, the way the glass tinted every so slightly.

"Please don't be sad," she said. "Please, it will make me cry."

"But I want to go to school, Mom," he said. "I want to play with other kids. What does being made of glass have to do with it?"

Because she loved the boy, because she wanted to make an impression on him that would last, she went to the cupboard and pulled out one of her most precious wine goblets.

"This is why," she said, and dropped it.

She could not be sure if the boy screamed after the glass shattered or in anticipation of it, but both sounds filled her ears at once. The shards skittered across the floor. The boy looked at her, horror stricken, then ran out of the room. As she swept up the remains of the goblet, she hated herself for making him feel that way, but she knew she had to keep him with her, where he was safe, where he was loved.

On the fifth day, he was more the size of a man, and too self-conscious to run around the house naked, so she rolled up her husband's old shirts and pants and let him wear those.

Coming into the room, she expected to see him sitting in the rocker, but he wasn't there. She called his name and there was no answer. She ran through the house and all the rooms were empty. When she passed the front door, she saw a note taped to it, a note written in his jagged penmanship, all straight lines and no curves:

MOM, WENT TO THE PARK TO PLAY WITH OTHER KIDS. DON'T WORRY. BE HOME SOON.

When she got there, she saw him in his oversized clothes atop the jungle gym. At first glance it looked like the clothes stood there by themselves, the orange and red leaves of the oaks behind him clearly visible through his head and arms. The other children, at least a dozen of them, had him surrounded. They were shaking the jungle gym, and her boy was clinging to the top.

Climbing out of the car, she heard them chanting.

"Shatterboy! Shatterboy! Shatterboy!"

She was going to shout, but before she could summon the words, he looked up. He saw her. He raised a hand, either a wave or a call for help, and when he did he lost his balance. Like the wine goblet she once dropped for him, he fell swift and straight. Her slim hope that he would be fine, that the bark chips were not as hard as they looked, shattered just as his body shattered into a dozen pieces.

The children scattered. She went to the pile, walking in a daze, and gathered up the broken pieces in her sweater. She took him home. She placed the pieces in the middle of her living room floor, her body shaking, and settled into the rocker. Her whole life stretched out before her, dark and unknown.

After only a few minutes, the shards trembled. They stirred, they slid, they moved together. There was a snapping and a dinging and a ringing and then it was all together—connected, totally whole, no seams or scars or signs of his accident. He rose unsteadily to his feet, her glass boy, almost a glass man.

"A miracle," she said.

She didn't know if it was pity or sadness she saw. He put his hand on her shoulder and stood there, a tall, gleaming, beautiful young man, then strode to the door. It had been left open, and the gray clouds in the gray sky shuttled through his body.

"I love you, Mother," he said.

"Don't go!" she said. "Please, I didn't know this would happen. I did it for you. I wanted to protect you. I wanted—"

He came back to her and silenced her with his smooth finger, and it was like the mouth of a wine bottle pressed against her lips. He turned and walked out and left her there in the rocking chair. She sat there long after he had gone, shaking, quivering, and somewhere nearby, somewhere close, hearing the sound of breaking glass.

It was only a moment before she realized that it was her own heart.

Heart of Stone

SHE HAD BEEN with Thomas a year when he told her he might be able to see again.

"It's a new procedure," he said, touching her hand across the glass table. "They can repair my retinas with lasers."

His rough, deeply tanned hands engulfed her tiny pale ones. They were alone in her sanctuary, as they always were when they were together, sitting at the table in the rotunda that overlooked the ocean. The windows, ceiling, and floor of the alcove were all tinted glass; on the other side, they were mirrors to keep out prying eyes. The half-eaten roast chicken sat between them, steam still rising from the meat. Mozart played faintly from the speakers in the other room.

Madeline heard the excitement in his voice, saw the hope on his rugged face, and felt her body go cold. She had never seen him look this way—small and afraid, like a little boy. This was not the man she had chosen, a fearless adventurer who had never let blindness stop him from enjoying life. He had raced sled dogs in the Alaskan Iditarod. He had climbed Mount Everest with a single guide, one who had not been trained to work with the blind. He had founded a multimillion dollar company by creating a revolutionary breakthrough in voice controlled computer interfaces.

"What is it?" he asked.

She pulled her fingers away. "You know what I am," she said, looking out through the windows. A seagull swooped over the rippling ocean waves, and far out on the horizon, a catamaran's yellow sail fluttered. "You know that if you do this, you'll never be able to see me again."

And while she spoke, the serpents on her head hissed and snapped at the empty air, as they always did when she was angry.

It was five thousand years before she decided to see if it was possible for someone to love her.

It was to be an experiment on her part, nothing more. Madeline knew she was the ugliest thing any living creature could ever look upon. It was not always so, but it had been that way for so long she could no longer remember what it felt like *not* to be ugly. At one time, she knew this bothered her, but she could not remember this either. She had accepted her ugliness, and her acceptance had given her strength. Rather than rage endlessly against the gap-toothed shaman who had doomed her because of her vanity, she had quickly focused her energy into accomplishing all that she could despite her limitations.

In the age of the Egyptian Pharaohs, she had made her living as a veiled fortune teller, never revealing an inch of her body. In the days of the Greeks, she had put bread on the table by working as a prostitute, never walking into her bedchamber until a man was blindfolded. In the Middle Ages, she had been a thief, wrapping her face in silk scarves, and only robbing houses and manors she knew to be empty. She tried not to turn anyone to stone, not because she cared one way or the other what happened to them, but only because it always brought a lot of unwanted attention.

Sometimes unwanted attention had spawned legends. Myths. Stories passed down through time. They could malign her all they wanted, it did not matter because it did not affect her own happiness. They had given her the name Medusa, among others, but she had always chosen her own based on the time.

And now she lived as Madeline Hogart, making her living as a stock investor, of all things, in a custom-designed mansion on a cliff that overlooked the Pacific Ocean. She liked this life the best, because it had made her richer than even a Pharaoh could have dreamed. Though she had no contact with people, living in the mirrorless interior of her mansion, with her army of servants giving her what she needed by carefully orchestrated transactions, she was content. A phone and Internet connection were all she needed to conduct her business.

She played the piano. She painted watercolors. She read all the world's great literature, always in the original language. And it was only after many decades that she began to wonder if someone could love her.

It was a challenge, and she had grown hungry for one.

THE DINNER was growing cold. Madeline looked at the ocean, thinking of all the hours she had wasted online searching for just the right man to lure into her bed. Even through the tinted glass, the glare on the dark blue water was so strong she had to squint.

It had taken two years to find Thomas. In the end it had not been in a support group for blind people, where she had first looked, but in a forum for windsurfers. It had taken another year of emails and phone calls until she was ready for him to meet her in person. There had still been a risk, of course, but she had played him well. When his hands found the snakes, he had recoiled at first, but it had not taken him long to overcome that initial reaction. She had to turn a few grasshoppers to stone for him to believe the rest of her story, but then he loved her even more. She had counted on that being the case. She knew that what he prized above all in a woman was her individuality, and no one could say she was not unique.

She looked at Thomas. He put down his silverware, and sat there with his hands clasped.

"Don't you love me?" she asked.

"Of course," he said, "you know that. Don't you want me to see?"

She hesitated. What was the right response? Everything she said to him was carefully calculated, designed to get him to love her. Honesty was never one of her talents, nor had she ever seen it as a necessity. "I want you to stay with me," she said.

"That's not up for debate," he said.

She pushed away from the table and stood, turning to face the window. Here was the ultimate test of his love. If it came down to a choice between her and his sight, what would he do?

"You know that's not true," she said. "You know what you'll become if you see me."

She allowed her voice to break at the end. It had the desired effect. She heard his chair scoot along the floor, heard him step up behind her, felt his heavy hands on her slim shoulders. He kissed her neck, and the snakes quieted.

"I love you more than anything," he said, "but you've got to understand, I've wanted this my entire life."

"But haven't you been happy as a blind person?"

His fingers bit into her shoulders. He felt his breath on her neck as he leaned forward.

"Of course!" he said. "I would not accept anything less. But this . . . this is sight! I want to be able to see the color of the sky. I want to see the mountains I have scaled. I want to look at the face of the woman I love and see her with eyes rather than my hands."

She let a tear fall, and then feigned a shuddering breath. "It will kill you."

"That won't happen to me," he said. "I love you too much. My love will overcome the curse."

"That's foolish sentimentalism. He turned her around to face him. His blue eyes, glassy and faded, looked beyond her, but they were filled with determination.

"No, it's not. I believe that is the way around your curse. If I love you enough, I won't turn to stone."

IN THE END, she could not dissuade him. She would not beg. That would render her experiment worthless. It was seven weeks before he had received enough training to be able to return home. She allowed a servant to let him into her sanctuary, while she waited on the white leather couch. The room was dark except for the flickering light of the fire, her overhead lights programmed to fade as the sun went down. She could not risk seeing her reflection in the windows.

When she heard the clicking of his cane on her marble floor just around the corner, she raised the hood of her black cloak.

"Madeline?" he said.

"Did it work?" she asked.

"Yes. It's amazing."

"But you're still using a cane."

"For a time, yes," he said. "My mind is still making sense of what it sees. Turn around. Face me."

She knew this moment was coming, and she had debated for a long time what to do. It was his choice, after all, and deep down inside she did hope he was right. Perhaps love would be enough to end the curse. She just needed to give him one more opportunity to walk away. One more opportunity to prove his love for her was genuine and deep.

"No," she said. "You need to leave now. I don't want to hurt you."

"I will not leave."

That was it. She had done all she could. Keeping her head bowed, she rose from the couch and turned to face him. Then, all at once, she lifted her head and threw off the hood. She felt the snakes stretch out briefly, then recoil at the sight of Thomas.

He inhaled sharply. His eyes, eyes that were no longer glazed and white, widened. His face contorted, his mouth shaping into a scream. But the sound never came. His body froze, all the color slipping away, a silent grayness starting at his eyes and spreading outward, down his neck and over his body, until all the flesh and clothing had been replaced by stone.

IT TOOK a great deal of her resources to arrange his disappearance, but she was confident that she had left no clues. The story was that he had gone windsurfing with some friends, fallen off and drowned. She paid a good deal of money to make sure there were witnesses who said this was so.

Knowing now that love was not enough, that it would never end her curse, she resigned to live the rest of eternity alone. She did not doubt Thomas loved her, so there was no point in duplicating the experiment.

But something unexpected happened.

Her breasts became tender and swollen, and her areolas darkened. She felt nauseous all the time. She was frequently tired. It wasn't until her belly began to bulge that she realized what was happening. Her first instinct was to get rid of it, but then she realized that here was another experience. Even if she brought it to term, it was likely the child would turn to stone once leaving her womb, but Madeline would still have the experience of childbirth. She would have to do it alone. It was a challenge that excited her.

She mastered it as she had mastered everything before, and then the day came when a child's cry broke the stillness of her sanctuary. Madeline lay naked on the floor in her bedroom, three layers of white satin sheets protecting her Persian rug. The pain was nothing—when you had lived five millennia, you had lived through far worse—and when it was over, she felt euphoric. For once, the snakes on her head were still.

She had not expected the child to even cry. She sat up, scooping the thing out of the mess of blood and other fluids that had soaked her sheets. It was a girl, and she had her father's looks—a few locks of curly chestnut hair, bright blue eyes, an olive complexion. Even now, wailing, she was beautiful.

Madeline waited for the change to come, but it never did. Flesh remained flesh. The baby went on crying.

"My, you do have lungs, don't you?" she said to it.

Then it occurred to her—of course, her father had been born blind. Maybe it was genetic. This girl might be blind, too.

If the babe was blind, Madeline could raise it for a time, see what it was like to have a child. It was something else to experience. And when she grew tired of the endeavor, she would give it up for adoption.

Madeline never expected to keep the baby. She turned out to be quite colicky, crying constantly, sleeping only in fits. After a month, Madeline was exhausted. Plus she was having a hard time keeping up with the markets, and she could not allow for any slippage. It had taken years of prudent buying and selling, and more years for the miracle of compound interest to work in her favor, for her to get to this point. She wasn't going to piss it all away because of another foolish experiment.

But a strange thing happened. Any time she thought about arranging for an underground adoption, she became short of breath. If she tried to imagine what life would be like without the babe, it wasn't long before she was in the bathroom throwing up. Even when she debated about arranging for a nanny to help her out a day or two a week, she felt queasy.

These reactions mystified her, and she kept putting off the day when Kali (she eventually had to give her a name, just for convenience) would leave for another month or two just to keep it out of her mind. Another month or two turned into another year or two, and soon giving Kali up didn't occur to her at all.

Kali was a beautiful, normal human child in all respects, and thankfully, it wasn't long before she had grown out of her colicky stage. Raising a blind child was hard enough as it was. Madeline relished all of the experiences of motherhood—breastfeeding, bathing, singing the child to sleep. Soon Kali was eating solid foods and smiling with delight. Next she was crawling, then walking, then attempting to mimic her mother's words.

The years passed quickly, much faster than any years Madeline had lived. She taught Madeline to read brail, to think deeply, to be strong as every modern woman needed to be—especially one who was blind. She home schooled her for as long as she could, but she knew for Kali to live a full and happy live (and that was what Madeline wished for her, above all else) she would need to experience the world in ways Madeline couldn't. She had already made certain that Kali didn't have her mother's curse, performing a few experiments with some goldfish, and so when the time came to put Kali in first grade, Madeline reluctantly did so.

But from the moment Kali left in the morning to the moment she returned in the afternoon, Madeline worried. There was so much that could go wrong in the world, so much that could hurt her. She was, after all, only an ordinary human being. Yet somehow Kali avoided all of life's pitfalls, except a few scrapes and bruises, and grew tall and beautiful.

There was only one last great pitfall left, and Madeline had been dreading its coming. Kali was fourteen when the moment finally arrived.

"There's this operation, mother," Kali said.

Of all the ironies—they were sitting in that same alcove where she and Thomas had sat when he had made his own announcement. Instead of dinner, though, Kali had been working her way through *The Great Gatsby* in brail. Madeline had been reading the Wall Street Journal. The sun had vanished under the sea, but the sky was still awash with crimson and golden light.

"What do you mean?" There was a quiver in Madeline's voice, and this time she was not faking it.

"You know what I mean," Kali said. "My father had the operation. You never told me about it."

Madeline swallowed. Kali had never learned the need to mask her emotions, and her face had darkened with a scowl.

"How did you find out?"

"I'm not dumb, mother. I did some checking. I also have friends at school who know how to get to records and stuff."

"I see."

"Why didn't you tell me? Why didn't you tell me there was a chance I could see? Don't you want me to see? Don't you want me to have a good life? Why, mother?"

Madeline put down the paper. There were so many ways to reply. What could she say that would not jeopardize her daughter's love? She could not bear the thought of her daughter not loving her.

She rose from the table. "Come with me."

"Where?" Kali said.

"Just come. I have to show you something."

Sighing, Kali stood and allowed her mother to guide her into the recesses of the mansion. They went down one flight of stairs, then another, until they came to a locked door. The air was cool and damp.

"You've never taken me here before," Kali said.

"I've never had a need," Madeline said.

Madeline unlocked the door and led her daughter into the basement, brushing the cobwebs out of their path. The air was stale and smelled of mold. The floor was soft dirt, the walls concrete. She flicked on the single hanging light bulb. There, in the center of the room, the only thing in the room, was a statue of a screaming man.

Thomas.

Madeline guided her daughter's hands, placing one hand on each cheek. At first touch, Kali yelped and jumped back.

"What is that? It felt like . . . like . . ."

"He is your father," Madeline said.

She felt no need for subtlety. It was the blunt shock of reality that Madeline hoped would do the trick. Kali had known since she was old enough to keep a secret about her mother's curse. The truth, as it turned out, was the easiest way to explain her mother's peculiar nature.

Kali swallowed hard. "My fa . . . But you said, you told me—"

"I told you he drowned at sea because I didn't want to upset you. But this is the truth. He had the same operation you want to have. I told him if he did he would have to leave, that he would never be able to see me again, but he didn't listen. This is what happened to him."

Kali was silent for a long time. Looking at her in the dim light, Madeline was struck by how much Kali looked like her father. She certainly acted like him—fearless to the point of foolishness, strong willed to the point of stubbornness. So it came as no surprise when Madeline heard echoes of Thomas in what Kali said next.

"That won't happen to me," she said. "I don't believe it. I love you too much for that. I love you even though you lied to me. My love is stronger than your curse. It can't turn me to stone. It *can't.*"

"You're wrong," Madeline said. "It's all happened before."

"Not to me," Kali said, shaking her head fiercely. "Not to me."

"You'll have to leave. You'll never . . . never . . . "

"No, mother."

" . . . be able to return."

Madeline was now on the ground, hugging her knees. What was happening to her? The world felt like it was collapsing, a tunnel of darkness swallowing her whole. Her snakes were wrapped so tightly around her head that it felt as if they were about to crush it. Was this the rapture she often wondered if she would live to see?

Then she felt Kali's arms wrapping around her, tightening, pulling her into the warmth of her embrace.

"No, mother," Kali whispered. "I will never leave you. *Never.*"

THIS TIME Madeline *did* beg. She pleaded. She cried. She wailed for her daughter to not go through with it. Kali had her own money, an account she had created herself for her unspent allowance, and there was nothing Madeline could do to stop her.

Kali was too much like her father. Once she had set her mind on something, nothing would detour her. And that was the problem.

Madeline worried about what would happen when her daughter was well enough to leave the hospital. She would want to come to her mother, of course. Madeline couldn't let that happen. She wanted Kali to live a long and full life, as long and full as any mortal's could ever be, and even the possibility that she might someday look upon her mother's face was too much for Madeline to bear.

She would have to run. She would have to find a place where her daughter could never find her.

Eventually, however, Madeline realized that there was still risk in running. She had raised her daughter too well. She was smart and resourceful. No matter where Madeline hid, there was a good chance Kali would find her.

So it was not enough to hide. Madeline would have to cease to be.

The thought of her own death had always greatly terrified her. There were times when the sheer hopelessness of her existence made her contemplate suicide, but she had always been too much of a coward to go through with it. But now she had no other choice. Still, it took her weeks to summon her courage, and it was not until she received a phone call from Kali, announcing her arrival that afternoon, that Madeline found the will to act.

She dressed in the same black cloak she had worn the day Thomas had come home from the hospital. She kept the hood up and her head bent low as she made her way across the sand toward her little rowboat. The noon sun blazed high overhead, and the breeze was still. She climbed into the boat and began to row. The current was strong and she had to work hard. It wasn't long before she was sweating profusely, but she refused to rest. Kali could be home at any moment.

Twenty minutes later, she finally stopped and allowed herself to look up. The shore was a jagged line of green and brown, the sky above it the most intense color of blue she had ever seen. She wondered if Kali was looking at the sky right now. She wondered what she thought of it.

While she was looking, a seagull swooped in front of her, glanced in her direction, then turned to stone and plummeted into the ocean's depths.

The cold splash of the water on her face was a stark reminder of what she had to do.

It was simple, really. She was going to look over the bow into the reflection in the water. When she saw her own face, and turned to stone, her own added weight would carry her forward. She would sink fast and deep. This was what she wanted. There was a chance that her body, even as stone, would still go on turning other creatures to stone who looked upon it, so she had to end up where no one would find her. But the longer she sat there, the harder it became to go through with it. She would not live to see Kali grow up. To see her go to college. Get married. Travel the world. Have a child. Or none of that and something else entirely. Something only Kali herself could dream.

The rowboat bobbed up and down, and the sun felt hot on top of her head. She didn't think she had been there long, but suddenly she heard a voice calling out to her.

"Mother!"

It was Kali. The boat had drifted slowly around, and Madeline had her back to the shore. She forced herself not to turn. She knew Kali was a strong rower and would be here in seconds.

"Mother! Don't!"

Closer now. But Madeline had finally found her courage.

She leaned over the side and looked down into the water.

She saw the bone-white skin, the oily heads of the snakes peeking out of her hood, the gaping shadows of her eyes . . . but something was wrong. The water was rippling. The image wasn't clear, and she didn't change into stone.

But her quick movement still tilted her off-balance.

She plunged into the cold saltwater, taking it into her mouth and into her nose. She had never learned to swim, never had a reason to, and she flailed about, gasping for air, constantly sinking under the surface. Her cloak, weighted by water, hung on her like a suit of chain mail. Then it occurred to her that this might also save her daughter. Perhaps she would die, or perhaps not, but maybe she would sink deep into the ocean and live out eternity.

She stopped struggling and started to sink.

Before she had gone far, a pair of hands closed about her waist and pulled her upward. She struggled, but soon they both broke the surface of the water, each of them gasping for air. After some amount of effort, Kali had pulled her mother into the rowboat.

Madeline's hood had fallen away, exposing her.

"No!" she cried, covering her face. "No! Turn away! Turn away quickly."

"Mother, look at me."

"No!"

Madeline felt her daughter's hands grip tightly to her wrists and yank her hands away from her face. Fearing the worst, she looked at her daughter. Kali was squinting so hard her eyes were tiny slits, but Madeline could still see a hint of blue in there. She kept waiting for the change to come, for the horrible crunch of flesh turning into stone, but it didn't. The sun was bright at her daughter's back.

"I'm still here," Madeline said. "I told you it wouldn't happen to me. I *told* you."

Madeline heard a sizzle, and then the snakes attached to her head popped free and slithered over the side and splashed into the water. She felt the warm rush of blood flowing into her skin. She felt the aches and pains of a mortal body returning to itself.

But all the while, she went on looking at her daughter's face. For the first time in five thousand years, Madeline saw her own reflection, and it was in Kali's face. She saw herself for who she was in that moment—not the physical reality, but who she had *become*. She was beautiful. And extraordinary. And unique. She knew then that both Madeline and Thomas had been right, and they had also been wrong.

Love had been powerful enough to overcome the curse, this was true. But it had not been because they loved *her*.

It had been because she had finally learned how to love someone else.

The Tiger in the Garden

AT PRECISELY NOON—not one minute earlier, not one minute later—the ship appeared in Regence's sky. It started as a black dot in a perfect canvas of cobalt, like a drop of ink carelessly spilled from a painter's brush. So small, so seemingly insignificant, and yet José felt his whole body tremor at the sight of it. The punctuality did not surprise him. Unless something had changed, this one was a Bal'ani, and they were said to obsess about such things. José had made certain to arrive a half hour early at the landing station. On their home world the Bal'ani were rumored to *eat* those who insulted them.

"Constable Valcorez," the attendant behind him said, "is that truly an Agent's ship?"

"Yes," José said. Hand raised to block the glare of the sun, he watched through the glass doors as the black dot grew quickly in size, soon filling almost his entire field of vision, until finally the ship's thrusters stirred up a fog of dust on the bone-colored ground. Behind the pulsing electric fence that surrounded the landing area, the desolate plains extended flat to the horizon, making the ship that much more stark an appearance. He had seen vids of Agent ships, of course, but seeing one up close was both more awful and awe-inspiring. There were three other ships outside, freighters which were not small themselves, and the Agent ship was at least as big as all of them *combined.*

The hand of death, José thought. That's what it looked like, with its black gleaming surface and five pincer-like landing gear. The hand of death descending on Regence.

"Do you . . . do you know why they've come, sir?" the attendant asked.

The edge in the man's voice was palpable. Ah, yes, it's already begun, José thought. This was what the Agents did, bringing out the fear in those who should have nothing to fear. He watched the ship touch down, then turned to the young man behind the counter. He could have been looking at a mirror image of himself, albeit one three moon-downs younger: a small man with a slender build, black hair, and deeply-bronzed skin. He was a Regence native, just like José. What was his name? José jogged his memory. He *should* remember. He had met this man before, and he prided himself on remembering people. It was one of the reasons he had risen to Constable at such a young age.

He smiled when the name came to him. "My dear, Philippe," he said, "you know as well as I that I could not tell you even if I knew."

"Yes, sir," Philippe said. "Thank you, sir. It's just . . . Well, you know, sir. No one . . . well, no one wants them here. It is not a good thing. It is *granza.*"

José nodded. *Granza.* A bad omen. If his years at the university at Kelton had not burned out his superstition, as well as created a distaste for Regence's common tongue, he might have been inclined to agree.

He lifted his hood and pushed through the glass doors. He felt the scorching slap of the sun even through fabric designed to shield him from the heat. A few steps and the landscape tinted. UV iris adaptation was a cheap mod, something anybody with even a bit of money could do. His salary as Constable did not allow him to afford the more expensive dust-repellant mod, however, so he squinted as he walked into the dust. He held his breath, but still he could taste the bitterness of the dirt on his lips. The ship's landing elevator was already humming down, three figures visible in the shadowy area beneath the ship.

As he approached, he thought he caught the silver gleam of the Bal'ani's teeth, and he forced himself to continue without hesitation. He could not show weakness. If he ever hoped to be hired off of Regence by the Unity Defense, he could not have a bad report from an Agent on his record. And if he was lucky enough, by the end of the day, to be personally thanked by one that was a Bal'ani—a race that considered praise, from one of their own, the highest compliment one could receive -- it would certainly serve him well.

"Agent Korin?" José said. Despite his best efforts, his voice still cracked.

"Only a fool would assume otherwise," the Bal'ani said, emerging from the mist.

José had memorized a greeting in the Bal'ani's language, but one look at his visitor and the words were lost. He had of course seen the alien on the vid when they had spoken the previous day, but in the harsh sunlight the creature looked so much more . . . terrifying. It was as if someone had taken two human faces, stretched them until the skin was about to tear, then smashed them against one another. There were four beady black eyes and two snout-like noses, each placed on the misshapen head as if by accident. Then there was the mouth. It was the Bal'ani's most defining feature, taking up half of its face, easily big enough to engulf a child's head in a single bite. The two fangs, encased in metal sheathing, as was the Bal'ani custom, extended past the stubbled chin. The alien wore a red robe that completely hid its lower body, leaving only the head and the gnarled, three-fingered hands exposed.

Norslim. The word sprung into José's mind. When he was a boy, there was a story that circulated among the children of a monster that emerged at night and dragged orphan children from their beds, muzzled their mouths with its clawed hands, and hauled its victims deep into the desert to bury them alive. He had not thought of the story in years, though at one time he trembled under his sheets at every creak and groan in an ancient building that produced endless creaks and groans.

Norslim . . . It was nothing but a foolish word. A Regence word. The Bal'ani may have been terrifying, but he was still an Agent. And Agents may have been terrifying themselves, able to stretch the law to fit their dark whims, but as much as they stretched it, they could not break it—at least as long as one remained vigil.

The two other figures were security robots of some kind, sleek bipedal things with a single red-glowing eye and massive shoulders. They were not like the awkward, jerky robots José was used to seeing. Despite their girth, these machines walked with grace.

"Welcome to Regence," José said, deciding to ignore the Bal'ani's condescending tone. "I am Constable Valcorez, and I'd like to offer my—"

"Let us assume we have exchanged the necessary pleasantries," Korin said, walking past him. "I assume you have a pod waiting?"

The robots had no trouble keeping up with Korin's brisk pace, but José did. "I have transportation," he said. "It is around the—"

"Here is my coded authorization card," Korin said, producing a thin blue wafer from within his robe. "I assume even on your world they are required?"

José took the wafer, slipping it into the inner pocket of his jacket. He knew right away that his handheld was too out of date to process such a recent card, though he did not want to admit it. It was likely the desk units in the terminal would also be too out of date, much to his embarrassment. "Thank you," he said. "Now would it be possible to tell me why you have come to Regence?"

"Not by my own choosing, of course," Korin said, both of his noses wrinkling. On someone else this gesture would have been comical; on the Bal'ani it was deeply disturbing. "It is hard to imagine there are still worlds with not a single Stepdock. To fly here was a considerable inconvenience."

"I'm sorry for that," José said. "We are a poor world with little resources, but there are plans to put a Stepdock—"

"Surely this is not the pod," Korin said.

They had rounded the terminal to the parking area, an open dirt lot empty except for José's six-wheeled vehicle, the wrap-around window cracked, the gray exterior spotted with rust. It was a true pod only in the sense that it *could* hover for short distances, but it was primarily a land vehicle, and a tiny one at that. It could hold all four of them, but it would be a tight squeeze considering the size of the Bal'ani and his robots.

"I'm afraid it's the only one I have," José said.

Korin looked at him. Just for a moment the Bal'ani's cool exterior fell away, exposing a murderous rage. It lasted a half second at most, but it was enough. There was no doubt in Jose's mind: if he gave the Bal'ani enough cause, and a few moments in a dark alley when the confining laws of the Unity Defense could be conveniently forgotten, Korin would kill him.

José felt his body go cold, but he maintained his composure and waved his hand over the hood of the pod.

"Access," he said.

The door on their side swung upward, cranking rhythmically. José started to back away to allow his guests to enter, but Korin was already pushing past him, the robots following. Korin took one side, the robots the other.

José had hoped he could sit next to a robot, but he wasn't about to say so. He squeezed into the pod, doing his best to melt against his side, but still his knees brushed against the Bal'ani's. He moved his legs away, but not before he felt himself shudder.

"Are you racist?" Korin asked.

José realized Korin had noticed the reaction, though there was nothing to do now but play ignorant. "I'm sorry?"

"You should be sorry," Korin said, "even if it is understandable. One does not expect civilized behavior from one of your upbringing."

José swallowed. "I really don't—"

"Of course you do," Korin said, "though it is irrelevant to our present situation. I will say this for your benefit, however, and I advise you to listen carefully. If you desire to ascend from your lowly beginnings, you must rise above your savage instincts. It is the only chance you have."

Even as his face burned, José bowed his head. They were only words. When he got off this dust speck, he would do his part to rid the Unity Worlds of the Agents, but for now he would bear the slight. "I'm sorry," he said, "I meant no—"

"Let us be on our way," Korin said. "Our destination is the Harmani Orphanage."

José flinched as if he had been pricked. It was the very place where had had been raised. "The Harmani?"

"Is there something wrong with your hearing, Constable?" Korin asked.

Feeling a bit shell-shocked, José spoke the address to the pod. The door clamped down, and then the pod, humming, rose up on its springs. Cool air hissed through the ceilings vents, somewhat masking the Bal'ani's strong, musky body odor. The pod headed straight into the main thoroughfare, jostling when it fell into the deep ruts. They were soon in the heart of the city, the mud-stained buildings casting their hard-edged shadows on shirtless children playing alongside the road. The children, and the dour-faced women watching from the glassless windows, gawked at them as they passed. They were so poor that even a dented old pod was the sign of great riches, and José couldn't help but feel ashamed of them. At least their brown skin made it harder from a distance to see the dirt and grime they were never able to wash away—no matter how hard they tried.

"Surely there can't be anyone you're seeking there," José said.

"Oh?" Korin said. "You are so certain? You are privy to information that has escaped the Agents?"

"No, I was only—"

"In my profession one does not rule out any possibility when searching for traitors, Constable. Do you know of a man who operates under the name Henry Wolheim?

José could instantly visualize the sallow-cheeked old man as if he was sitting next to them, his white hair fluttering, a worn leather book under his arm. Books. There were probably less than a hundred actual printed books on Regence, and half of them were owned by a gardener—one of the man's many paradoxes. Henry Wolheim had come to Regence during José's last year, and José had spent many hours in the garden as punishment for his constant misbehavior. He had always hoped that if he misbehaved badly enough, they would hold him back a year. It was the old gardener, and a non-native at that, who made him see the benefit of getting an education. Of using that education to do something meaningful with his life. José used to visit with the old man at least a couple times year, though it had been over a year since his last visit.

"Yes," I said. "But certainly you're not insinuating—"

"Did your law enforcement ever perform a genetic scan on him?"

José pulled out his handheld and punched in Henry's name. "That was before my time, of course, but it looks like we had no reason. His authorization card checked out."

Korin wrinkled his twin noses. "A pity. You see, if you had we would have caught him the day he arrived. When his genetic sample was recently sent to Earth, our interceptor identified him as Henry Thomas. I assume you know of whom I speak?"

José shook his head. "I'm afraid—"

"If you stayed current with the Registry, you would know he is a notorious computer hacker who was of great assistance to the terrorists attempting to undermine the Unity Defense. He earned the nickname Tiger Thomas because he left a digital holo of a tiger in whatever system he hacked, and he hacked many. In fact, if not for his interference, we surely would have destroyed the terrorist networks years ago."

José found it hard to believe the kindly old man he knew could have been part of the terrorist group—or the Resistance, as they were known among those who sympathized with their cause. José did not despise them as so many of the pro-Unity Worlds crowd did, because he truly did believe they had a point, that the Unity Worlds were only a means for the rich and powerful to control the poor and powerless, but he also didn't believe their methods were justified. They had killed in the name of their cause, targeting politicians mostly, but complete bystanders had been killed as well. He could not see Henry, not gentle Henry, participating in such acts.

José turned to the window. They were passing through one of the worst neighborhoods—there were no *good* neighborhoods on Regence, only bad and worse—and the haggard, emaciated people sitting listlessly in the doorways watched him with their shadowed sockets. It was like being watched by the dead. Why would a man like that come to Regence? He could have hidden anywhere. "There must be a mistake," José said.

"I do not make mistakes," Korin said. He paused. "I have, of course, read your file. I know you were at the Harmani Orphanage. Though your file does not specify it, I conclude based on your response that you developed some attachment to Wolheim. Perhaps he was some sort of father figure?"

The comment, both in its bluntness and utter accuracy, made José stiffen. He had never thought of Henry as a father, at least not consciously, but it was fair to say that he had treated him as such. Like many of the children, he had referred to the gardener as *valda*, meaning old, lovable man, a term that often *was* used when speaking of one's father. José felt a flash of anger at the Bal'ani for making him remember something that now embarrassed him greatly.

He decided to deflect Korin's question by changing the subject. "You said a genetic sample had been sent to Earth. Why?"

"Irrelevant," Korin said. "What is relevant is we have located a traitor to the Unity Worlds, and he will be convicted and tried accordingly. And of course, I expect your complete assistance."

There was a tone that José didn't like, as if Korin was implying José might be a hindrance.

"I will of course do everything within the law to make sure justice is done," José said curtly.

They arrived at the Harmani a few minutes later. The orphanage, and the Church of Unification across the street, were some of the oldest buildings on Regence, boxy, stone and mortar structures built by the earliest settlers. The monks had worked tirelessly over the years to make sure the buildings remained respectable, and the fresh blue paint and the bright flowers under the windows spoke to their efforts. But the many cracks in the walls, like wrinkles under heavy makeup, were dead giveaways to the true state of the buildings.

Some orphanage boys—distinct in their blue uniforms—were playing flipdisc in the street, and they scurried away as the pod parked in front of the wooden door. When José stepped out into the heat, raising his hood, the front door opened and a portly man in a yellow and blue Unification robe stepped out to greet him. He was shaved bald except for his white sideburns.

"Hello, Father Jansen," José said.

"*Trenda!*" the monk exclaimed, smiling. "My boy, José! It is so good to see you . . ." His voice, as well as his smile, faded when he laid eyes on who was emerging from the pod. He swallowed. "Who are your guests?"

"I am Agent Korin," the Bal'ani said, stepping up next to José, his shadow engulfing the monk. "These are my sentries, unsentient robots who do not need to be referred to directly. Please take us to Henry Wolheim."

Jansen looked at José, confusion in his eyes. "Henry? But why?"

"That is not your concern," Korin replied, before José had a chance to answer. "Can you lead us to him, or should my sentries search the premises?"

"Please, Father," José said, "we don't want to alarm the children."

"Well, I imagine he's in the back garden, as he always is," Jansen said, turning back to the door.

José followed the monk into the building, Korin and the robots following. They walked down a narrow hall lit by candles, the robots' metal feet clicking on the cobblestone floor. The place, especially its familiar musty odor, brought back a flood of memories for José. A few boys appeared at the other end, stopped dead in their tracks when they saw who was approaching, then scurried back the way they had come.

Though José could have easily taken them to the garden himself, he allowed Father Jansen to lead them to the double glass doors. The glass was opaque, but the green color was everywhere. They stepped through the doorway into a garden surrounded by ugly brown buildings. It should not have been a place to grow a garden, the shadows too deep, and yet the place was brimming with plants, the air heavy and moist, the smell of life invigorating. A red brick path wove its way through the rich soil.

A man was humming. Jansen led them to the source of the voice, and there was Henry, down on all fours planting violet flowers along the back wall. His hair was a bit whiter, his shoulders a bit bonier, but otherwise he was as José remembered: a spindly man who was more arms and legs than torso, skin much paler than a native's.

"Henry," Father Jansen said, "there are some people here to see you."

The gardener continued humming, working on his flowers as if he had not heard. José noticed that his green jumpsuit, spotted with dirt, appeared to be on backwards.

"We have no time for such foolishness," Korin said. He looked at his sentries. "Apprehend him."

"Wait," Father Jansen said.

But the robots had already moved, one on each side of Henry, and together they grabbed his arms. Henry cried out as he was hauled to his feet. As the robots turned him around, Henry struggled.

"Monsters!" he cried. "There are monsters in my garden! Let me go! *Trenda! Ipsin!*"

The hysterical behavior startled José. He had never seen Henry behave this way. The man had always been the epitome of calm, regardless of the circumstances.

"Don't hurt him," Father Jansen pleaded. "He doesn't know what he's doing. He's . . ."

The monk trailed off, as Henry's body had suddenly gone slack.

He was staring at José, his gaze so fixated that José felt his cheeks burn with shame. He hated that he was doing this.

"My boy," he said. "I know you. Yes, yes . . . They say I have forgotten, but I have not forgotten *you*."

All at once José understood why Henry's genetic sample had been sent to Earth, and he felt a sinking feeling in his stomach when the realization hit him. He looked at Jansen. "Trident's?" he said.

Father Jansen bowed his head. "I'm afraid so. The laboratory on Earth confirmed it."

"My boy, my boy," Henry said, pulling against his captors, trying to move toward José. "Why did you bring these monsters into my garden? Why?"

José swallowed. Trident's Disease had been around since the Stepdock first came into use, a neurological disorder that struck the elderly, and over a period of ten years caused madness and eventually death. A small percentage were genetically predisposed to get it if they used the Stepdocks, which was why a genetic sample was now required before anyone could use the system. But that was now. In the early days no one knew about Trident's, and someone like Henry would have used the instantaneous transportation devices in ignorance of their possible side effects.

Korin had pulled a handheld out of his robe and was pointing it at Henry. "There is a match," he said, turning and walking back along the path, his red robe billowing behind him. "Bring him."

The robots followed, dragging Henry along with them. The old man was beginning to thrash about again.

"Please, boy! Don't let the monsters take me!"

"What is his crime?" Father Jansen called after Korin. "You must tell me his crime!"

But Korin didn't break stride and José heard the glass door open. The robots carried the screaming gardener out of his sanctuary. Father Jansen made a move to follow, and José grabbed his arm.

"Don't make it worse, Father," he said. "Henry was once part of the Resistance, a man known as Tiger Thomas. There's nothing we can do."

Father Jansen jerked his arm away, his face flushed. "Impossible! Not the Henry I know!"

"I'm afraid the evidence is there."

Father Jansen shook his head. "Even if it is true, even if it is . . . Look at him. Just look at him. What's the point in taking him now? He doesn't even remember what he's done. Hasn't he suffered enough?"

José didn't know what to say, and he didn't want Korin to leave him behind. "I'm sorry," he said, running after them.

When he stepped into the building, he heard Henry's distant screaming echoing off the stone walls. As he ran, he passed dozens of orphans who were gathered at the doorways, their eyes wide and fearful. He wished he could say something to comfort them, but there was no time.

The door to his pod was already closing when José reached it, and he dived inside. All the seats were occupied, and so he squatted in the middle, catching his breath. There wasn't much space, knees pressing up against him in all sides.

"He's come to rescue me!" Henry shouted. The robot next to him pinned him against the seat. Henry struggled but to no avail.

"You may stay if you wish," Korin said to José. "I believe the situation is causing you emotional distress."

"I'm fine," José snapped, and instructed the pod to take them to the landing port.

The pod rose up on its wheels and rumbled back down the street. José glanced through the back window and saw Father Jansen at the curb, dozens of children gathered around him, faces forlorn. "José!" Henry cried. "See, see! I do remember. I remember lots of things. I remember the time you came to my garden and you were crying. Do you remember? You said you hated Regence. You were quite upset, oh so many tears. Yes, that was you. I remember it perfectly."

"Please, Henry," José said. "Just be quiet. We'll be to the landing port soon."

"Oh, Henry, is it?" the old man said, looking hurt. "You didn't use to call me Henry. You called me something else. It was a word of your world. What was it? I can't . . . No . . ." He started crying. "So many words, lost."

Valda, José thought. But he wouldn't say the word aloud. He had to be strong. It wasn't his fault that Henry had gotten into this situation.

"What a quaint sentimental display," Korin said, stroking the metal sheathing surrounding his fangs. "On our world we sometimes observe your theatrical presentations so we might better understand your peculiar emotional defects, but it is so much more vivid when seeing them in person."

José said nothing. Henry started humming again, and José realized it wasn't one song but parts of many jumbled together. They were all songs of Regence, songs Henry sung to the children sick in the infirmary. He had sung them to José more than once.

As the pod wound its way through the desolate streets, José agonized about what was happening. The old man may have been guilty of a crime, or he may have been a hero, it all depended on your point of view, but whatever the case it would do no good punishing him now. He was nothing but a shell of who he was.

And yet, even if José *could* do something, was he willing to sacrifice his career, maybe even his life, to help Henry?

He had a future. Even Henry—if he had all of his faculties intact—would have told him not to sacrifice himself. Hadn't the old man said as much on the day of José's graduation? *There are times when a man of conscience must do what's in his own interest, even if it is not in the interest of his people, though it pains him greatly*. José realized now that Henry had probably been trying to console himself for abandoning the Resistance. If he had done what was right for himself, why shouldn't José?

But as the pod came to an abrupt halt, José still felt like he was making a mistake. Abandoning the Resistance and abandoning an old mentor were not at all the same. The robots carried the gardener out of the pod and around the terminal, Korin following. José's eyes tinted, but he did not raise his hood. Since Henry wore none, he did not feel he should either. Henry's feet barely touched the ground, stirring up dust. When the Agent's ominous ship came into view, Henry whimpered.

"Your presence is no longer required," Korin said, looking at José. "Thank you for your assistance. I assume you will send along my authorization card when you have a chance to process it."

The Bal'ani's thank you only made José feel worse. And as he stopped on the sun-baked ground, so bright it was like a mirror, he realized he could no longer pretend he was doing the right thing. It did not matter that it was the law. It did not matter that if he acted, his ambitions would turn to dust. He sensed that if he did not act, that if he did nothing now, when it mattered most, his very self would be lost.

And Korin's mention of the authorization card gave him a flash of inspiration.

"I'm afraid I can't let you take him just yet," José said.

Korin, who had already walked a dozen paces away, stopped and turned. José noticed for the first time that the Bal'ani's robe was the same color as human blood.

"Excuse me?"

With Korin's hideousness completely exposed under the glare of the sun, the word *norslim* again jumped into José's mind. This time he did not force it away. Yes, the Agent was a *norslim*. It had nothing to do with his appearance and everything to do with what he represented. He was also *granza*. José would not deny either of these things, but neither would he fear them.

"Is there something wrong with your hearing?" he said, smiling.

"I heard you perfectly, Constable," Korin said curtly. "What I don't understand is what kind of game you are playing."

"It is no game," José said. Despite his pounding heart, he walked toward the Bal'ani. "And unless you want to commit a serious violation of Unity law, I would suggest you tell your minions to take Henry no farther."

Korin stared at José another beat, his eyes full of wrath, then turned and ordered his robots to stop. They froze, about to step onto the landing elevator. Only Henry, who was screaming and flailing, showed any movement. Korin looked back at José.

"Explain yourself," he said. "And I warn you, if I find that you are attempting to —"

"Spare me your warnings," José said, producing the Bal'ani's authorization card from his jacket. "You see, sir, your authorization card has not been processed. We are but a poor world with little resources, and we have no equipment that can process such a modern card. We of course will obtain that equipment, but it will take some time."

"This is bureaucratic nonsense!" Korin cried. "You know as well as I that my card will check out!"

"Oh?" José said. "You have some information I am not privy to, sir? I'm afraid I must follow the law, and the law clearly states that your authorization card must be cleared before you can act on behalf of the Unity Defense. Unless, of course, you wish to *violate* the law . . ."

Korin fumed silently, his face twitching as if he was about to burst. There was a moment when José thought Korin was going to dispense with the law and kill José on the spot, but after a few seconds Korin signaled his sentries to return.

"You realize you are only delaying the inevitable," he said. "Once I clear this matter up with your superiors, I shall return and apprehend Thomas."

José nodded. "Perhaps," he said, taking his time, realizing that despite the danger, he was truly enjoying watching the Bal'ani squirm. "But you don't really think a man with Trident's is a flight risk, do you? Are you afraid he'll die before you get a chance to convict him?" And what he thought but didn't say was: who knew what would happen between now and then? It was entirely possible that when the Agent returned, Henry would be missing. It was also more than likely that if he *was* missing, he would not be found.

Korin shook his head, ordered the robots to leave Henry, then turned and walked toward his ship. He didn't go far without offering one parting shot.

"You are throwing away your future for a traitor," he said.

To this, José said nothing. He watched the Agent and his robots ride the elevator into their black ship. It was quite possible Korin was right. It may have been the greatest thing he had ever done, or it may have been the worst.

"The monsters are leaving," Henry said, his head bobbing. "They are leaving, José. Watch them go."

Standing side by side as the ship lifted into the sky, that's exactly what they did. They watched as the hand of death soon became a tiny black dot, something small, something insignificant, until it was gone altogether, leaving the sky once again a perfect canvas of cobalt. José knew there was much to do before the Agents returned—communiqués to send to reporters, complaints to file with the appropriate authorities. He would make very certain that the Agents would be under heavy scrutiny when they returned. None of it would probably help José's future, but it would help spare Regence from the worst of the Agents' wrath.

But that was tomorrow's work.

When the dust cleared, José took his old mentor by the arm and led him back toward the pod.

"Let's get you home, *Valda*," he said. "Your garden needs you."

Directions to Mourning's Deep

LIKE ME, YOU SUFFERED a tragedy too great to bear. You lost a father or a mother or a brother or a spouse. You loved and you lost, and how it haunts you, stays with you, only you know. If this is the first time you have experienced such loss, if you feel as though hope has fled and will never return, then listen. My words are for the virgins of sorrow.

There is a bar known as Mourning's Deep. In this bar is a man who can give you hope again.

Here is how you get there:

Get in your car and drive downtown. You can do it in this city or another, it does not matter. Simply drive to where the tallest buildings block the sun. It must be a cool and shadowy place, and if it is grimy and grungy like so many of our biggest cities, all the better. If vagrants scrounge the dumpsters, if ravenous dogs fight over leftovers from a Chinese restaurant, if businessmen in limos drive past, their faces obscured by smoked glass, this is preferred. But it is not necessary.

Any city of decent size will do.

With your mind firmly on the person you lost, circle the block five times, then turn and go five times the other way. If it is a one-way street, do it anyway, and ignore the blaring horns. Find the darkest alley between two buildings and put your car in reverse. With your eyes closed, and they must be closed, back into it for five seconds. One Mississippi . . . Two Mississippi . . . Do not open your eyes! If you give in to temptation, you will have to start over.

I see that you do not believe me. You think this is nonsense. But I ask you, have you ever done it?

When you open your eyes, and if you have done as I said, you will see a plain metal door set in a red brick wall. There will be no sign, but the name of the place has been scratched on the door with a knife:

Mourning's Deep.

Leave the car running. You will find the door unlocked. Go inside. It will be smoky and dim, as all such bars are, and a somber tune will be playing from the jukebox. Pay no attention to the figures in tattered black cloaks at the mahogany bar. If they look at you, do not look back! Walk quickly past the pool table, and do not be alarmed if the pool balls are moving of their own accord. Push through the swinging doors to the room in the back.

Only a faint orange glow from the fireplace will guide your way. You will see him, a slim, shadowy figure in the corner, sitting at a small round table. He will be wearing a cloak like the others, but his will be gray, not black, and out of his sleeves will come fingers yellowed and dry like old newspaper. He will be the only one in this room. He may have a beer in front of him or he may not, but he won't drink while you are there. Do not put wood on the fire! It must be kept dark so you can't see him.

Sit at the table. Tell him your suffering, tell him of this first, deep loss that threatens to destroy you, and do not to look at him. When you are done, put your hand on the table, palm upward. The wood, stained with years of spilt beer, may stick to your skin, but leave it there. If you are honest, if you hold nothing back, he may chance to reach out and touch you. His fingers will be as cold as the ocean's deep. The touch will last only a moment, but you may feel lightheaded. This will pass.

When he pulls his hand away, rise and walk out of the bar. The cloaked figures will not look at you, for you have nothing for them now.

Go through the door back to your car. Leave the alley. Merge with traffic and drive where you must.

Soon you will be able to think of the person you lost and feel nothing. You will be able to look at the events from afar, dispassionately, as if they happened to someone else. You will have hope again. It will not take long. An hour perhaps.

Finally, and this is of utmost importance, you must never go back. No matter who you love and lose the rest of your days, do not return to *Mourning's Deep*. If you do, if you burden him with your agony once again, he will touch you, but this time all you forgot will come rushing back, and it will be worse than before. And if you plead with him, if you beg, if you cry out for him to have mercy, he will only laugh and call for the cloaked ones to throw you on the street. Once outside, the door will be gone, and you may search the rest of your days in all the cities of the world, and you will never find it.

So do not give into temptation. Be satisfied he gave you hope again. If you go back, you may lose it forever, and spend eternity looking for it.

I would know.

Motivational Speaker

THE OVERHEAD FLOURESCENT lights flashed, signaling that Mart-Co would be closing in five minutes. Craig had spent the better part of an hour scrutinizing the fine print specs on the back of the Tek-King universal remote, and yet he still hadn't decided whether to buy it or not. He was leaning toward buying it, maybe eighty-five percent there, close to ninety percent, really, but he still wasn't sure it was the right one for him.

He could always come back another day. Or just live without a remote, as he had done for the past three years. With a sigh, he hung it in its clear plastic packaging on the metal rod and turned to go. His tennis shoes, wet from the afternoon rain, squeaked on the tiles.

"Oh, just buy the damn thing, already," a woman said.

Craig jumped. The voice had come from right behind him. But when he whirled around, there was no one in the aisle but him.

"Hello?" he said.

"You heard me."

The voice seemed to be coming from the stereo system on the

shelf right next to the remotes. It was a vaguely familiar voice, though he couldn't say where he'd heard it before. There was also a very faint beeping noise in the background. *Beep . . . Beep . . . Beep.*

"Okay, very funny," he said. "Somebody's piping in through a microphone. Ha Ha."

"Don't be a flipping idiot, Craig. Just buy the remote and go home. What more do you need, a sign from God? I've never known someone as wishy-washy as you."

Craig frowned. They knew his name, meaning this was something they had been planning. "Okay," he said loudly, "whoever you are, you can come out now. The fun's over."

A clerk in a green apron poked his head around the corner. His buzz of blond was an unnatural color of yellow, like polished gold. He had a diamond stud earring on his nose. "Need help, dude?" he said.

Craig pointed at the stereo. "You think this is funny?"

"You lost me, man."

"I don't think he can hear me," the woman said.

"There! There!" Craig cried. "You hear that?"

"Hear what?" the clerk said.

Craig crossed his arms and stared at the clerk. "You mean you didn't just hear all of that?"

The clerk shook his head. "Dude, I don't know what you're going on about, but we're closing in about two minutes."

"All right, fine," Craig said tersely, "I've had enough of this. Great practical joke. Ha, ha!"

Feeling a rush of blood to his face, Craig started down the aisle, accidentally knocking off a package of batteries along the way. Being the butt of a joke brought back fresh memories from high school, even though it had been five years since his graduation.

"Wait," the woman said.

She said the word with such a pleading tone that Craig stopped.

"Please," the woman begged. "Don't go."

She sounded more like a lonely little girl now than the confident young woman he had made her out to be. Either that, or she was a very good actress. He looked at the clerk again, who just shook his head and walked away.

Craig made his way back to the stereo system. It was just a cheap boom box—black and silver plastic, with two tape decks and a single-disc CD player. It was maybe a foot tall and two feet wide, the speakers detachable. A yellow clearance sticker listed a price just under twenty dollars, marked down from twenty-five.

Then he noticed that the power was turned off. Not only that, but the stereo wasn't plugged into an outlet. He turned it over, popped open the battery compartment, and saw that it was empty as well.

He felt a cold chill.

"Who are you?" he said quietly.

The woman didn't answer. The beeping continued.

"Game over?" he said.

"No," she said softly. "I just . . . don't remember."

"Okay," Craig said, "let me get this straight. You're somebody talking to me through this stereo who . . . has amnesia?"

She was silent a moment. "I don't know. I guess I *am* the stereo. Or at least I'm trapped inside it. I don't know . . . . I can't remember anything before today."

"What do you want from me?" he said.

"What does any woman want?"

"Huh?"

"Humor, Craig. *Gallows* humor, specifically. Helps me deal with the reality of being a disembodied voice trapped inside a bit of plastic and wires."

"How do you even know you're in a radio? You don't have eyes."

"I don't know how I can see things. I just do. I mean, I don't have a brain either, but it's obvious I can think, right?"

"Hmm . . ."

"Buy me, Craig. Take me home. I don't know how things will go beyond that, but it's a start. Come on, come on, what do you say? We're talking twenty bucks here. Geez, you can always return me if things don't work out."

She had a point. Mart-Co had a very liberal return policy.

"Okay," he said, surprising himself.

"Great," she said. "Just one thing. I'm not listening to any country music."

AN EVENING BREEZE rattled the leaves of the giant oak that took up most of the yard of the ten-unit complex. The light was fading, and the lamplights mounted on black poles glowed a faint yellow.

He set her up on the carpet in the corner of his living room, away from the sunlight and the heating vent, both of which might damage her. Since she didn't actually require any power, he wasn't sure if she *could* be damaged, but he figured it was better to play it safe.

Craig realized there was a practical matter he needed to resolve right away. "What should I call you?" he asked.

"What do you mean?"

"I mean, do you know your name?"

"Hmm . . . How about Lucky? Call me Lucky. I'm sure I'll bring good luck for you."

While he was making dinner—macaroni and cheese, what he made for himself every Tuesday—Lucky asked him a few questions, and gradually he relaxed and talked a little more freely. Had he been married? No. Engaged? No, just dated a little bit, the longest was a woman named Anne who he saw for four months. What were his parents like? His mother, who died of breast cancer ten years back, had been a stay-at-home mom and something of a zealous Catholic. His father, a silent man, had worked as a CPA for the government. These days, he saw his Dad once a year, at Christmas, but neither of them had much to say.

Craig was never very comfortable talking about himself with a real person, but somehow it was easier when it was just a voice inside a stereo system.

The next few days, they settled into a routine, talking during the meals and watching television together in the evenings. Craig hadn't lived with anyone since he left his parents' home—and he wasn't even sure if this qualified—but he was beginning to enjoy having her around. He even opened up to her about his problems making decisions.

"It's just so hard," he said, while he was spooning up some spaghetti, Thursday night's meal. "It's like I just freeze up. Even about the smallest things."

He looked at her across the table, where he now placed her anytime he was having a meal. He wished there was some way to read her reactions.

"Yeah, you really have a problem with that," she said. "Has it always been that way?"

He paused mid-bite, the steam rising off the noodles, smelling of garlic and cooked tomatoes. "Well . . . no. I was never much of a go-getter, I guess, but I didn't have this problem."

"When did it start? He thought about it. "When I was in college, I think."

"Uh huh. And when did your Mom die?"

"Right before college." He laughed sharply. "What, are you going to do a Freud routine and tell me my problem has to do with my mother?"

"Well?"

He dropped his fork, which clattered against the porcelain plate. "Oh, for Christ's sake . . ."

"Okay, okay," she said. "You don't have to talk about it. Hey, let's do something, huh? Let's go for a drive."

He frowned. "Where?"

"Anywhere! Cruise the town. Roll down the windows and whoop. Anything. Just get out of this condo."

"But where?"

She sighed. "Just get your keys."

* * * * *

At first, he clenched the steering wheel so hard his knuckles turned white, but by the end of the drive he was whistling the *Chips* theme song along with Lucky. And that night, when he lay in bed staring at the white ceiling and walls, he thought she might have been right about his mother.

But over the next few days, Lucky's suggestions began to wear on him. She wanted to know what his goals were, and when he said he didn't have any, she kept pressing him until he admitted that he had always dreamed of doing computer programming for a gaming company. Then she kept giving him suggestions on how he could make his dream a reality—taking classes, looking for jobs more closely related to what he wanted. She kept pressing him to try new things—go scuba diving, take a dancing class, fly a kite at the coast—and he always put her off.

"I'm just trying to shake you out of your doldrums," she explained.

He sprinkled the chopped green pepper into the sizzling frying pan. He was making an omelet—on a Saturday, something he had only previously done on Thursdays—as his way of showing her he could do new things.

"Maybe I'm happy in my doldrums."

"Nobody's happy that way. You just need somebody to show you a way out."

He knew she was right, that he wasn't happy, but the more she pushed him, the more uneasy he became. He couldn't sleep. His appetite disappeared. He still loved spending the evenings talking to her, but he was beginning to depend on her, and he didn't like that. What pushed him over the edge, though, was when she asked him to take her out to dinner.

"What?" he said.

He was on his knees in the living room, eating sushi on a TV tray and watching a Bruce Lee movie—none of which he had done before. Well, except for getting on his knees. He had done that plenty of times when he used to attend Mass.

Lucky was perched on a matching TV tray—one that pictured

Elvis in his white suit and tinted glasses. Craig had picked them up while "antiquing" the previous Saturday, an activity Lucky had encouraged him to do when he said that going with his mother to antique shops had been something he enjoyed as a child.

"I'd just like to be treated to a night out once in a while," Lucky said. "I think I deserve that."

He laughed.

"What?" she said.

"Well," he began, trying to find the most tactful way to put it, "you're . . . a stereo."

"So?"

"Don't you think it would look a little odd, me having dinner with a cheap piece of plastic made in China?"

"There's no reason to be cruel."

"But you get my point, right?"

"No. I don't see why you can't treat me like a lady once in a while."

"You're not a lady!"

She started making sniffling sounds, punctuated by bursts of static, which made him feel both useless and awful. He felt awful because he knew he had made her feel this way, and he felt useless because he didn't know how to comfort her. It didn't matter that she was a stereo system, either, because he felt equally helpless around flesh and blood women when they cried.

Back when Mom was alive, he remembered hearing her cry sometimes. She cried a lot, and she could never give any reason. His father never said a word when she cried. He just sat in the corner and read his paper. When he got older, he learned that his mother was bipolar, and that she got that way when she was off her medication.

That's when he realized how much Lucky's crying reminded him of his mother. And then something occurred to him, something that seemed obvious but had eluded him until now. There was a distinct possibility that all of this was in his mind. There *was* mental illness in his family. It all added up.

He knew, then, what he had to do.

*****

SINCE THEY often went for drives in the evening, and she had no reason to suspect anything was unusual about their drive until he pulled into the Mart-Co parking lot.

She fell silent. Then, softly, she said, "What are we doing here?"

He parked in the same spot he always did when it was available, the one right between the cart rack and the island with the maple tree. It was almost ten o'clock. Fog hung in the air, and the parking lot lights formed golden halos through which he saw tiny streaks of rain.

"Craig?" she said.

He got out of the car, walked around to the other side, the air misting his face, and got her out of the car. He held her with both arms, so neither of the speakers would fall off.

"Craig, please answer me," she said.

"I'm sorry," he said, starting for the door.

"You're taking me back."

"Yes."

She started crying. "Why?"

"I can't do this any more."

"I thought things were going well. I . . . I thought we were good together."

He shook his head. A young couple holding hands passed him, giving him a curious glance, but he didn't care. He could be crazy one more night.

"You're not real," he said.

"What?!" The word was barely audible, lost in fury of static. Don't be a flipping idiot! I'm real, Craig! I'm a real person in here! I don't know why I'm in here, but I'm not imaginary!"

"You're a voice that no one else but me can hear, Lucky. I think it's safe to say you're not real."

She kept pleading with him, but he didn't answer. His mother had often given in to her madness, but he wouldn't. He took Lucky inside and returned her at the Customer Service desk, having a hard time hearing the clerk over Lucky's stream of profanity.

With Lucky still yelling at him, he turned and walked toward the door, a crisp twenty now gracing his wallet.

He couldn't sleep that night, and the entire next day at work was miserable. It took him four hours to install a new sound card in someone's computer, a job that usually took him twenty minutes. He didn't eat, but he still managed to throw up three times. The last time, he didn't even make it to the bathroom, throwing up in the secretary's waste basket. His boss witnessed the incident and sent him home for the day.

When he got home, all he could think about was Lucky.

It was a little after five o'clock when he reached Mart-Co. The store was bustling with the after-work crowd. He had hoped that she would still be at the Customer Service counter, but they told them that the stereo system had been re-shelved. He went straight to the place in Electronics where he had originally found her. The same yellow discounted price tag hung from the metal shelf, but the stereo itself was gone. He felt lightheaded, and steadied himself with a hand on the shelf.

"Help you, man?"

It was the same clerk from before, the kid with the buzz of blond hair and the stud nose ring. When Craig looked at him, the kid's eyes widened with recognition.

Craig pointed. "The stereo that was here . . . you sold it?"

"Oh. Yeah! Just a few minutes ago."

Craig felt a new surge of hope. "Do you know what the person looked like?"

"Uh . . ."

"Please. It's very important that I see that stereo again." He fumbled for his wallet. "I can make it worth your while."

"Aw, man, that's all right. He was Asian, short, with thick black glasses. Maybe sixty."

Craig shook the kid's hand. "Thank you!"

"Yeah, no problem. Too bad Lucy's not here, or she might even tell you the guy's name."

Craig was already a half dozen steps down the aisle when what the kid said lassoed him to a stop. He turned and looked at him. "Who?"

"Lucy. Lucy Redding. She used to work here until about a month ago. She really liked talking to the customers. Knew a lot of them by name."

Craig felt a tremor of excitement. Lucy. *Lucky.* It couldn't have been a coincidence. He had a vague memory of her, a tall, thin girl with blond hair and a quick smile. And the voice. That might have been why he thought Lucky sounded familiar when he first heard her.

"What happened to her?" he asked.

The kid shook his head. "Motorcycle accident."

"Did she die?"

"No, worse, man. She's in a coma."

Craig took off at a run toward the front of the store. In a coma. Of course. He thought about the beeping noise, and that made sense. It must have been a heart monitor.

He scanned the checkout registers, didn't see anyone who looked as the kid described, then burst through the double doors into the parking lot. The sky was gray and a fine mist hung in the air. He ran from one row in the parking lot to the next, not seeing anyone who looked remotely Asian, and felt the heavy weight of despair settling over him. He headed back to the store, shoulders slumped.

He was nearly there when an older Asian man in purple turtleneck emerged through the automatic doors pushing a cart.

Craig froze. He was short and somewhat round, his skin pale, his hair thinning and gray. His turtleneck was too tight for him, and pinched at his rather bulky neck, as well as pulled taut around his belly. His dark-rimmed glasses fogged up, and he paused to wipe them on his shirt.

There were two items in the shopping cart: the stereo, and a large box of diapers.

"Lucky?" Craig said, his heart beating so hard he was afraid he might pass out. "Lucky, is that you?"

The stereo didn't make a sound, but the man looked at him, his eyebrows arching.

"Sorry?" He had a slight Japanese accent.

"The stereo," Craig said. "I'd like to buy it."

The man looked confused, then smiled. "Ah, I see. A joke. Excuse me, I must go."

He hurried away, his cart rattling over the black asphalt. Craig followed.

"I'd really like to buy it off of you," he said.

The man wouldn't look at him now, and he doubled his pace. "Bought it for my granddaughter. Very nice. I don't want to sell. Sorry."

Craig pulled out his wallet, leafing through the bills. "A hundred and twenty-seven dollars," he said.

The man stopped, staring at him with a perplexed expression.

"I really want that stereo," Craig explained.

Craig closed the door of his car and looked over at her on his passenger seat. She hadn't said a word yet, but the beeping noise continued.

"You still in there?" he said.

There was no reply.

"Come on, I know you're mad, but I did come back for you."

There was nothing for a moment, and then finally she spoke softly. "I hate you."

"You have every reason to be mad," he said.

"You're a bastard."

"Yes."

"A jerk."

"Definitely. But I think I know who you are, and maybe how to get you back."

"You're the worst sort of scum—what'd you say?"

"I know who you are."

"Really?"

"Yes."

"Oh God, I love you." And then, after a pause. "You're still a bastard, though."

WHILE HE HEADED for the hospital, he told her what he had learned. The gray sky was going dark, and droplets of water beaded on the front window. There was a part of him that was desperately afraid that if she managed to get back into her own body, a girl like her, she would never want to be with him. But he couldn't withhold the information. More than anything, he wanted her to be happy.

"Lucy Redding," she said, trying out the name.

He looked at her, the gray and black plastic in the passenger seat, encircled by a seat belt. "Anything come back to you?" he asked.

"No, but I get a weird sort of electric charge when I say it."

They drove in silence. The hospital was only a few minutes away.

He cleared his throat. "Listen, I'm sorry about leaving you. I think . . . I think I was scared."

He hoped for some encouragement, but she said nothing.

"And—and I think you're not going to want to have anything to do with me when you're back in your body."

"Don't be ridiculous."

"Why would you? A guy like me?"

She snorted. "You ever think that maybe a guy like you is exactly what a girl like me needs? Huh?"

Despite the edge in her voice, he felt encouraged. Pretending to be a cousin, he managed to cajole Lucy Redding's room number out of the reception clerk, and then he rode up the elevator with the stereo Lucy cradled under his arm. He stepped off onto polished gray tiles, the place smelling of antiseptic. The room wasn't far away, and the name written on the sign next to the door confirmed it was her. He pushed open the door.

The room was lit only by the crack of light coming from the partially open bathroom door. Still, he saw her at once, lying prone on the bed, her forehead bandaged, her body hooked up to various machines. A feeding tube hung from the corner of her mouth. He heard the same beeping noise, only louder, that he had been hearing from the stereo.

"Who the hell are you?"

Craig didn't see the man until he spoke. He sat in the corner, a grizzled middle-aged man with a bald head and a stubble of gray beard, dressed in a rumpled blue uniform that was stained with grease.

"It's Dad," Lucy said. "I . . . remember him."

"I'm a friend of Lucy's," Craig said. "I—I brought her something." He lifted the stereo.

Craig expected more resistance, but the man just nodded, eyes glassy and dead. Craig took the stereo and placed it on the table next to her, carefully making room for it next to the bouquet of yellow roses in the glass vase. Craig looked down at her face, and though it was marred by bruises and cuts, one of the eyes badly swollen, he thought her stunningly beautiful.

"Gonna play something for her?" her dad said.

In truth, he hadn't planned to do any such thing, but it seemed the right thing to do. He plugged in the stereo. He found a modern rock station, something he thought she might like. He kept waiting for something to happen, for her to open her eyes and look up at him, but she went on sleeping.

"I'm still in this box," Lucy said, sounding irritated. "But I remember. I remember everything, Craig."

"That's great," Craig said.

"Huh?" her dad said.

"Oh, this song," Craig said. "I think she liked this one a lot."

"Oh."

They listened to the rest of the song without saying a word.

"Still here," Lucy said.

"Damn, something's gotta work," Craig said.

"What are you talking about?" her dad said.

"Oh, I just . . . something's got to wake her up, you know. She can't go on like this forever."

The man's eyes turned watery, and when he spoke, the words were strangled. "Something," he said, nodding. "You know, I told her that damn motorcycle would get her killed unless she slowed down. It's the way she did everything—too fast, all the time."

"He was always a worrier," Lucy said. She was silent a moment. "He was right, though. I think . . . I think I know why I ended up in the stereo. It was the pain. There was just so much pain. I had to get out—but I didn't want to leave. Not completely."

"Wait!" Craig said excitedly, remembering something Lucy had said to him when he first brought her home. "I need to find a country western station."

"But I hate country!" Lucy said.

"But she hates country," her dad said.

Craig turned the dial, searching. "Exactly! It's just the kind of thing that might force her back into her body."

"What in the hell are you talking about?" her dad said. Blotchy red spots appeared on his cheeks. "Just who the hell are you again?"

Craig found a station that was currently playing a Garth Brooks song and cranked up the volume. Her Dad covered his ears with his hands and bolted to his feet. Lucy shrieked—a long, high-pitched noise that started in the stereo, and then, suddenly, was coming from the real Lucy on the bed. Her eyes popped open, and her own hands flew to her ears.

Craig clicked off the stereo.

"What in the hall—" her dad began, and then stopped short when he saw Lucy's eyes. He moved to her bedside.

"Daddy?" she said, her gaze darting back and forth. Her voice was garbled by the feeding tube in her mouth, and she coughed a few times. She pulled the cord out of her mouth, gagging. Finally, she saw her father, and she began to cry. "Daddy, where am I?"

Her father put his hand on her forehead. "In the hospital, sweetheart."

"It hurts, Daddy."

Now the father was crying, too. Craig felt embarrassed, intruding on a private family moment. Lucy looked over at him, and his heart skipped.

"Who are you?" she asked.

"I'm—I'm Craig."

She blinked a few times. "Do I know you?"

Of all the reactions she could have had, he hadn't expected her not to remember him. It was devastating. He was nothing more than a stranger to her—worse than a stranger, a stranger who had intruded upon her life at the worst possible time. He had feared that the real Lucy, this beautiful girl who lay broken in bed, would have no reason ever to fall in love with him. His only hope had been that she had already gotten to know him, and that might count for something, but now that hope was gone too.

"Oh," he said, back away toward the door, "I was one of your customers . . . just somebody who, um . . ."

Her eyes began to dim. He couldn't go out like this, full of indecision and doubt. She may have forgotten him, but there was something positive in that, too: she had also forgotten how he had abandoned her. If he got the chance, he could prove himself more worthy of her. He could really be there for her when she needed him.

He cleared his throat. "I want . . . I want to ask you out."

Her eyebrows raised. Her father frowned.

"Let me get this straight," she said. "You came here to ask me out when I'm all beat up, tubes sticking out of me, wasting away in a hospital bed?"

Craig fought the impulse to apologize. It was time to be bold. "Yes," he said. "That's exactly right."

She looked at him for a long moment, and then she smiled. Despite her condition, it was the most beautiful smile he had ever seen, the way it lit up her whole face. He wanted to make her smile again. He wanted the chance.

"Wow," she said.

Craig smiled back. He didn't know if that was a yes, but for the first time in his life, he was sure about something: she *definitely* hadn't said no.

It was a place to begin, and that was all he needed.

The Time Traveler's Wife

YEARS LATER, when the history books were written about the only known time travel experiment, it was said that Yolanda Green was not at all like her husband.

Yolanda was an even-keeled, mostly content person, who hummed her way through life. The ambitious Dr. Horace Green, known world over for his improvements to the subatomic laser, was usually depressed and irritable, and he never, ever hummed. Yolanda had a stress-free job as church secretary, spent her free time knitting sweaters for her nephews and playing bridge with the Evergreen Women's Club, and her only true aim in life was to have a house full of children.

This goal, however, required the participation of her husband, whose desire to start a family ranked somewhere below his desire to spend more time on university committees. Still, she needled him with suggestions, tried to plant the seeds of it in his mind—"Oh, this backyard will be great for our kids, one day!"—all the while, waiting patiently for him to capitulate.

All her fancies seemed to blow out like candles in the wind one day when he made his announcement at dinner.

"We've done it," he said. "Three times with a mouse and five times with a monkey. The university has approved my request for a manned test run. We're going into the future!"

He had the gleam of excitement in his eyes and the flush of pink on his baby-smooth cheeks. When they were fifteen, it was his enthusiasm that made her fall in love with him.

"I'm proud of you, dear," she said. "Who will be the lucky time traveler?" And her voice cracked because she already anticipated his answer. He looked down at his egg salad and responded in the voice of a child: "Why, me, dear."

"You? But you're the project leader. Wouldn't one of the grad students be a better choice?"

"I can't make them take that risk. Besides, I've worked all of my life on this." He reached across the table and took her hand. "You've seen what's happening. I've got to believe that in a hundred years all our problems—poverty, war, disease—will be solved. So I'm doing this for us, dear, for our unborn children. I've got to give them a vision of the world the way it will be. "

"You'll come back, won't you?"

"Of course, dear! I would never leave you behind. I'll be back for dinner as usual."

OF COURSE, Dr. Green did not show up for dinner as usual. Instead, a portly man in a gray suit showed up at her door with the news that her husband had not returned according to schedule, and the schedule, when it came to time travel, was everything. There was no guarantee he wouldn't show up at some point, but it was also possible that something prevented him from returning.

The news of the experiment leaked out, and all the tabloids ran with it. "Scientist Vaporizes Himself in Attempt to See Buck Rogers." Her friends gave her sympathetic looks which were unbearable—unbearable because they knew, like her, that she would never have children unless she had them with another man. Since she had never loved anyone else, this thought was unthinkable to Yolanda.

Eventually the public's interest in her faded. Since the insurance money provided more than enough money to take care of all of her needs, she spent her days knitting socks her husband would never wear, and her nights listening to the old grandfather clock ticking away the hours. She watched in grim silence as her husband's fears about the world were confirmed. Violence, poverty, starvation, plague—all of these became facts of life, and each year it worsened.

To escape from witnessing such despair, Yolanda began to read.

She had never read much before, so she her skills were limited. Her husband had an extensive library, so her choices were varied. She read Dickens, Alcott, Bronte and Austen. Her skills improved and she tackled Faulkner, then Conrad and Camus. She had never been educated beyond the eighth grade, and with each book her understanding of the world deepened. She worked her way through their set of Britannicas, then moved on to Plato, Aristotle, Nietzsche, and Marx. Soon she had exhausted her husband's collection and she began to visit the library. The librarians soon knew her by name.

The years passed and one day Yolanda received an official-looking letter in the mail. It bore the Presidential seal.

Mrs. Green,

Congratulations on reaching the graceful age of one hundred years!

It bore the President's signature, a stamp she was sure, but it still thrilled her. What astonished her more was her age, for she hadn't given it a second thought.

She had little time to enjoy it. The next day the United States went to war. Yolanda decided right from the start that people needed a message of hope. She started small, with peace sittings in her own city, and letters to her congressman, but her efforts spread. No one knew who she was or even her last name. To those who asked her age, she said simply, "I'm older than most."

When the war finally ended, Yolanda was asked to give speeches everywhere, and she did not disappoint. She called people her children, and she asked them not to shirk their responsibilities. She told them, "If this little old lady can do it, so can you."

Finally, she allowed herself to fade quietly into the background, and made her plans to die. But strangely, the end did not come.

When she arrived at the university, she saw that an oversized grandfather clock had been mounted next to the red-carpeted stage. As the time approached, everyone counted down the seconds. With a voice hoarse from years of giving speeches, Yolanda counted with them. At precisely zero, the egg-shaped metal contraption appeared. No fanfare, no smoke, no lights. The stage was simply bare one moment, then there the time machine sat. The crowd cheered. The hatch popped open and her husband emerged.

He had not aged one day since she last saw him. Dressed in a blue jump suit, he smiled and waved to the crowd. Scientists and journalists immediately converged on him, assailing him with questions.

Yolanda moved toward him, nudging her way through the crowd like a needle through a soft fabric. Soon she stood near her husband, just outside a circle of people.

"Horace, it's me, dear," she said.

The circle around him parted. When he saw her, his eyes widened, and he moved to her instantly, putting his arms on her shoulders.

"Yolanda?" he asked, incredulous.

"Yes, dear." There was a strange tremor in her heart.

He looked her up and down. "My God," he said, "what kept you going?"

She smiled and slumped into his arms. Her immortal and endless strength had finally deserted her. The people in the crowd—her children, her many children—fell silent, so all could hear her final words.

"Someone had to give you the future," she said.

And she realized, finally, why he never came back.

Epic, The

March 15, 2005

Dear Mr. Moles and Ms. Groppi,

I am writing to ask you if it would be possible to get an extension on your deadline of March 21.

When I heard about your *Twenty Epics* anthology, I have to admit that I found the idea of writing an epic in under ten thousand words a bit daunting. I mean, brevity has never been my strong suit! So I decided to pass on the project and work on something more fitting of my particular talents, some erotica hard science fiction, perhaps. At least, that was my original intention before I met the man in the white suit.

I am the middle of a feverish work session right now, but I wanted to at least whip out this letter to plead with you for a short extension. A few weeks, at most. I guarantee you it will be worth it. I'll give you more details when I get a chance, but for now, please consider this letter a placeholder in your slush pile. The real manuscript, which I am now writing under the working title of "The Epic" (or "Epic, The" if you want to file your titles alphabetically), will be on your desk as soon as humanly possible. Perhaps even faster.

My stories have appeared or will shortly appear in *Analog*, *Weird Tales*, *Crimewave*, and *Cicada*, among other places.

Sincerely,
Scott William Carter

~ | ~

April 2, 2005

Dear Mr. Moles and Ms. Groppi,

Though I haven't heard back from you on my first letter, I'm operating under the assumption that my request for an extension has been granted. I certainly hope so, because the story is coming along nicely.

You deserve a better explanation of why I wasn't more on the ball with getting you the story by your deadline, and I finally have a moment (while my co-writer is out on the back porch, taking a "brandy break" as he calls them) to explain.

On the day I wrote you the last letter, I was out on a noon walk here at the university where I work. We've had some unseasonably warm weather here in the Willamette Valley and the sun shined brightly in a perfect blue sky. The scent of freshly mowed grass was strong in the air. As I wandered the neighborhoods behind the school, I passed the Woodland Park that was just on this side of the highway. The park was empty except for an old man in a white suit and fedora who sat on the bench near the swings. He had a belly that hung out over his belt, a full white beard, and a face weathered and pockmarked as if he had lived a hard life. He looked like a mix between Jerry Garcia and Santa Claus.

As I walked past, I nodded to him. He said something back to me, but there was an eighteen wheeler rumbling past on the highway on the other side of the pine trees.

"What was that?" I asked. I expected him to tell me it was a nice day or something similar.

"Have a nice day or something similar," he said.

I gaped at him. "Sorry?"

He laughed. It was a high-pitched pig squeal, not at all what I expected from such a large man. "You're a writer, aren't you?"

"Ah . . yes." I was beginning to wonder what institution had allowed him to escape. The State Mental Hospital in Salem had closed years ago. I have a website, and my picture is on it, so it was possible he had looked me up and placed himself here because he guessed I would be walking by. Though I was a new writer with only a few credits, I knew it was possible I already had my first crazy fan.

I kept my distance.

"And," he said, "there was an anthology being called *Twenty Epics* you were thinking of writing for but ultimately decided against it?"

"How did you know that? What kind of game is this?"

"No game. I'm offering you a chance of a lifetime."

Then he went on to tell me that he had an idea for an epic short story so revolutionary and so groundbreaking that it would forever change the face of literature. He said he wasn't a writer, however, and he needed a capable young talent to partner with him to get the story onto the page. Would I like to help? Well, I figured I'd humor him for a few minutes, since he had been kind enough to flatter me (although I still kept my distance). He smiled and tipped his hat back on his head.

Then, his breath smelling of some sweet alcohol, he told me the story idea.

And he was right. Just the essence of it, a few sentences told in the jumbled fashion of a man who had no idea how to construct a story, moved me more than any piece of writing since *Flowers of Algernon*. And this, if it was handled right, would be even greater. It would be an epic of astonishing grace and beauty, adventure and heartache, romance and bravery—all in a mere five thousand words.

When he was finished, there was a long moment of silence. The world seemed different to me, clearer somehow. I took a deep breath, then told him I would use every ounce of my ability to make sure the story was told right. I knew that if I handled it correctly, both of our names would be linked with greatness no matter what we did the rest of our lives.

So he told me he would meet me at my house later in the day and we would begin. That's where we have been ever since. I have been burning up my sick leave (under the pretense of having a bad case of the flu) to work on this day and night. My wife has not been happy, but I told her it's all for art.

Whitey and I (Whitey being what I have taken to calling my Idea Man in the White Suit, since he still refuses to give me a name) are making good progress. Please, please be patient with us. Greatness, as Whitey has said to me more than once, can't be rushed.

My stories have appeared or will shortly appear in a number of magazines and anthologies. Though I haven't yet sold to *The New Yorker, Playboy, Esquire,* and *GQ*, I plan to appear in those prestigious markets in the near future.

Sincerely,
Scott William Carter

~|~

May 15, 2005

Dear David and Susan,

I hope you don't mind me calling you by your first names. I've spent so much time working on this project I almost feel like I know you by now.

Alas, it is my unfortunate duty to inform you that I have hit an impasse. I'm afraid all our hard work was for naught, and there's a good chance the story won't be finished.

Both my sick leave and my vacation have been completely exhausted, my boss has been leaving messages on my machine telling me I need to report to work or there will be consequences, and my wife and daughter are now staying at my mother-in-law's house. Whitey and I finished the first draft of The Epic two days ago It clocked in at 1,567,986 words. My fingertips have been bleeding from the constant, round-the-clock typing, I have blisters on my bottom, and I've been averaging only three hours of sleep a night, but yes, the draft is done. I was a bit concerned at the word count, but Whitey assured me that this was part of the process to get to the true greatness of the story. Look at most of the multi-volume epics being published today, he insisted. Aren't they far too long? Couldn't they be pared down? Well, the five thousand word work of genius was now waiting for us in that million and a half words. We just had to find it.

There is only one problem. It's Whitey. I was napping on the couch at three in the morning three days ago when I heard a door slam. Whitey never sleeps himself, instead waits impatiently for me by the computer when my body demands a rest, so I was surprised not to see him when I woke. I looked everywhere in the house, but he wasn't there. It's been three days. Where is he? He needs to come back. He has to come back. If he doesn't come back, it won't be finished.

Scott William Carter, who has been working on a yet to be published epic of staggering scope and depth, makes his home in Oregon. He has a two cats. More about his work can be found by doing a Web search under his name. His website currently has Google ranking of 3.

Yours Truly,
Scott

~ | ~

May 15, 2005

Dear Dave and Susie,

All hope is not lost! Immediately after dropping my last letter into the blue mailbox on my corner, I discovered a clue to Whitey's whereabouts. Frustrated at the thought of not finishing The Epic, and the terrible loss this would be the future of literature, I picked up my monitor to hurl it across the room. There, in an inch of dust and cobwebs, was an empty bottle of Alize Red Passion. There was a crumpled piece of white paper inside.

I put down the monitor and retrieved the bottle. Using a pencil, I fished out the paper, which now smelled of cranberries and was red-stained at the edges. Smoothing it out, I saw that there were magazine pictures of various celebrities that had been pasted to it. There was Richard Gere, Brad Pitt, Harrison Ford, Adam Yauch, Steven Segal, Martin Scorcese, and Cindy Crawford, among other faces I didn't recognize. Dozens of them, wrinkled and bent, one overlapping the other.

I had no idea how these ideas people were related, so I punched all of their names into a few Web searches to see what came up. It took a bit of surfing, but it soon became very clear what linked them. They had all, at one time or another, supported a free Tibet. Nothing else made sense!

So I now believe that Whitey wants me to follow him to Tibet. For some reason he must believe that only there can The Epic be finished. I am going to dig out my passport, then arrange a flight. I'll be taking my laptop computer, plenty of spare batteries, and the entire manuscript in printed form. I will not stop until we have finished this story once and for all.

I don't even have to worry about my job any more. I was informed in a letter yesterday that I no longer have it.

All my best,
Scotty

~ | ~

August 19, 2005

Dear David Groppi and Susan Moles

I have heard some disturbing rumors that you have already chosen your stories for XX Epix. I hope this is not true. I believe I have located Whitey, and soon we will once again be hard at worke.

It wasn't until last month that I finally found him. Months searching. Was growing desperte. No one in Tibet had heard of him. Finally I bumped into a spindly old man in the lobby of the Da Ji Jinjiang Hotel in Lhasa, the captiol of Tibet. He had thick glasses and gray sideburns as big and furry as mice. He said his name was Isaac and he had been in China since 1992. He had just gotten back from a tour of the Jokaang Temple. He talked and talked and I must be honest I thought he was a blowhard. Finally, when I was about to tell him I kneaded to get back to my room, he asked me why I was there. too tired to lie, I told him the truth. And then he said something amazeing. He told me knew the man I was talking about.

I told him to help me, but I must have seem too exited. He says to calm down and then asked me to dinner, and we ate there in the restarnat. He tolde me he was once a writer of some stature himself, tho he never wrote any of that fantasy crap, and he had used the man I called Whitey (he had his own name for him) many, many times in his career. Much of his success was based on Whitey's help, in fact.

But where could he be found, I said asked.

And that's when he tolde me the long and boring history of the

Drepung Loseling monastery. Started in Lhasa in 1416 or something. The second Dalai Lama lived there. The Chinise in 1959 invated and burned all the monk places, and then a bunch of monks from Loseling escaped all the buchering and started over again in Karnataka State. Thats in South India. And over time it became real poplar and lot sof new monks lerned there. Isaac said go there. Thats where Whitey will be waiting.

So that's what Im doing. I will will write again when I find Whiteyy.

[put impressive cretits here]

Sin seerly,
Scott Robert Jordan

P.S. Something strage is happning to me.

~|~

September 2 , 2005

Dear Gardner Moles and Ellen Groppi

I right to you frum India. I found Whitey. Isaac was rite. He was in the[do research make sure names splet right] new Drepung Loseling monastery. He was medatating outside the main shrine, on his knees, still in his white suite, sipping from a bottle French Cognac. he had been waiting for me and was very angry that it took me so longe to find him. He said to meet him the nex morning outin the quart yard.

So I did as he says but he doesn't show. Come to find out he dies in his sleep that night. They had a very big thing here for him. Lots of chanting and wearing fancy clotheing with feathers and brite colours.

But now I have to finish The Epic on my own. I dont know if I can do it but the monks here says I shud try. The say it is the jurney of my life to do this. so I am going to. I am going to stay and finish.

It is very hot here. I wish I had better clotheses. My wife, tho, won't send any and says only on the phone that I neede to call her lawer.

Trulee,
Scott Wm. Carter, Esq.

~ | ~

Knowvember 31, 2005

Dear Etitors,

It has now become a parent to Scott Robert Jordan Tolkein Wm. Carter, Esp. (who shall be refered to thenseforth as The Writer) that the manuscript in question (Epic, The) shall not be finished buy designaded time. The Writer wants the esteemed etitors of the soon to be published anthalogee to know that The Writer shall continue to worke on the story until it is finished, breaking only briefly to eat, sleep, meditate, or performe the chores required of all Monks here in XXX. This may take the reste of his life, since he has only the guide dance that the Budda chooses to inlighten him with, and his Mentor, Whitey, the Idea Man in the White Suite, is gone forever. the Writer is alone. afraid. but bravely he goes on.

The Writer's worke has been collected in such things as *The Bible*, *The Best of Elvis Presley*, and *The Kama Sutra*. U can find out more about Him by burnin cinnamon in sense.

Currrently makeing a mandala to cree ate world harmonee,
The Wrider

Happy Time

WHEN DALE THOUGHT BACK on their encounter, he often wondered what would have happened if he had been more alert. Would he have seen the girl coming? Would he have been able to avoid bumping into her? If he hadn't been tired from squinting at a monitor all day, if Portland's pollen-thick air hadn't given him a splitting headache, if he hadn't been lightheaded from the evening's bourbon, then maybe, just maybe, he would have noticed her before stepping out of his doorway.

Then everything would have been different.

But he *didn't* see her, and he *did* step, ice bucket in hand, out into the Phoenix Inn's blue-carpeted hall. He always refilled his ice before he went to bed. It was one of his rituals. If he woke up thirsty, he liked having ice in his water. Behind him, he heard the rain pelting the parking lot outside his open window. It had been raining since his plane touched down three days earlier, except for twenty minutes that first morning when it hailed. The hall was warmer and more humid than his room. Dale always kept his room cool. Sixty-two degrees. That's how he liked it.

Pinching the bridge of his nose, he turned to head to the ice machine, and that's when he saw the little black girl cart wheeling into him.

Routine will save you. Whenever a new guy tagged along on a job—which, thankfully, wasn't all that often—that's what Dale told him. No matter what city you land in, no matter how much the clients fucked up their network, you can find solace and comfort in the daily rhythms of your own routine. When you land in Denver, get your shoes shined before you take a taxi to the Hilton. Before bed, have a half of glass of bourbon with half of glass of Coke, one ice cube, while catching a full cycle of CNN. In Chicago, eat breakfast at the Iron Skillet and order the mandarin crepes, light on the whipping cream. Have your cup of coffee with two sugars. Read the local paper, front page first, then sports, then financial. Scan the obituaries. If you're feeling down, you can compare your life to some poor bastard who died younger than you and say to yourself, "Shit, it can't be too bad. I could have been *him*."

After five years as a traveling network engineer for Benco Industries, Dale had found that these carefully constructed habits acted as a shield against the occasional melancholy. If the new guy asked, and he often did, whether Dale liked his job, whether it made him happy, he said sure. You make sixty grand a year and you get to see the country. Do you get lonely? Sure, you do. It's normal. It's part of the job. That's why you need routine. It keeps you from thinking about things that don't matter. And if you have needs, as all men have needs, there are places to go to take care of that.

Sure beats having a wife and a couple of brats to anchor you down, he'd say. A lot of guys, they get lonely, and they go out and do something stupid like get married. But if you just wait until the feeling passes, if you use routine to insulate yourself from the depression, then the next thing you know you're having a steak, medium rare, in the Space Needle in Seattle at sunset, a new Grisham hardback open on the table next to a glass of white wine, and a feeling of total contentment swells up inside of you. That's when you know it, man. That's when you know life just can't get any better.

Right before he collided with the girl, Dale heard a shout from the other end of the hall— a man with a high, sharp voice: "*Eunice!*" But it was too late. The girl's feet plowed into Dale's chest, both of them going down, the ice bucket flying out of his hand and bouncing off the Van Gogh print on the wall. She landed on top of him, crushing the air out of him, her brown eyes inches in front of his own, wide and terrified. Her black braided pony tail fell against his neck.

At first, other than a sharp pain in his tailbone, he felt only mild irritation—mostly at himself, for failing to look before stepping out into the hall. It was only when the girl touched him, inadvertently on the arm as she scrambled back to her feet, that he felt the most powerful surge of loneliness he had ever felt in his life.

It was like drowning in cold water.

Then, for just a few seconds, he remembered a life he had never lived.

The chance encounter with Susan happened in an Atlanta grocery store three years earlier. Jingle Bells played faintly in the background and red and green streamers decorated the aisles, which just didn't seem right when his collar was soaked with sweat from walking five blocks from the hotel in the balmy heat. He was stooping to pick up a package of shaving cream when he saw her pass his aisle, pushing a squeaky cart. Since they had attended high school three thousand miles away in Los Angeles, he told himself it couldn't have been her—not the same blond Susan who sat next to him in American History, the Susan with a locker three down from his, the Susan who smiled and said hello to him when most people looked through him as if he was made of glass.

His heart beating harder, he followed the direction of her cart to the produce section, peering cautiously through a wine rack. And there she was, her hair cut shorter than he remembered, a little heavier around the middle maybe, but still gorgeous in cut off jeans and a white T-shirt with the words "Bean Counting Babe" across the front in bold black letters. She was picking out organic apples.

Dale, pretending to look at a bottle of merlot, wondered if he should say hello. What would he say? You know, I always had a crush on you. And she would say, what, gee, you look kinda familiar . . . She dropped a couple of apples in a plastic bag, sealed them with a twisty tie, and then rolled her cart away. Going, going . . .

Realizing she was about to disappear from his life, Dale stepped from behind the wine rack.

(No, Dale thought. That's not what happened. I never approached her. I walked away, never saw her again . . .)

"Susan?" he called.

She turned, and when she saw him, her face lit up with a smile.

She knew his name, she remembered him, God, how wonderful that she remembered him. She said she always wished she knew him better. They got to talking and it came out that she was recently divorced, finishing her accounting degree so she could make something of her life. He told her he was there on a job and she said, hey, no sense in eating alone.

They ate at a smoky Italian place around the corner. The lump in his throat wouldn't go away, and all the words that came out of his mouth didn't seem to form into sentences, but she still laughed and smiled at the right times. You remember Mister Trindle? The Biology teacher who couldn't go through a class without breaking a test tube? You remember that prank our senior year, when we came to school and found the principal's car on the front lawn with all the tires missing? When they finished, she gave him her phone number. Hey, if you're ever in Atlanta . . . And two weeks later, he *was* in Atlanta and they did dinner again. They made love that night, and everything went wrong because he'd never done it with anyone but hookers, but she didn't care. After that, he called her from the road, and whenever he got time off he spent it with her. A year later they married. A year after that they had their first child— a little blond girl named Francine.

(None of this happened. I never saw her. I heard from a friend a couple years later who saw her at the reunion. She was with her husband, a doctor, and she had a little boy . . .)

Francine took her first tottering steps at eleven months and said Daddy for the first time at thirteen months when he was reading her a bedtime story. She had said it before, but this time she looked right at him and he knew she meant it. Then Susan was pregnant again, and he quit his job and took one for half the money with the State of Georgia explaining to frustrated people why their mouse wouldn't work or just how exactly to attach a file to an email. It wasn't great work, but it didn't matter.

He was happy, happier than he had ever thought possible.

ONCE, AT THE URGING of a roommate back in college, Dale had dropped some acid, and he remembered the head-spinning craziness that followed. For a moment he thought that's what had happened—the girl must have stuck him with a needle. But in seconds the wooziness passed, leaving him just as sober as he was before, and all that remained was the aching loneliness.

And all those memories . . .

The black girl, wringing her hands together, peered down at him. She wore a yellow tank top and blue shorts, a Band-Aid on one of her bony knees. Her face—there was something familiar about her. A tall, sandy-haired white man in a brown suede jacket appeared next to her. He looked down at Dale gravely, his eyes partially hidden behind hazel-tinted glasses. The beginnings of a patchy beard decorated the man's face. He was young, an air of intelligence about him. He looked like somebody who spent his free nights reciting poetry in coffee shops. A gray duffel bag was slung over his shoulder.

"What—what—" Dale stammered.

"Sorry about that," the man said, reaching down and taking hold of Dale's hand. He had small, delicate fingers, cold. Dale froze, wondering if what happened before would happen again. But as the man pulled Dale to his feet, nothing happened. The blood rushed to his head, and he felt dizzy, but that was normal. That happened to him all the time. He was a man with a slow heart.

Susan . . .

"I'm sorry," Dale said, looking for his ice bucket, and, finding it, hurriedly picking it off the floor. "I should have looked—"

"You have nothing to be sorry about," the man said, giving the black girl a scolding look. "She gets a little hyper sometimes. Are you all right?"

The man looked at him with concern. Dale, who was trembling, stumbled to his door. "Fine," he said. "I just . . . need to sit down."

The man was opening his mouth to say something else when Dale shut the door. He leaned his back against the cool wood and let out a long trembling breath. He was still trying to make sense of what he had seen. A vision? A dream? It was so real, so vivid. Looking at his empty room, the perfectly made queen bed, the spotless carpet, the absolute lack of anything personal except for his single brown suitcase sitting on the dresser, the top open, everything inside neatly packed, his loneliness deepened.

He had a baby girl. Her name was Francine. When they played music for her, she waved her arms in time to the beat.

No, he reminded himself, he didn't. It was a fantasy. Susan had married someone else. Dale had never married, never planned to marry, never thought there was anything in it for him.

The air conditioner kicked on, its droning hum filling the room, and Dale shivered. So cold. He had never felt this cold before. He moved to the air conditioner, and as he reached to turn the dial, the black girl's face popped into his mind again. There was definitely something familiar about her. He had seen her somewhere. Then it came to him—the paper. He retrieved the day's *Oregonian* from the bathroom, rifled through the news section until he found it: a small blurb inside, the girl's picture right there in black and white. Definitely the same girl. "Foster Child Kidnapped From Los Angeles Home" was the headline. A man had kidnapped the girl, ten-year old Eunice Harkins, during dinner. He was wearing a ski mask, but they knew he was white because they could see his neck. He had a gun.

Dale felt a cold feeling of dread settle over him. A gun.

Swallowing, he stepped over to the phone. Intending to call 9-1-1, he picked up the receiver.

That's when his door swung open.

Dale froze. The sandy-haired man stepped inside, and as he shut the door behind him, he pulled his hand out of his pocket. He had a revolver, and he pointed it at Dale. The man's face was pinched, his cheeks pale. He looked like he might throw up.

"Please don't," the man said.

Dale put down the receiver. His mind raced through what he might do. He could scream. Maybe the man, frightened of being caught, would bolt.

"Don't even think of making a sound," the man said, stepping closer. Dale saw that the man's gun hand was shaking. "I can't let you call the police."

"I wasn't going to," Dale lied. He wondered how the man knew.

"Just shut up," the man said. "Sit on the bed."

Dale obeyed, feeling the cushion sink beneath him. The man, shaking his head, stepped up to him.

"I thought we could sneak in," he said. "Damn. Damn." He went on pointing the gun at Dale for a few seconds, then closed his eyes and dropped his gun arm to his side. "I can't do this. I can't. I'm not a killer." He opened his eyes and glared at Dale. "Why did you have to be coming out right then, huh? Now we've got this mess. They can't know we're here—they can't."

"If you let me go, I promise I won't call them," Dale said.

The man leaned against the opposite wall. "You can't lie to me," he said quietly.

"I'm not lying."

The man laughed. "What I mean is, you *can't*. How do you think I knew you were going to call the police, huh? I heard your thoughts. I can hear them if I'm close. Walls don't matter."

"You what?"

The man was about to say something when the door opened again and the black girl stepped into the room.

"You're not going to hurt him none are you, Tom?" she said.

"Go back to the room, Eunice," the man said sharply.

"No! Not till you promise you won't hurt him none. You said we wouldn't hurt nobody."

"I'm not going to hurt him," Tom said, looking at Dale.

Dale was confused. Eunice seemed to be with the man willingly. He had gotten the impression from the article that the girl had been taken from her family against her will.

"No, she came of her own free will," Tom said. When Dale jumped, he added, "I told you—I can hear thoughts."

Dale was beginning to believe it. "What number am I thinking of?" he asked, imagining the number fifty-eight.

"Fifty eight," Tom replied immediately. "It's also how old your father was when he died, which is what you thought just now. You're also thinking that your father was alone when he died. He divorced your mom when you were still in high school, and he never married again. He—"

"Stop!" Dale said, terrified. It was true, all of it. He felt naked before this man. "Who are you people? What—what did she do to me?"

Sighing, Tom stuck the gun back in his pocket. He motioned for Eunice to shut the door, and after she did, he pulled the chair out from under the little table and sat in it across from Dale. Eunice, her hands clasped behind her, stood next to Tom.

"Look," the man said, "I'm not supposed to tell you. It could get me in a lot of trouble, understand? But I'm going to. Maybe if you know, you'll understand why you shouldn't call the police. Eunice, she's one of the gifted. There's lots of us out there, and when we find one, we watch them. If they're in trouble, we make contact. We give them the choice of living with us."

"Where?" Dale asked.

"I'll just say we were on our way north to get there."

Dale looked at the girl. "And what happened to me, what I saw, she did it?"

"Yes," Tom said.

"What was it?"

"Your happy life," Eunice said quickly. She briefly locked eyes with Dale, then looked at the floor.

"Eunice has a unique gift," Tom said. "She hasn't learned to control it yet, and that's why you felt what you did. If she touches you, you get a glimpse of your best possible life."

"Your happy time," Eunice said again.

"That's right," Tom said. "Every choice you make over the course of your life has consequences. One thing leads to another. A thousand paths diverge, another thousand from those, and on and on. Eunice shows you the path of choices that would have lead to your happiest life. It is her gift. Her foster parents didn't see it that way, though. They had no idea what was going on, and they couldn't stand touching her. The memories were too painful. She spent most of her time locked in a closet."

It sounded crazy, but because of what Dale had seen, what he had felt, he believed it. He also understood how the memories could drive the foster parents to act so cruel.

"I'm glad you believe us," Tom said.

Dale nodded. How could he ever go back to his solitary life after what he had seen? He had thought he was happy, but now he knew it was only the shadow of happiness. He had never known real happiness.

"Can she take it away?" Dale asked, looking at Eunice. "Can she put me back the way I was?"

"Yes," Tom said. "With my help, she can. But—"

"Do it," Dale said.

Tom shook his head. "Are you sure?"

"Yes, yes. Please. It's all I ask. If you do that for me, I won't call the police. I promise. Just take it away. Take away what I've seen."

"It doesn't have to be a curse," Tom said.

Dale looked over at the open window, watched the rain flashing in and out of the light. "No?" he said, feeling his throat constrict. "Susan married someone else. You want me to be a home wrecker? I can't have that life. I missed it. I don't want to be reminded of it every day. At least, before, I was fine. I didn't know. That's what I want. I want to go back to not knowing."

"But you can have other happy times," Eunice said, and Dale saw that she was fighting back tears. When she went on, she was nearly shouting. "Everybody always has the chance of having other happy times. That's why it's not so bad, no matter what I see. If I touch you now, it might be different. If I touch you tomorrow, even more different. Another happy time. Always more chances. Always . . ."

The girl was talking in a rush, words spilling out one on top of the other, and Tom took her hand. She quieted and looked at the floor.

"I just don't want him to be sad," Eunice said.

Tom nodded and looked at Dale. "You've got to understand, what you saw was only the happiest you would have been *up to this point.* Who knows what the future could bring?"

"It hurts so much," Dale said.

"I know," Tom said. "Believe me, man, I know. I'm a loner, too." He smiled weakly. "You're not the only one who saw something he can't have. But like I said, it doesn't have to be a curse. For guys like us, it can be a reminder—a reminder to open your eyes. To take a chance. To not let life pass you by."

Dale wasn't sure he could live with that memory haunting him. "What if that's the best it can ever be?"

"What if it isn't?" Tom said.

* * * * *

It was after midnight when Dale left the hotel, and the only restaurant open was a Denny's four blocks over. When he stepped inside, his rain slicker dripping on the gray slate tiles, there was a sign that said, "Seat Yourself." The place was empty except for a couple of kids in tie-dye talking heatedly and a burly trucker-type in the corner reading a magazine. Dale took a booth in the back.

The waitress who approached his table, a lanky brunette, smiled at him. She didn't look a thing like Susan, but he liked her smile. There was no ring on her finger.

"Need a menu?" she asked.

"Just some coffee," he said, smiling back. It felt strange to smile. He rarely smiled.

"Sugar or cream?"

"Yes, p—" he began, and then shook his head. How easy it was to fall back into his old routine. "No," he said. "No, I'll just have it black this time."

"Gotcha," she said, and started to turn away.

"Say," Dale said, and when the waitress turned back, eyebrows raised, his heart started racing. A lump formed in his throat. "Do you, ah . . . do you get a break?"

"Yes," she said, eyes narrowing slightly, though the smile was still there. "Why?"

He swallowed. He didn't realize it would be so hard. "How would you like to have coffee with me?"

For a moment, she didn't answer, and Dale looked at her expectantly. He was a man without the comfort of his routine and he was scared. But excited too. Every choice had consequences. A thousand paths diverged, another thousand from those. Would she say yes? Would she say no? And then he realized that it didn't really matter.

All that mattered was that he had asked.

The Grand Mal Reaper

SHE STOOD ACROSS FROM ME, hands tucked into the armpits of her jean jacket, the tear in her nylon stocking looking garish in the pale yellow light. When she glanced at me through the fogging breaths and cigarette smoke, my heart did the skids.

Five of us huddled on the snow-covered sidewalk outside the restaurant, Lenny the manager, a couple of waitresses in addition to Rita, and me, a thirty-year old busboy who'd only been in Oregon a month. The conversation had turned to our plans for the holiday, and while Lenny and the other waitresses chatted animatedly about turkey dinners with annoying relatives and last-minute shopping for hard-to-find toys, Rita and I hadn't said a word.

We'd been exchanging glances a lot the last couple of weeks, the kind of glances that often lead to buying condoms and beer from the mini-mart in the middle of the night, but I hadn't thought about pursuing her until that moment. I was sure my own eyes had the same look, a what the hell am I doing here sort of a look. I didn't know squat about Rita, nothing except that she was about my age and that she lived on the south side of Rexton out by the golf course, but after that glance I wanted to know everything about her. I wanted to know where she grew up and what movies she liked and why she never smiled. The conversation was winding down, everybody doing the slow sidestep toward their cars, and I was thinking don't let her go, ask her stupid, do it now, but then came the death-tugging. Like an invisible cord pulling at my chest.

At first I thought it was a small one. The last year or so I had been getting three to five small ones per day and I had gotten pretty good at suppressing them. But then everything took on an azure glow and I knew that in ten seconds I would be on the ground frothing at the mouth. I abruptly said goodbye and turned to go, thinking maybe I could make it around the corner, behind the juniper bushes where nobody would see me, but I hadn't made it three steps when the world went dark.

I WAS PULLED over black asphalt and along a double yellow line straight into a pair of bright lights. I didn't recognize them as headlights at first because they were stacked on top of another, but as I neared I saw the shape of a black minivan turned on its side. I passed two out-of-focus bodies before I came to an old woman lying flat on her back in the middle of the road, her legs twisted at an awkward angle. A piece of glass was embedded in her forehead and blood was gushing from it, covering her face as if she wore a red mask. She blinked up through the blood.

"The grandchildren," she said, coughing.

"I'm sorry," I said, "I can't help you. I'm not really here—"

"Please . . ."

"You're the only one who can hear me or see me," I insisted, saying the words I had said hundreds of times before. "There's nothing I can do. It sucks. I know. I'm really sorry."

I had long since learned there was no sense in trying to walk away, but I *could* turn, and once I stopped moving I faced the other direction, focusing my eyes on the place where the edge of the road blurred into white fog. There were other voices too, people yelling at one another down the road. She kept talking to me, begging me to tell her if her grandchildren were all right, if they were alive, her voice sounding more gurgled and strained until finally she stopped talking.

I would have covered my ears, but I knew from experience that it would have made no difference. My hands wouldn't block the sound.

THE SNOW FELT cold and wet on the back of my head. When I opened my eyes, the first thing I saw was Rita. She was leaning over me, the streetlamp creating yellow halo around her curly black hair. I saw Lenny and the others behind her, looking down at me with that particular mix of revulsion and relief I had seen plenty of times throughout my life. I wondered how long it would be before Lenny found a reason to fire me.

"I'm—I'm all right," I said, starting to sit up.

Rita gently placed a hand on my chest. For a small woman she had a surprising amount of strength. "Take it easy, Jimmy," she said.

"Man oh man," Lenny said excitedly, "you gave us quite a scare, Jimbo. I thought maybe I was going to have to give you mouth to mouth but Rita said to just leave you be and it would pass. Shit, you almost gave us a heart attack but she was right." He laughed. "You've got her to thank or you might have had a rude awakening. And everybody around here would have thought I was queer."

He said it as if he expected people to laugh, but nobody did. I imagined kissing Lenny's cigarette-stained lips and had to stifle an urge to retch. It was bad enough with the taste of bile in my mouth as it was. My legs and arms burned as if I had just spent all day in the gym. Rita helped me to a sitting position, and that's when I saw the worst part: the stain in my crotch.

"You're not wearing a bracelet," Rita said.

I couldn't look her in the eyes. "Guess I forgot it," I mumbled. Quickly, I stood and started for the street. "See y'all after the holiday."

I took three steps before the world started to tilt. Rita was there, a hand on my arm.

"I'm giving you a ride," she said.

"No, it's all right," I said. "I can—"

"I wasn't asking," she said.

I WAS FOURTEEN when I had my first seizure, staying the summer in New Ulm, Minnesota. It was one of those sweltering days when you can feel the sweat sticking to your eyelids. Me and Ray Pullman, the red-headed kid who lived next door to my grandparents, were hiding out in his basement playing penny ante poker and drinking Coca Cola out of glass bottles. Having just cleaned Jimmy out of his comic book money, I asked him if he wanted me to keep a tab on his losses.

"Asshole," he said, smiling. He never showed his teeth long because of his braces. "That's you, asshole Peter Parker with the Imperfect Pecker."

I leaned back in the folding chair, feeling the metal stick to my bare back. It was too damn hot for shirts. "And you're asshole Clark Kent with the Boner of Steel," I said. "You can't even walk because your boner is so big."

It was a game we'd been playing all summer. Ray had been a big fan of Superman ever since John Byrne came out with his rerelease of the Superman origin story when we were in fourth grade; Ray had every issue since carefully sealed in plastic bags and backed by cardboard. He wouldn't even let me read them unless I washed my hands first, and even then he watched me the way my father watched me when I was washing his Mercedes. Ray liked Superman, a.k.a. Clark Kent, because the guy was pretty much invincible.

Me, I said that's exactly what made Superman boring. Peter Parker had problems just like the rest of us. You could beat him straight up in battle even if you didn't have some stupid green rock. It was *because* he was imperfect that we could relate to him.

"Well, what do you know," Ray said. "Anybody who leaves their comics sitting all over the floor, getting ripped up and the cats chewing and pissing on them and stuff isn't somebody who knows anything."

That was Ray's way of ending any dispute. A true comic book collector protected his comics and according to Ray only a true comic book collector could know anything for certain about comics. Since just about everything we talked about came back to comics eventually, that line of reasoning pretty much ensured Ray won every argument.

"This is dumb," I said, putting down the cards. "Wanna go to Baker's Pond?"

Ray shrugged. "Beats smelling your stink all day, I guess."

Twenty minutes later we were in our swimsuits and standing on the grassy bank twenty feet above the pond, the oaks casting a fishnet of shadows over us. Some little kids were on the shallow side playing with a dirty beach ball, but otherwise we had the pond to ourselves. We came there two or three times a week most summers, and every time we always started with a big jump off the bank.

"Tall buildings in a single bound!" Ray shouted and jumped, cannon-ball style, his red hair making him look like a ball of fire.

His splash was like a mushroom cloud. The little kids screeched and swam for the shore. I wanted to splash the little kiddies too, but I knew better than to jump before Ray surfaced. I had done that once two summers earlier and nearly broken Ray's jaw.

I waited, but Ray didn't show. It wasn't like him. Usually he was up and laughing, swimming hard for the near shore. Thirty seconds passed and still no Ray.

"Yo, Superman!" I shouted. "Stop kidding around!"

As the ripples faded, my pulse quickened. The kiddies were watching me. I was debating about what to do when finally I saw a bit of red hair coming up through the water, and I breathed a sigh of relief.

Then I realized that he was face down. And there was blood gleaming on the back of his head.

"Ray!" I screamed.

It would have taken me two or three minutes to navigate the narrow, rock-strewn path down to him, so I decided to jump. I knew there was risk of hitting whatever he had hit, but I thought that if I backed up and gave it a good running start I would land far past him. But as I turned around, something happened—the sun flashed through a crack in the leaves. A lot of people who suffer regular seizures say there's usually a trigger of some sort, flashing lights and pulsing sounds being the key culprits, but this would be the only time I could pinpoint an outside cause. It was nothing, a blip of white light, but I felt the world spinning and going dark. I never felt myself hit the ground.

Suddenly I was hovering directly over the pond. Everything except Ray was blurry and out of focus, fading into a white fog. I heard the little kids screaming. Something tugged at my chest, pulling me downward. As I plummeted toward Ray, I instinctively raised my arms; I had no cause for concern because I passed right through him.

Now I was under the surface of the pond, tiny particles floating in the murky green water. I didn't feel wet or cold. I held my breath, though I would find out later that there was no need for me to do so since I was no longer in my body. The first thing I saw was a couple of black oil drums stacked on top of one another, inches from my feet. The last time we came to the pond, they hadn't been there.

I looked up and there was Ray, eyes closed, blood trickling from his mouth into the water. I reached for him but my hand passed right through.

"Ray!" I shouted.

He didn't move. I shouted his name another dozen times but he never stirred.

RITA DROVE a blue Tercel, a manual transmission that jerked when she shifted and fishtailed when we hit an icy stretch. There were empty cans of Dr. Pepper and a mud-stained copy of *Vogue* on the floor. The piss in my crotch was going cold, my shorts sticking to my thighs. She had one of those funky tree-shaped air fresheners, and it must have been fairly new because the inside of the car smelled strongly of pine. I was glad.

"You want to listen to some music?" she said, breaking the stillness.

"Sure," I said, though I really didn't. I was thinking about the old woman on the highway. The images flared up in my mind and I forced them away. There was no rhyme or reason to who I saw die or why. She could have been anyone, anywhere. It didn't matter.

When Rita leaned over to turn on the radio, I stole a glance at her. The lines on her face were deeply drawn, but she was pretty in a rugged, worn sort of way.

She asked me where I lived. I told her where my apartment complex was. She started to make small talk about living in Rexton, about the upcoming election, and about other trivial things that people talk about when they don't know what to say, and I nodded and said uh-huh, uh-huh, knowing full well that any chance of us getting romantic then or at any point in the future had died outside the restaurant. This saddened me, and when she eased into the parking spot in front of my apartment, I started to open the car door so I could make a quick getaway. Down the street, a couple of kids threw snowballs at one another under a flickering streetlamp.

"Well, thanks," I said.

"Hey now," she said, placing a hand on my arm.

At her touch I felt a warm shiver pass through my body. I turned and looked at her and saw the way she was looking at me, her brown eyes wide, her lips slightly parted, and it wasn't a brush-off look I was seeing. It was the same kind of look she had been giving me the last few weeks.

"Do you want me to come in?" she asked.

"I'll be all right," I said, still figuring I must have been misreading her intent as one of concern.

"I thought you might not want to be alone."

I laughed. "I spend most of my life alone. It's no biggee. Really."

"Are you sure? Because I don't have anywhere else I have to be. I could—"

"Do you really want to do this?" I said abruptly.

She looked as if I had slapped her across the face. "What do you mean?"

I paused, knowing there was no easy way out now. "I mean, are you sure you want to get mixed up with a guy like me?"

"I was just asking if you wanted some company—"

"We both know where this is leading."

She sighed. "Why does it have to lead somewhere?"

"A guy like me, with my problem, you don't want to get mixed up with that. You have no idea what you're getting into."

"I know exactly what I'm getting into," she said sharply. And when I looked at her in surprise, she added, "I was married to an epileptic."

IN THE BEGINNING the seizures came once or twice a week. A little old lady in a nursing home passed in her sleep. A six-year-old boy accidentally shot by his older brother flat-lined on an operating room table. They talked to me and I talked back, but I didn't know if the deaths were real or all in my mind until I watched a pair of hikers freeze to death on a mountain, and then the next day saw the article in the paper with their picture.

Two Die on Oregon's Mount Hood.

That's when I knew I had been given an extraordinary power.

That's when I thought I was becoming the world's first real superhero.

The first few dozen deaths I witnessed with complete fascination. While my parents dragged me to one doctor after another, subjecting me to EEGs, blood tests, and every unpronounceable drug imaginable all in an effort to "cure" my seizures, I kept silent about my power. Someday, I figured, I would be a full-fledged superhero, and when that time came I probably wouldn't want anyone to know my true identity. The fact that I couldn't physically affect anything when I was having one of my visions, or that I couldn't interact with anyone other than the person dying, didn't bother me because I thought my powers were just beginning to develop.

But they didn't.

And the more I watched people die, the more I knew for certain that my ability wasn't a gift at all.

It was a curse.

AGAINST MY better judgment, I invited Rita up for coffee. While I threw on some new clothes in the next room, she complimented me on my décor. I laughed at my glorified lawn furniture and said yeah, the Salvation Army comes in handy. I asked her about her husband, but she demurred, telling me it was a long time ago. We talked about movies, books, and places we had been. Turned out Rita had been living out of a suitcase almost as much as me.

"Sounds like you're running from something," I said.

She looked at me over her coffee cup, steam rising in front of her eyes. "Why don't you wear a bracelet?"

"Maybe I don't want the seizures to define me. What happened to your husband?"

"Maybe I don't want my past to define me. You doing anything tomorrow?"

The next two weeks, Rita and I saw each other almost every night. I learned a little about her past. She had been born in Iowa, her parents were farmers. She had gone to school and become a nurse, though she didn't say why she wasn't doing that now. She didn't say anything about her husband. I had one more seizure at work, seeing a naked black woman with a grotesquely swollen belly die moaning inside a bamboo hut, but otherwise I fought off the rest. Lenny wouldn't look me in the eyes any longer and I figured my pink slip would be forthcoming.

I had no intention of telling Rita about my power, but then New Year's Eve we were at her apartment watching the ball drop in New York, and I felt a death-tugging ripping at my insides. I fought it off, clamping down hard on Rita's hand. When the feeling passed, my face was drenched with sweat and my heart was pounding, but I felt exhilarated because it was the strongest one yet I had suppressed.

"Are you all right?" Rita asked.

I looked at her, suddenly feeling more alone than I had ever felt. Nat King Cole crooned out *Dreaming of a White Christmas* from the boom box on her bookshelf, a bookshelf that was bare except for a couple of beat-up paperbacks and some wilted carnations in a cheap plastic vase. Outside, someone was setting off firecrackers.

"I want to tell you something," I said, and told her everything, starting with Ray's death. I told her of my time in and out of drug treatment for methamphetamines, of leaving home at seventeen and never looking back, and about the wacky support groups I had tried over the years, including ones that focused on astral projection and near death experiences. I told her the more painful the death was for the person dying, the stronger the pull on me, meaning that the deaths I did see were usually excruciating to watch.

I expected bafflement or skepticism, but she just leaned forward and kissed me. I was strong until that moment, but then I was in her arms, burying my face in her chest, her stroking my hair and telling me everything would be all right. We went upstairs and made love on her creaky futon, the ceiling fan droning above us. When it was done, she lay naked on top of me, her breasts pressed against my chest, her head nestled under my chin. Her hair smelled the way the air smelled after a thunderstorm.

"I always wanted to have super powers," I said, "but I never imagined it would be like this." I laughed. "I'm the Grand Mal Reaper. Watch out, because if I get the shakes it might be your time. And don't bother begging for mercy, because there ain't squat I can do about it."

She didn't say anything for a long time, lazily tracing circles on my chest with her fingernail. "Maybe there is some good you can do."

"Like what?"

I felt her shrug. "I don't know. But I can't believe you would be given a power that was completely useless."

I extricated myself from her arms, sitting up on the edge of the bed. "You've got to be kidding."

She sat up beside me, pulling the sheets up so they wrapped around her lower body. "I just thought you might find some positives out of it," she said.

"Positives?" I said. The word was like a douse of cold water. I stood, still naked, and faced her. "Do you know the kind of crap I've seen? Life shits on you and then you die. That's just the way it is."

"You don't really believe that."

"Oh yes, I do."

She sighed. "Jimmy, things happen for a reason."

"That's just the kind of crap we tell ourselves so we don't have to think about how meaningless life is."

She nodded sadly. I was shaking, and only partly because of the sweat cooling on my body. I pulled on my clothes. She didn't say anything until I was tying my shoes.

"Crap has happened to me, too," she said.

"Oh yeah, like what?"

"Like my divorce."

She looked small and fragile on the end of the bed, hunched over with her hands wrapped in the sheets, her breasts exposed. Until that moment I hadn't even noticed she was wearing a necklace with a tiny cross.

"Ben was just a goofball," she said. "We grew up together, and he was always hanging around the farm. He had voices for all the animals, and he could make me laugh." She shook her head. "You know the story, right? High school sweethearts and all that. We were married right after high school, and we had a plan. Ben was going to work to put me through school, and then I'd return the favor. And that first year at the University of Iowa, everything seemed to be fine. Then Ben had his first seizure."

I didn't know quite what to say. "How bad was it?"

"Bad. Three or four times a week, at least. But that wasn't the worst part. The worst part was when he was diagnosed with schizophrenia. I dropped out of school to take care of him. He wasn't even the same person. In the span of five seconds he could go from calling me a whore to calling me his special flower."

"So he left you?"

She laughed sharply. "No, that's the crappy part, see. I was selfish. I didn't want to spend my life taking care of him. He's back home with his parents now. They write me sometimes. They say he asks about me." Her eyes were glistening. "But I still believe that there's a purpose to things, Jimmy. I mean, it *can't* be any other way. It just *can't.*"

All at once I understood why she was with me, or at least I thought I did, and I couldn't stop myself from saying so. "Look, I really am sorry about what happened, but if you're looking for closure by being with me it's not going to work. I don't want to be somebody's therapeutic tool."

She swallowed and looked at the floor. "If you think that's why I'm with you, then I think you should go."

I didn't want to go. I wanted to take her in my arms and make love to her and tell her I understood her pain.

But instead I turned and walked out.

While I was washing dishes the next morning at the restaurant, I felt a couple of death-tuggings and I successfully fought them off. I was beginning to think that maybe I had finally beaten the thing. Maybe I could settle down and have a real life. I knew I had been too harsh with Rita and while I scrubbed the grease-stained pans I thought about how I could make it up to her. But she didn't come in at noon when she was due, and I started to think that maybe she had skipped on to another town.

At a quarter to one Lenny, ashen-faced, entered the kitchen with a clipboard in hand. I thought, here it is, he's finally worked up the nerve to fire me.

"It's Rita," he said. "Somebody just called from the hospital . . ."

He told me her car had been hit by a drunk driver, some fool who had been out partying on New Year's Eve, and she died in the ambulance. I leaned against the counter. He went on to tell me how great a person Rita was, but his voice sounded like it was coming from far away. I was thinking about the death-tuggings I had felt that morning.

How many had there been? Five? Six? I wondered if she had been one of them.

"Was anybody with her?" I asked.

He shook his head. "She was alone."

And I didn't need him to tell me that. I knew the answer when I asked the question.

Some things you just *know.*

THE OLD MAN had an IV attached to his arm and a breathing tube taped under his nose. The equipment next to him wheezed and beeped, but the old man himself seemed to make no sound. The room was dark except for the triangle of light from the bathroom that spilled onto his bed. His wasted body barely caused a rise in the sheets. As I stepped up to the bed, his eyes cracked open.

"Who are you?" he asked softly.

I knew from how gentle the tugging had been that he wasn't in a lot of pain, and I was glad for that. His eyes moved, following me, but he didn't turn his head.

"My name's Jimmy," I said.

"Are you a doctor?"

"No."

"Good. I'm sick of doctors. They always want to stick something up your ass." He stared at me for a moment. "There's something funny about the way you look. You're all shadowy-like. Are you an angel?"

"No."

"Who are you then?"

"Just somebody sent to be with you."

"Sent? Sent by who? God?"

I laughed. I hadn't intended any religious connection by what I had said, but now I wondered if my subconscious had other ideas. "I don't know."

"Do you believe in God?"

I thought about it for a moment. I realized then that I wasn't doing this just because nobody should die alone, although that was part of it. I was also doing it for me. I was doing it because I had been given a power, and if there was some good I could do with it, even a little, that meant there might have been a reason I had it. I wanted there to be a reason. "I'd like to," I said. "I'm just not sure I can."

He closed his eyes, and I knew, the way I always knew these things, that it would be for the last time.

"Me either," he said.

The World in Primary Colors

THE SIGN was quite clear—*No Adults Allowed. Thank you.* Like an afterthought, it was affixed to the red plastic tunnel with masking tape, slightly askew, handwritten on a white sheet of paper with a black marker. The paper had started to yellow and bubble with age, which was strange, because Doug didn't remember the sign being there last time—and that had been only a few weeks earlier. Of course Rosie had never asked him to take her into the plaything before, preferring simply to watch other kids, so he may not have noticed.

Rosie tugged on his hand. "Go in, Da-ee? Go in wid Wosie?"

The room smelled faintly of baking pizza. Her small hand felt slightly sweaty. Doug adjusted his glasses and leaned closer to the sign, hoping for some small print addendum that might let him pass. As a corporate tax accountant, he was trained to look for such addendums—loopholes, exceptions, and special circumstances to turn what was illegal into what was merely inconvenient—and he often found himself doing this in his private life, too. But in this case, no such luck.

The screeching and laughter of the children echoed all around them. The play equipment at Locomotion Pizza was in a separate room, its walls and ceiling almost entirely glass. Outside, mere inches from where children played, a steady pulse of traffic passed on Roosevelt Boulevard, but the glass was thick enough that it muted most of the noise. On the wall connecting them to the main part of the restaurant was a mural of an old steam engine passing through the mountains. The ceiling had been painted a perfect blue, but the real sky outside was a metallic gray, like the dull side of aluminum foil.

Doug's mood always rose and fell a little with the weather, but the overcast skies didn't seem to affect the kids one bit. They crowded eagerly around the video games in the corner, bounded through thousands of plastic balls in the area covered with black netting, and clambered after one another through the huge, castle-like structure of interconnecting tunnels.

The castle was the crown jewel of the play area, and the thing Rosie talked about incessantly for days after a visit—as big as a small house, each tunnel a different solid color, red, yellow, blue, with plastic bubble windows at various junctures and three different slides, some straight, some that curled like twisty fries. If only they had toys like *that* when he was growing up. But of course, he knew he had been a little timid, like Rosie, perhaps even more so.

He squatted down next to her. Children's laughter echoed inside the tunnel.

"I'm sorry, honey," he said, squeezing her hand. "It says I can't. But *you* can go in. I'll watch you."

Her face darkened—lips compressing to a horizontal line, dark eyebrows bowing into the mirror image of checkmarks. It was an expression he had seen on Autumn's face many times. Rosie was the spitting image of her mother—round, brown eyes, fair, freckled skin, hair like dark chocolate and tied in a pony tail. *Oh, she looks so much like you, Autumn! She could be your clone*! Doug had heard that more times than he could count. What he hated was not the comment, but how people would always gave him this *look*, like they were either feeling sorry for him because she was physically so different—with his sandy hair, blue eyes, and darker skin, really more of an opposite—or they were just a tiny bit suspicious that the child was not, in fact, his.

She wore a white dress over a red and blue plaid shirt, his favorite outfit, one that made her look a little like Raggedy Anne. She fiddled with the hem. "But I wan you go in Da-ee!" she insisted.

He smiled. "I know that, dear. But it's against the rules."

"Wules?"

"That's right. You know . . . Kind of like how Mommy tells you not to kick the table at dinner time. That's a rule. Well, this is a rule, too. Daddies can't go in there. It's just for kids."

"Tids?"

"That's right, dear."

She hesitated a moment, gears turning, before saying with even more gusto than before: "But I wan you go in, Da-ee!"

Doug sighed. It was May, with the long days of tax season behind him, and he'd taken the afternoon off just to make her happy. He hadn't been spending nearly enough time with her lately, getting home long after she went to bed, and the guilt had been gnawing at him. This was their first stop. So what if he had a bad back and tendonitis in his wrists? He'd survive. It might even be fun. Break a few rules, be a rebel.

"All right," he said reluctantly. "You go first."

Swallowing, she started inside, only having to hunch a little. Doug followed on his hands and knees, glancing over his shoulder right before he went into the tunnel. Sure enough, just as he feared, a woman pushed through the double glass doors into the play area right at that moment. She was short and mousy, but she had a mean frown, the way his middle school librarian Mrs. Hampton frowned when she caught someone sticking gum under the card catalog. He smiled weakly, then followed Rosie.

The plastic felt gritty, like the plastic bowls at home felt, the ones they'd had since college. Years of sweaty hands had given the tunnel the musty smell of a locker room. Rosie hesitated where the tunnel started up, and Doug encouraged her, holding her waist as she climbed. "Step here," he said. "Use the footholds." With each step, she gained confidence. Doug had a little more trouble, his leather shoes slipping. Eventually they reached a landing, where the color went from red to bright yellow. Tiny plastic bubbles above let in light, and other than a glimpse of the blue ceiling, he couldn't see anything outside.

Rosie was nearly at the next tunnel, one that went up another forty-five degree angle. Doug, however, was already winded.

"Wait a minute," he said, leaning against the wall.

"But I wan go dere, Da-ee!"

"I know, dear. But just . . . wait a second. Isn't this neat? We're way up here, in this castle."

She stared at him, brown eyes blinking. Sometimes talking with her, he felt like he was Mission Control and she was on the Space Shuttle, and he had to wait for his signal to bridge the vast distance between them.

"Way up ere?" she said.

"Right. Way up here."

The next tunnel was blue, the next one after that green, twisting left and right, sometimes straight, sometimes climbing. Rosie chattered excitedly, repeatedly saying, "Way up, Da-ee, way up ere." She got a little ahead of Doug, and then when he rounded a sharp bend, entering another blue tunnel, she was already out of sight. He heard the sounds of shoes squeaking and thumping, but they seemed as if they were coming from a long ways off.

"Rosie?" he said.

When she didn't answer, a vicious panic took hold of him. The tunnel darkened, going from blue to black, pressing in on him, tightening. He put his hands against the sides, as if he could hold the vise at bay, but the feeling persisted. There was pressure on his lungs, as if someone was sitting on his chest. Each breath came short and quick, and he felt sweat break out all over—on his back, his forehead, his neck. He'd never felt such intense anxiety in all his life—the only time he'd felt anything even remotely similar was when his father died years ago—and he told himself it was foolish. She was just a little ahead. Christ. Calm down. *Calm.*

He was still sitting there trying to get a hold of himself when a brown-skinned boy in a blue baseball cap scooted around the bend, coming from the direction Rosie had gone. He gave Doug a curious look.

"It's okay," Doug said. "I'm with her."

The kid frowned, then passed without a word and continued down, a little faster than he had been moving before. Great. Kid was probably going to complain to Mommy that some adult was up here.

"Da-ee?" Rosie called from up ahead.

Relief flooded through him. "Coming, dear," he said. "Just wait, okay?"

When he caught up to her, she was crouching by a round window, one that bubbled outward as if they were on the inside of an eye looking out. She faced away from him, tiny fingers pressed up against the scuffed plastic. There were actually four windows, one on all three sides, plus on above. Just beyond the area, a blue tunnel continued upward, and another, a short green one, ended at the beginning of a slide.

"Look, Da-ee! Look!" Rosie said.

"You really shouldn't go ahead of me like that, Rosie," Doug said, crawling up next to her. Sweat glued his polo shirt to his back. "Daddy likes to be able to see you, and if you . . ."

He trailed off, having gotten a glimpse of the play area down below. He saw something, something black moving along the wall, that didn't seem quite right. He moved closer to the window and looked beyond the tiny fingerprints and the scratch marks and saw the mural of the train—but it wasn't just a mural anymore. The train was *moving*, white puffs rising from its smokestack, the whole thing chugging along the wall, as if it wasn't a wall at all but a giant television screen. And that wasn't all. The train had changed, now less realistic and more a cartoon, shorter, more compact, and with giant yellow wheels. Then he recognized it. It looked like the toy train Rosie had at home.

"Look!" Rosie said again. "Look!"

He looked where she was pointing and saw that the green plastic floor was no longer plastic, but real grass, at least a foot high. The doors to the restaurant were huge and crooked. The restaurant through the glass windows was out of focus. He saw the shapes of people, but he couldn't make out any of their features. Two squealing boys ran past, and their faces were clear but huge; their heads were at least twice the size they should have been, bulging as if someone had inflated them with air.

Doug blinked a few times, but nothing changed. "That's odd," he said. He cleaned his glasses on his shirt, but this didn't do the trick either.

Rosie smiled at him. "We up eye!"

It took him a moment to realize what she meant. "Yes," he said. "We're very high. Honey . . . what do you see out there?"

She stared. Earth to Space Shuttle, waiting . . .

"Dere?"

"Yes. Do things . . . do they look different?"

She looked at him a moment longer, then clambered past him. "Look, Da-ee! Side! Go side now!"

Doug looked back at the window. Surely if she saw the same thing, she would have said something . . . He looked more closely at the clear plastic, wondering if it was some kind of trick, a projection maybe, but he didn't see any equipment.

His heart racing, he joined Rosie. She glanced at the slide and bit down on her lower lip. The green plastic angled downward steeply. He didn't like heights much. He also didn't like going fast. A bad combination.

"Why don't you get on my lap, honey," he said. He sat at the edge of the slide, his legs extended in front of him.

She hesitated.

"It's okay, dear," he said. "You'll be with me."

Slowly, she moved onto his lap. She was no longer a little feather, and he stifled a groan when the full weight of her settled onto him. But when she clutched onto the scruff of his slacks and leaned into him, her back warm against his chest, he felt a tingle up his spine. He placed his arms lightly around her and scooted forward. For just a second, before he pushed off, he saw them from the outside, a snapshot of father and daughter, and he told himself to remember it. This moment here. Put it in the scrapbook of his mind.

They zoomed around the curves, picking up speed as they raced over the green plastic, each of them laughing. He felt the rush of air on his face. It lasted only a moment, and then they were at the bottom, his long legs skidding on the grass.

Real grass.

Giggling, Rosie hopped off his lap and headed back for the tunnel's entrance. "Side!' she cried. "Go side!"

Doug rose, so mystified he barely noticed the ache in his knees. The room . . . The grass felt soft beneath his shoes. The locomotive grinded and screeched along its tracks. Big-headed children dressed in solid blues and greens ran past, laughing, and the few adults around the room were looking at Doug with out of focus faces. He glanced at the castle and saw that it was a real castle now, with towers and parapets, although still painted in alternating solid colors.

Rosie stood by the tunnel waiting for him, but it was no longer a tunnel; it was an arched entryway that crossed a moat of sparkling blue water.

"Sir," a young man said.

Doug looked in the direction of the voice and saw a scarecrow with black button eyes, only he wore black jeans and the yellow polo shirt with the black train on it, the shirt the employees wore. His straw body shimmered like gold.

"You really shouldn't be in here, sir," the scarecrow said. And for just a moment, his real face came into view—a face with acne scars and patchy facial hair, a textured face of shadows and hues and imperfections.

Rosie protested, but Doug didn't want to make a scene, so they headed for the car. But it wasn't his car, not exactly. His Ford Explorer was now solid blue, tires and all, and it bulged like an inflated beach toy. All the cars were like that. The tall pines around the restaurant had been replaced by giant, two-dimensional Christmas trees, like something Rosie might make at daycare with butcher paper. All the buildings lining the street were made of blocks, some plastic with notches on the top, some wood with numbers and letters on the side. Inside the passing cars, Doug saw not people, but giant stuffed animals and life-size dolls.

Unlocking the car, he saw that his keys were no longer metal, but red and rubbery like a child's eraser. He lifted Rosie into the back seat, and instead of her car seat, found a purple octopus. She climbed into it, and he lowered the tentacled arms over her.

"Go ome, Da-ee?" Rosie said.

"Yes, dear," he said, and it was as if someone else was speaking. Home. Yes, home. Get his bearings. But even as he thought this, the world shimmered. Some of the cars changed to real cars. Driving home, paper trees turned to real trees, and blue sky became gray. Rosie sang happily, oblivious, but Doug gripped the steering wheel so hard his knuckles turned white. A small green brontosaurus, walking upright and pulling a red wagon, changed to a homeless man in army fatigues pushing a rusted shopping cart.

By the time he reached his house, the world was back to normal and he saw the house as it was—a one-story ranch with flaking gray paint, piles of rotting leaves in the driveway, a lawn going to seed. After pulling into the cluttered garage, he retrieved Rosie and carried her into the house. He passed through the galley kitchen, which stank of rotten milk, the sink full of dishes. When he rounded the corner into the family room, he saw Autumn sitting in the rocking chair inches from the television. Some talk show was on, but she stared blankly ahead, her eyes glassy. The shades were drawn, and the room flickered along with the television.

"Mommy!" Rosie cried.

"Oh," Doug said, putting Rosie down. "I didn't know you'd be home."

Rosie ran to her side, gripping the armrest, but Autumn didn't look at her. Her hair, more gray than brown these days, drooped over her wan face. She still wore her blue hospital scrubs, and he saw a tiny spot of blood on her sleeve. She had been a phlebotomist for nearly ten years, and it was the first time he could remember seeing blood on her clothes. Usually, she was quick to wash it off, as she said even a little stain could alarm the patients.

"I was tired," Autumn said.

"Are you sick?"

She didn't answer.

"Did something happen at work?" he pressed.

"Doug, please," she said quietly.

Rosie jumped up and down. "Da-ee and Wosie go side, Mommy!" she cried. "Side!"

Closing her eyes, Autumn leaned her head back against the rocking chair. For a moment, she looked like her mother looked the last time Doug saw her, back in the nursing home when she was in the full clutches of Alzheimer's, her face stretched and pale. "Can you just leave me alone for a while, please?" she said, her voice dying to a whisper.

Doug was going to tell her about the amazing thing that just happened to him, but the impulse dissolved in his anger. Lately she'd been having more and more of these moody phases, and he was sick of it. It's one thing to ignore him, but another to ignore Rosie. "What's happened to you, anyway?"

But when she answered, it wasn't with words. Her eyes remained closed, but tears streaked down her face. Rosie looked alarmed, and started to reach for her mother, but Doug didn't want her to see Autumn like this. He guided Rosie to her bedroom and shut the door just as Autumn began sobbing. The wood was thick, but he could still hear her. He turned on Rosie's CD player, a song about counting animals.

He looked at Rosie. She stood in front of her toddler bed, clasping her hands and biting down on her lower lip. The rest of the house may have been a mess, but Rosie's room was perfect, the bed neatly made, all the books and toys on their shelves, all the tops of the dressers clean. Doug kept it that way.

"Mommy sad, Da-ee?" Rosie said. "Mommy ha tears?"

Doug swallowed away the lump in his throat. "Yes, dear. Mommy's a little sad right now."

"Mommy ha ow-ee?"

"No, not exactly."

"Why Mommy sad, Da-ee?"

He kneeled in front of her and tried to smile, though his face felt like dried wax. "Sometimes," he began, and had to start over when his throat constricted. "Sometimes people are just sad, honey. Sometimes . . . there is no reason why. But Mommy will get better. I promise. We just need to give her time."

She looked unconvinced, but he managed to distract her with a toy fire engine, and soon she was laughing again.

THE STRANGE THING that happened didn't happen the next day, or the next, and he was too afraid to go back to the pizza place. But on the weekend, when he was pushing Rosie on a tire swing at the park, it happened again. The swing changed to a red crop duster with a bright yellow propeller. Rosie swooped around in a circle, her head bent low in the cockpit and her pony tail flapping behind her. The jungle gym turned into a blue rocket ship with yellow fins. Two kids in white spacesuits looked out from the hatch.

This time, Doug wasn't scared. In fact, he realized he had been secretly hoping it would happen again. The grit and grime of reality returned on the walk home, but he was left with a pleasant feeling, like the buzz from a good brandy. He took the following Wednesday off and took Rosie to the zoo, and while they were there, the concrete walkways faded and they found themselves in a lush jungle, surrounded by animals, but not animals that could bite or claw. These animals were big, fluffy, and friendly, like the animals from her picture books.

Doug decided he liked Rosie's world. He started taking off early in the day to do things with her—the mall, where every shop was a toy shop with toys that talked back, the riverfront carousel, where there were horses with manes like silk and hides like satin, and the beach, where dolphins dressed in tuxedos emerged from the surf to tell them stories of the undersea world. The more he did, the longer this wonderful new reality lasted. He saw all of Rosie's friends brought to life—Marmar, Slow Joe, Big Cat, Little Cat, and thousands of others he didn't know by name. He was burning through his vacation days, and he wanted more.

Three weeks after that first experience at Locomotion Pizza, Doug was crunching numbers on a spreadsheet when his boss, Gabe, stopped by his cubicle.

"You wanted to see me, old buddy?" he said.

Doug saved the file and swiveled in his chair to face him. Gabe had both hands on the edge of the cubicle and was peering around it, as if he had been passing and remembered Doug's email at the last moment. They had been friends for years, playing racquetball before their knees gave out, playing board games with their wives before their children devoured their evenings, until now they rarely saw each other outside the office. Autumn used to say—back when she and Doug used to do things like talk—that Gabe looked like a repressed hippy. He wore a white shirt and dark slacks, but his personality still showed in his pony tail, his thick mustache, and his trippy rainbow tie. His glasses had a slight red tint.

The sounds of the office surrounded them: clicking keyboards, humming printers, and the steady background drone of people speaking on phones. It was a gray world, with gray walls and gray carpet. Even the fluorescent light seemed flaccid and dull.

"Yes," Doug said. "I was wondering . . . Well, I was thinking . . ." He didn't realize this would be so hard. "I was thinking, if it's all right with you, that, that I'd like to take a leave of absence. Unpaid, of course."

Gabe had watery blue eyes, the kind of eyes that used to get him laid all the time back in college, or so he said, but they looked purple through the glasses. He narrowed them. "You're serious?"

"Yes."

"How much time we talking about here?"

"Um . . . I don't know. A month?"

Gabe sighed and stepped around into the cubicle. He reached for a door, but there was no door, so he turned and sat on Doug's metal desk. Gabe's tie-dye socks had the same swirl of colors as his tie. When Gabe spoke, he lowered his voice to just above a whisper.

"I talked to Autumn," he said.

Doug didn't understand where he was going with this. "Yeah?"

"She's worried about you, man."

"Worried about *me?*"

"That's right. She said you've been acting strange."

Doug felt the cubicle walls collapsing in on him, the same feeling he had back at Locomotion Pizza, but this time it only lasted a second before it was replaced with his rising anger. He felt his jaw grow tight. "She said *I'm* acting strange? What about her? She's the one going through some weird, delayed version of postpartum depression."

"Doug—"

"If anybody's acting strange, it's her. She . . . she should see someone. Get some help. It's ruining our family, what's she's doing. She—"

Gabe placed his hand on Doug's shoulder, silencing him. "She *is,* man. She is seeing someone."

The comment derailed Doug. "What?"

Gabe looked at Doug for a long time with sad eyes, the way someone looks at an old family dog that has started snapping at invisible squirrels. Did he know about Rosie's world? Doug hadn't told anyone yet, not even Autumn.

Finally, Gabe sighed and headed out of the cubicle. When he'd reached the hall, he glanced over his shoulder.

"Take all the time you need, Doug," he said. "But you guys should talk. *Really.*"

* * * * *

On the way home, moving from one stoplight to another in a slow waltz with hundreds of other cars, Doug thought about what Gabe said. He knew he needed to talk to Autumn, that their marriage was disintegrating in a barrage of silent moments, but he just couldn't bring himself to care about that now. He wanted to spend more time with Rosie. He wanted smiling purple bears and magic carpet rides, not therapists who talked in monotones and loud arguments about how neither of them knew what the other was feeling. He wanted a world of soft edges and primary colors, not one with sharp corners and a little gray in everything.

Then, as he was turning onto their street, one lined with pin oaks and leafy maples, the most amazing thing happened. The world changed. It changed, and Rosie wasn't even with him. The cars parked on the street became green and yellow tugboats, the road a bright blue river twisting through banks lined with palm trees. He turned where their house should be, but it wasn't a house; it was a white spaceship shaped like a half-inflated beach ball. A door opened in the ship, a ramp extended, and he motored his boat inside. But it wasn't a boat. It was a motorcycle. It was a horse. It was a leather bound book with feathered white wings.

The doors whisked open and he walked into an igloo, the walls made not of ice, but white shiny blocks. Passing the dining room, he saw a sparkling beach and six monkeys in pink dresses having tea around a picnic table. He heard Rosie's music coming from her room, and her singing along with it. He was turning toward the hall, now a rope bridge across a deep canyon, when Autumn called out to him.

"Doug," she said.

Her voice sounded like it was coming from the living room. He turned in that direction and he was walking along the deck of a sailboat. The sails fluttered, and he smelled salt water on the breeze. He knew Rosie's world was becoming more real to him, and he was exhilarated by it. But then he saw Autumn, head bowed, waiting for him at the aft of the ship, and the world around her was the old world, fuzzy at the edges. She sat in their old burgundy couch, piles of unfolded laundry on either side of her. He saw the scratches and the smudges in the off-white walls. He saw the lint and dirt in the taupe carpet at her feet. Autumn—dressed in a gray sweat pants and sweat shirt, holes in the knees—looked up at him and frowned.

He stopped a few paces away, afraid to go closer. "Something amazing is happening to me," he said.

Sighing, Autumn closed her eyes and brought her hands up to her face as if to pray. She breathed deeply for a moment, then stood. When she looked at him, he saw that the shadows under her eyes were so deep they could have been carved with a knife.

"This has to end, Doug," she said.

"What has to end?"

"This! This . . . *thing* you're doing."

"I don't know what you're talking about. I'm changing, Autumn. I'm changing and I like what's happening. I'm—I'm seeing what Rosie sees."

She bit down on her lower lip, the perfect imitation of her daughter, and closed her eyes again. She tucked her arms around herself in a tight hug. When she opened her eyes, there was moisture in them, and when she spoke, her voice was so strained it didn't sound like her own.

"Doug," she said. "Doug . . . I let you pretend. I thought it would help you. But it's got to stop now. It's been six months."

The fuzzy edges of the grungy living room pushed outward, enveloping a few more feet of the sailboat and the ocean. Doug felt a clamp tightening on his chest, and he took a step backward.

"What are you talking about?" he said.

"Doug, listen to me—"

"Why are you doing this?"

"I want you—"

"Can't you let me be happy? I'm happy. I'm—"

"Stop!" she cried. More burgundy couch appeared, more dirty

carpet. "Just stop! Christ, don't you remember what happened at the pizza place? For God's sake, it was in the paper . . . It happened so fast, you said, just turned around a second . . . just a *second* . . ." Her voice choked on the words. The scuffed walls extended, and he saw crooked paintings and cobwebs in the corner. "Don't you remember the trial, Doug? Don't you remember how you screamed at him? Jesus, don't you remember the *funeral*?!"

The boat faded and flickered and then he was just standing in a dim living room, the curtains half open, the weak light cutting across the easy chair and the carpet like a wall between them. And the harsh memories started to return, like unwanted houseguests, and he tried to close the doors of his mind closed.

"She's . . . she's not . . ." he began.

"She is!" she said fiercely.

"But she can't . . . I've seen . . ."

"Doug," she said, with a little more gentleness. "Doug, I know it's been hard. Especially for you. But—but we can't . . . We can't go on like this. You've got to face what happened, Doug. You've got to accept it. You've *got* to. You've . . . You've . . ."

But the rest was lost in a fit of sobbing. She turned away from him, and he stared helplessly, watching the way her shoulders shook. In a daze, he turned away from her, heading back through the living room to the dark hall. Rosie. He had to see Rosie. He saw the flaking paint along the trim, the dead fly inside the opaque light fixture. The walls closed in on him, tightening, squeezing the air out of his lungs. He stumbled, sliding against the wall and knocking off a framed picture of Rosie. When it struck the carpet, the glass cracked. His temple throbbed, pain flaring behind his eyes, but he pushed on, staggering into her room.

"Da-ee?"

He blinked away the sweat in his eyes and saw her standing by her bookshelf, wearing her white dress with the red and blue plaid shirt, the Raggedy Anne outfit, his favorite. The one she was wearing the day they went to Locomotion Pizza. It was going to be their day, a special day. She clutched her favorite stuffed animal against her chest, a blue rabbit, and looked up at him with worry. The room around her was clean and tidy. He kept it that way. The rest of the house was a disaster, but not this room. *Not this room.*

Behind him, he heard Autumn sobbing in the living room, and he turned and closed the door. He leaned his head against the wood, his pulse like a raging river in his ears. Autumn was right. He had to deal with this. They couldn't go on this way. He had to be a man now—accept what he'd lost, what he could never get back.

"Mommy sad, Da-ee?" Rosie said behind him. "Mommy ha tears?"

He turned and looked at her, and just for a moment, in the time it took to blink, he saw the Rosie when they found her in that man's van—a dark gash along her forehead, blood covering half her face, her dress covered with red spatters. Then it was gone, and she looked as she had before, only with tears in her eyes. She wrung the rabbit in her little hands.

"That's right, honey," he said. "Mommy's sad."

"Why Mommy sad, Da-ee?" she said. "Why?"

He opened his mouth to speak but no words came. He felt a cold chill, the coldest he'd ever felt in his life, and he shuddered violently. She rushed to him, hugging his legs. He patted her hair. She was so warm and solid he couldn't see how she could possibly be fake. He dropped down to her and pulled her away from him, looking into her moist eyes. There were worlds in those eyes. He had seen them.

"Sometimes," he began, and he was planning on saying the rest. *Sometimes,* he was going to say, *there is no why.* But before he could, her room changed. He saw the rumpled sheets in her bed, the same as they had been the day she left. He saw the books stacked haphazardly on the carpet, the pile of toys by the closet, the dirty clothes in front of the changing table. He saw the dust on the blinds and a spider camped out in the corner. And the smell—the staleness of the air, how it had lost the scent of her over time and now only smelled like death. Even this, he thought. Even this is taken from me.

He hugged her violently against him. He had to deal with this. But it wasn't about dealing. It was about *deciding.* And then he knew what he had to do. He picked up Rosie and ran with her through the house. When he passed the living room, Autumn called out to him, but he kept going. He rushed into the garage, hit the button, and quickly buckled Rosie into her car seat. Never felt forget to buckle. *Never.*

"We going, Da-ee?" she said.

"Yes, dear," he said. "We're going."

And then he was in his Ford Explorer, starting the engine. As he was backing out of the garage, Autumn appeared at the door, her face red, filled with confusion. She said something, but he couldn't hear her over the engine. He was in the street, and he shifted into gear. Autumn followed him, shouting, and now he could hear her. *We've got to deal with this! Don't run away!* But he pressed down on the gas pedal and sped away from her. He glanced in the rearview mirror and saw her in the middle of the street, running after him. Only it wasn't her anymore. It was the horrible vibrating ball that Rosie hated, the one someone had given to her on her birthday. It bounded after them, but they were too fast. They were getting away.

"Where we going, Da-ee?" Rosie asked.

Instead of answering, he stepped on the gas, speeding up the car. Only it wasn't a car. It was a giant eagle, but plush, with feathers as soft as Rosie's hair. The wings flapped and they leaned low, racing over the road. Only it wasn't a road. It was a runway, with a bright yellow control tower at the end, a smiling blue cat inside giving them the thumbs up. The eagle lifted them up into the sky, high up over the neighborhood. Only it wasn't the neighborhood. It was Rosie's world—a world with soft edges and primary colors, a world with no gray in it at all.

Father Hagerman's Dog

ROUNDING A BEND on the gravel road, the low sun momentarily blinding him, Marty finally came to the white picket fence that was the edge of Father Hagerman's farm. Everybody called it a farm even though it was only a few acres, because that's what Father Hagerman wanted it called, and nobody in their right mind contradicted Father Hagerman.

Marty's collar was damp with perspiration. The dashboard fan blasted a steady stream of warm air. Turning onto the dirt drive, he saw a white cottage nestled among a grove of birch trees. A dozen chickens pecked at the ground next to a large, fenced-in garden full of corn, cabbage, and other vegetables. He remembered picking pumpkins there every October with his mother, back when they lived down the road.

He killed the engine. The Gonzo curled in the passenger seat—nobody would be able to tell it apart from a golden retriever at a glance—opened its eyes and perked up its ears. Marty checked his appearance in the mirror, straightening his tie and brushing his unruly black hair out of his eyes. He frowned, thinking about the con artist who got him into this mess. *The Gonzos sell themselves! You'll not only make enough money for college, you'll be able to buy a house!* What a bunch of garbage. After a month of trying, he was just hoping to break even on his investment.

He got out of the van, smiling his salesman's smile, and looked up as the screen door banged open.

His smiled faded when he saw that Father Hagerman was dressed in nothing but white jockey undershorts.

The old man, over six feet tall and as thin and tan as a copper wire, held his hand over his eyes to block the sun. Then he threw his arms wide.

"Marty!"

He bounded down the wooden steps. Mortified, Marty used the van door as a shield, thrusting out his hand in the hopes that no other physical contact would be required.

Hagerman pumped Marty's hand furiously, his thick glasses glinting in the sunlight. "Marty, my boy," he said.

"Hello, Father," Marty said.

Even though Hagerman had been kicked out the seminary for seducing nuns some fifty years back, he still insisted on being called Father. He was bald on top, but the hair on his chest was thick and white. When Hagerman opened his mouth, Marty saw that most of his teeth had been capped with gold. The last Marty had heard, Father Hagerman was worth over ten million dollars, all of it inherited from his parents' oil drilling days. His chief occupation the last fifty years, other than playing at being a farmer, had been writing angry letters to the local *Two Spoons Gazette.*

Hagerman finally stopped shaking Marty's hand, stepping back and appraising Marty as if he were livestock up for auction. Marty did his best to keep his gaze at eye level.

"I remember you when you was just a pup," Hagerman said, and put his hand out, waist-high. "Got kids yet?"

Marty laughed. "No, sir. I'm only twenty-one. Still in college."

"Well, *sheeoot*," Hagerman said, which was something Marty remembering him saying often. "That don't stop most kids these days.

How about this weather? Too damn hot for clothes, I'll tell you that. What brings you here?"

Marty was trying to decide the best way to answer that question when a mangy gray mutt, as fat as Hagerman was thin, pushed open the screen door and slumped onto the porch. The animal's mixture was impossible to guess. It looked out at Marty with glassy eyes, a line of slobber dribbling from its mouth. The mutt's fur was patchy and thin, and one ear was missing.

Marty smiled. If this was his competition, then selling the Gonzo was gong to be easy.

"Well, sir," he said, "I've got a little something I'd like to show you."

Hagerman's thin white eyebrows arched. Marty wasn't sure how the old man was going to react when he found out why Marty was there. He remembered the time Hagerman chased off a pair of Mormon missionaries with a shotgun.

"Well, I see you have yourself a dog," Marty said, warming into his sales persona. "Now what I've brought with me—"

"That there is Chib," Hagerman chirped.

"That's an interesting name. What I also think you'll find interesting—"

"Stands for Cold Hearted Insane Bitch. If you spend five minutes with her, I think you'll agree it's fitting."

Marty lost his train of thought. "Er . . ."

"Hell, you look positively piqued, boy," Hagerman said. "Why don't you come in and have some lemonade? I'll read you some scripture. I'm doing Mathew."

He turned to the house. His bony back was even tanner than the rest of him.

"Sir," Marty said, realizing he was going to have to be more direct, "I've come to see if you might like to buy a Gonzo 450."

The old man had put one foot on the creaking porch. He turned, confusion registering on his face.

Marty cleared his throat. "A Gonzo . . ."

"I heard you. What is it?"

Hagerman's lips were pressed into a thin line. Marty wondered if he was making a mistake. This was, after all, the man who had challenged the local postman to a duel after the postman informed him the price of stamps had gone up three cents.

"Well, sir, it's a dog," Marty said. "Not just any dog, mind you. A special kind of—"

"I got a dog," Hagerman snapped. "Yes, sir. I see that, sir. But this—"

"So you came all the way here to sell me a dog?"

"No, no. I came to see *you*. But this isn't an ordinary—"

"How long has it been since you've been here? Four, five years? And you come trying to sell me a dog. I've always had one dog. I'm always going to have one dog. No need for more."

Frustrated, Marty turned to the still-open van. "Gonzo, come!" he shouted.

The robot leapt out of the car, landing gracefully next to Marty. It wagged its tail but otherwise stood motionless. Chib raised her head for a moment, then slumped back onto the porch.

"Nice retriever," Hagerman said. He squatted next to the robot, scratching it behind the ears. "Obeys well. But I'm still not buying it."

"It does more than obey well," Marty said. "It obeys perfectly."

Hagerman stood. "All dogs crap on the carpet once in a while."

"As I was trying to say, sir, the Gonzo 450 isn't an ordinary dog. It's a robot."

Hagerman laughed. "A robot dog?"

"That's right."

"Kind of like them metallic-looking bag boys at the grocery store?"

"You got it. Only these robots are made to look and act like the real thing, only better."

"Hell, I wouldn't have known unless you said so. I read about these in the paper. How do I know you ain't joshing me?"

Marty looked back at the Gonzo 450. "Roll onto your back, Gonzo," he said. The dog complied, putting all four feet in the air.

Marty got down on his knees and popped open the chest compartment, revealing the battery. He pulled out the plug, holding it up so Hagerman could see it.

"You recharge him every night," Marty said. "It's the only way to know he isn't real."

"Looks like a her."

"Oh, well, yeah. They come standard as females, but you can get males, too."

"With little peckers and everything?"

"Um . . . yes, sir. That's right."

Hagerman slapped his knee. "Well, *sheeoot*. What will they think of next? A robot dog with a pecker. I thought I had seen it all. They don't hump other dogs, do they?"

Marty felt a flush spread across his face. "No, sir. No, they don't need to do that."

"Could you program them to do it?"

"Ah . . . "

"Just kidding," Hagerman said, punching Marty so hard in the arm that Marty stumbled back against the van. "So you drove all the way up here to sell me a robot dog? They out of robot vacuum cleaners or something? Look, son, you know I'm not going to buy one, so I'm sorry to waste your time. You say hello to your Mom and Dad for me."

He turned to go. Marty knew he needed to go for broke.

"Okay sir," he said. "Sorry to bother you and all. I'm just trying to earn some money for college."

The old man turned and looked at him, his expression softening. Marty hated using the sympathy angle, but the truth was, he needed any help he could get. If he didn't sell at least one of the Gonzos, he wouldn't be going to school that September at all. He climbed into the van as if he was going to leave.

"Isn't your Daddy helping you?" Hagerman asked.

"Come Gonzo," Marty said. The dog leaped onto his lap and stepped across him into the passenger seat. Marty looked up at

Hagerman. "He's trying. His company almost went under and he's digging out from under a lot of loans."

"So you thought you'd sell robot dogs to pay your way through college?"

"Among other things," Marty said. "I work during the school year, too. But because my father's income was good until lately, it's almost impossible for me to get financial aid."

Marty started the car. The electric engine buzzed, then settled into a quiet purr.

"Well, I better be going," Marty said. "I'll use the daylight while I have it."

Hagerman sighed. "Hold on now."

"Sir?"

"Come on and give me your sales pitch. I'll listen." He leveled a bony finger at Marty. "But no promises, you hear?"

Marty smiled. "Sure, but I tell you, the Gonzo sells itself."

Hagerman grunted. Marty killed the engine and climbed out of the car, then called for the Gonzo to follow. In the fading light, the color of the pine trees was deepening from green to black. Yet there was still enough light that Marty spotted a stick on the ground by the porch. He picked it up, tossing it as far he could down the drive. Chib raised his head but didn't move. Neither did the Gonzo, but Marty knew that was because of the programming.

"Fetch, Gonzo," he said.

The robot burst into a run, kicking up gravel in its wake. Its graceful stride was a beautiful thing to watch.

"Fast," Hagerman marveled.

"You got that right," Marty said. "All the models can run about three times faster than their biological counterparts. Not only that, but imagine having a dog that doesn't need to eat, sleep, or produce waste. You plug it in nightly as a rule, but it's got a two-week charge. You want to pull an all-nighter, your Gonzo is right there with you."

The Gonzo returned, placing the stick at Marty's feet. He picked it up and tossed it again. The robot took off after it. Chib got up and sauntered down the porch, settling in the tall grass at the edge of the gravel. It never once glanced at the stick.

"Notice how I didn't have to issue the command again," Marty said. "The robots have an intuitive understanding of what is expected of them. But only the good things. This dog won't bite children or tear up your drapes. It won't run in front of a car chasing a squirrel. Plus they adapt easily. You want it to pick up your newspaper, you only need to show it once."

The robot came back, depositing the stick. This time Marty ignored it.

"Sleep, Gonzo," Marty said.

The dog sank too its belly and closed its eyes.

"It'll stay like that all day if I let it," Marty said.

"Heck," Hagerman said, "Chib will do that right now."

Marty ignored the comment. "They're programmed initially with over two hundred tricks. Most of these commands are intuitive—sit, roll over, shake—but there's a guidebook included, too. Here's the kicker. With the 450, the programmers have made a breakthrough. The robots are now able to adapt to your needs in ways they never could before. In time, this dog will fit you just as well as your . . . er, personality." He was going to say clothes, then realized how stupid that would sound since Hagerman wasn't wearing any.

The old man scratched the hair on his chest. The sky above the trees was going purple.

"They like being petted and all that?" Hagerman asked.

"Sure," Marty said. "They respond to affection."

"Respond . . . But do they like it?"

"I'm not sure I see the difference."

Hagerman shrugged. "How much they cost?"

Marty told him. Hagerman whistled.

"I know it seems like a lot," Marty said, "but it's really about the cost of a two-week vacation. Plus Gonzo Incorporated backs every product with a hundred percent guarantee. If you don't find this to be the most perfect dog you've ever had, just send him in within ninety days, and they'll give you your money back."

Hagerman made a noncommittal sound. He looked at Marty a moment, then gazed at his vegetable garden.

"Maybe you'd like to come up and get a pumpkin this year," Hagerman said.

Marty tried to keep the impatience out of his voice. "That might be nice," he said.

"No charge, of course."

"That's very generous."

Hagerman looked down at the Gonzo. "Well, I guess you convinced me. I'll be right back."

Hagerman headed into the house. His feet left footprints in the dust on the porch. Chib yawned but didn't get up.

Marty felt like crying out with joy. It was true that Father Hagerman was probably doing it out of pity, but Marty didn't care.

"You won't regret it at all," he called after him.

The old man returned a few seconds later. Marty's smile vanished. Hagerman was carrying a black, double-barreled shotgun.

The old man stopped on the porch, the gun held loosely at his side. It was a rusted-out thing, something that must have been passed down to Hagerman through the generations.

"Sir . . ." Marty said, his voice cracking. He couldn't get himself to say anything else. His lungs refused to take in air.

When Hagerman came down the steps, Marty realized that he had underestimated the insanity of the old man. If only the Gonzo's self-defense protocols weren't turned off until a sale was made. . .

Just when Marty was about to run, Hagerman suddenly swung toward his scrawny dog lying in the grass. He pointed the shotgun at the dog's head, the fading sunlight glinting off the black metal.

"Got to be done," he said, cocking the hammer.

"Sir!" Marty cried.

Raising an eyebrow, Hagerman looked at him. "I told you I only need one dog," he said.

Marty swallowed. The lump in his throat felt as big as one of

Hagerman's pumpkins. The mouth of the barrel was only inches from Chib's head.

"But sir," he said, realizing he had to tread lightly here, "you can't just . . . kill her."

"Why not? Your dog is better in every single way."

He pressed the gun down on Chib's head, flattening the coarse fur. One of Chib's eyelids opened a crack, then shut.

"Please," Marty said. "You can't do this . . . I mean, don't you care about her?"

Hagerman turned to Marty, and for the first time, Marty realized it was all an act. There was a gleam of amusement in Hagerman's eyes. He lowered the rifle.

"So there's another reason to have a dog then?" he said, cracking a gold-toothed smile.

It was a strange mix of emotions that Marty felt—relief that there would be no gunshot, and disappointment that he was not going to make a sale.

"You see, son," Hagerman said, "it's hard to love a dog unless there's a chance it don't love you back." He opened up the barrel and turned it to face Marty. "Empty. Just in case you were wondering."

Marty nodded. His heart was still racing, but he attempted a smile. "I appreciate you're letting me talk to you," he said, and turned back to the van. The drive home suddenly seemed much longer. It would be all right, he told himself. He would just have to work two jobs all year.

"Where you going, son?" Hagerman asked.

"Home," Marty sighed, opening the door. He was about to call the Gonzo, which was still sitting quietly.

"Well, aren't you going to sell me the dog first?"

Marty looked at Hagerman. The old man didn't appear to be joking.

"Sir?"

"You heard me."

"But . . . what about . . . I thought you only needed one?"

Hagerman nodded. "That's right. I've got Chib. But I still need someone to watch my garden."

There was no doubt in Marty's mind that Father Hagerman was insane. It didn't matter. He wasn't going to argue.

Hagerman went into the house to get his money, returning with a wad of cash. Hardly anyone used real money these days, but it didn't surprise Marty that Hagerman did. The old man filled out the necessary paperwork. Then, after issuing the proper voice commands to program the dog to respond to Hagerman, the transaction was done.

"I'm really grateful," Marty said.

"Don't thank me," Hagerman said. "You just get on back here in October and get yourself a pumpkin, all right?"

They shook hands. Hagerman turned to the house, the Gonzo following on his heels. Marty climbed into his van. He realized he had forgotten to give Hagerman his user manual.

He rolled down the window. "Oh, Father!" he called, holding up the manual with the other hand. "This is yours."

"Keep it," Hagerman said.

It wasn't until Marty returned on a cool Saturday in October that he realized what Father Hagerman meant. Coming up the drive, he saw that nestled among the tall cornstalks and the plump, shiny pumpkins was the Gonzo. Marty almost didn't recognize it. It was standing on its hind legs, braced against a wooden post. It was dressed in a red plaid shirt, rolled up blue overalls, and a straw hat. Marty knew, from how still it was, that the battery had long since died.

There wasn't a crow in sight.

With Dignity

So SPERM meets egg and ! my life starts with an exclamation point and it's strange having one in the middle of a sentence but we're always born in the middle of something and I'm a living but not yet breathing being and my fetus grows inside my mother's womb and I get arms and legs and a head so I can think and then I have a soul:

that's the colon which is the beginning of consciousness and everything's still a jumble but my life is really going and I can taste and touch and feel and I want out of that warm place so I can see and hear too and I kick and kick—

and with a dash I'm out in the world and my lungs fill with air and I wail to let everyone know that there's someone else that wants to live and my parents take me home and raise me and I start to have memories;

now my semi-adult mind forms and I will remember with commas because my mind wants to order it all, going to preschool and biting the teacher's toe, kissing little Jenny behind the monkey bars in second grade, seeing the Grand Canyon with my Mom and Dad, pissing on the neighbor's house, going to my Grandpa's funeral when I'm twelve and seeing my Mom cry and cry, and now my body feels strange . and

with the period everything comes to a stop because I feel all these odd sexual urges and I play with myself and feel ashamed and I make love to my first girl at age fifteen and she's got these great breasts I love to play with and dream about and now life starts to speed up and I go to college and get a job and meet a woman and get married and this all goes so fast I hardly have time to blink much less think and then this wonderful thing happens ? and my God

I have a child which is a mystery I can't comprehend and I know that if nothing else that one thing will put my mark on history and then this terrible things happens and during the night when that child is two it stops breathing and my life

(turns into a parenthetical mess without even conjunctions to keep things straight I am so depressed lonely lost I lose my job I get a divorce I live with my parents I take the revolver one night from Dad's sock drawer to kill myself only Dad finds me stops me please God forgive me)

and the rest of my life blurs by and now I'm old and wrinkled and I spend my days on the golf course and there's not much time left but I know I must lift up my chin and face the end with dignity and when it comes I set it off with quotation marks as if saying

"my mind is mush and there's not much order any more I wonder when those next quotation marks are going to come along I can almost see them I'm a little afraid then the fear goes away I'm only curious curious curious I wonder what will come after those last . . . "

A Christmas in Amber

THE SNOWFLAKES BARELY touched the glass before they melted, the moisture swept aside by his humming windshield wipers, but Alan was still mesmerized. Not a word had been said about snow on any of the Evacuation Updates. Rain had been the forecast. Lots and lots of rain. It had been many years since he had seen real snow—twenty or thirty at least, back when Janis was still alive. And that had been at a ski resort, not Los Angeles. The last time he could remember it snowing in Los Angeles was when he was still in his twenties, some fifty years back, and he could *never* remember it snowing on Christmas Day.

The snowflakes wafted through the golden halos surrounding the streetlights before they vanished on the glistening pavement. He was amazed at how deserted the streets were. *That* never would have happened if not for the evacuation. There'd be gobs of kids outside trying to make snowballs. Every house in the subdivision looked the same, with gabled windows and brick facades, posh and expensive in every respect, so identical Alan was surprised when the autopilot turned the van into a driveway. He had been to the house lots of times, but still he couldn't tell it apart from the others. Only when he saw Michelle's face pressed against the bay window, hands cupped on either side, did he know he was in the right place.

She wore the purple A's baseball cap he had bought her when they attended the game the previous year. The blinking holiday lights around the window made her face green one moment, red the next. When she saw him, she waved excitedly and disappeared through the part in the curtains. So they hadn't told her. If they had told her, he doubted she would be smiling.

A sharp sadness stabbed at his heart. For a moment, he wondered if this was a good idea.

"Open all doors," he said.

The van's computer beeped in acknowledgement. The two front doors, the sliding side door, and the back doors all popped open. In his haste to get to his son's house on time, he had forgotten his jacket, and the chill wind sliced right through his thin cotton sweater. If Janis was still alive, he knew what she would say. Stepping out onto the pavement, he could hear her voice.

You trying to get pneumonia, Alan? Is that what you want?

"It's not like it matters now, dear," he said, catching himself when he realized he was speaking out loud. He had been hearing her a lot lately, and he had been trying hard not to answer. If the kids heard him, they'd worry.

The driveway was lit by two lamps, one on either side of the garage. The air smelled like the old pines that lined the street. The front door to the house slid open and Rick emerged, bulging brown leather suitcases under each arm. His hands were covered with thick mittens. He was dressed in the type of heavy blue parka somebody on an expedition up Mount Everest might wear, as well as bright red ski pants, a brown wool cap with ear flaps, and yellow rain boots, all of which looked brand new. Under all that garb his face was tanned a deep bronze, which Alan knew was a requirement of the part Rick had been playing—a professional surfer on that soap opera. This amused Alan to no end; as far as he knew, Rick had never been surfing. He hated both swimming and the ocean.

An image of Rick surfing in his current outfit flashed through Alan's mind, and he chuckled.

"What's so funny?" Rick asked, breath fogging. His curly black hair ruffled in the breeze. Janis had always called him muffin head because of his dome-like hair.

"Nothing," Alan said.

"It's cold."

"Yes, it is."

He made a motion to take the bags, but Rick shook his head and walked past. Katherine came out next, also dressed in a heavy coat and pants, also carrying bulging suitcases. The difference was that her clothes matched: they were solid white, hugging her model-thin body, and stylishly designed. Her blond hair was pulled back into a braided pony tail, sticking out the side of her Russian-style fur hat. Michelle came out right behind her, dressed in the same coat as her mother, but otherwise in rumpled jeans faded in the knees, dirty tennis shoes, and of course, the baseball cap. He knew her hair was as blond as her mother's, but it was cut so short you couldn't see it underneath the hat. A black backpack was slung over her shoulders, and he saw the eyepiece of her microscope jutting out the top.

How her parents had ever ended up with a child so dissimilar to them Alan couldn't say, but he was glad for it. She was more like him than his son had ever been. She was even saying she wanted to grow up to be a paleontologist. The thought of that made his chest tighten, and he forced it away.

"I'll help you," he said to Katherine, taking one of her bags.

"Oh, thank you," Katherine said, breathing a sigh. Up close, he saw that she was perspiring, her cheeks pink. Alan wondered if she had lifted anything that heavy in years. It must have been hard being without servants, he thought sarcastically, and then felt guilty for thinking it. He and Katherine had never gotten along great—hell, he and Rick had never gotten along great—but he needed to be positive now

"*Dear*," Rick said from behind the van, "think of his back."

"I'm fine," Alan said, but he did feel a twinge. Damn thing had been bothering him for years.

Rick made a noise that sounded like *hummmph*. It was a sound Janis used to make, a sort of disgusted resignation. Janis had been in the business, too, a television director. They had always been close, Janis and Rick. They had a bond that Alan could never understand Kind of like he and Michelle.

"Hey, sport," he said to her.

She beamed up at him, smiling with sealed lips. He knew she was embarrassed about the gap in her teeth. She had lost them a few months earlier, a couple days shy of her sixth birthday. He also remembered that her parents, obsessed with the preparations they needed to make after they received winning lottery numbers, had forgotten to put money under her pillow. Grandpa had given her a ten, telling her the tooth fairy had come to his house by mistake. She was a smart kid, too smart to believe this, but she had nodded just the same.

The snowflakes dotted the brim of her cap before turning into dark watermarks.

"You all packed, huh?" he said.

"Yeah," she said. "Hey Grandpa, guess what? We get to go on a spaceship!"

"I know," Alan said.

As if Alan might drop the bag at any moment, Rick quickly snatched the bag from him, scooting it into the van. Then he helped Katherine with her other bag. Alan helped his granddaughter take off her backpack, all while she chatted nonstop.

"Mommy says only a few people get to take a ride on the spaceship and we're lucky," she said. "She says we're going to be gone a while so I better take all the stuff I want to play with, so I made sure to bring my microscope."

"I see that," Alan said. "You bring any of your fossils?"

"No," she answered glumly. "Mommy says they're too heavy."

"Well, she's probably right."

"But I do have this!"

She reached into her pocket and pulled out an object that fit into the palm of her hand. When the lamps shined on the yellowish plastic, he knew what it was. He had bought it for her when they visited the California Academy of Sciences in June. The plastic looked more yellow than honey-colored; it was meant to look like amber, a facsimile of a new species of termite that had been found in Columbia, encased in amber, perfectly preserved after sixty million years. He had offered to buy her a t-shirt, but she had insisted on the little keepsake.

"Ah," he said, and for a moment he couldn't speak.

With the luggage secured, they boarded the van, everyone absorbed in grim silence. Except for Michelle. She talked about how she had never been in a spaceship and how it would be so much fun to tell everyone at school about it—when she started going to school again, whenever that was. Alan punched in the coordinates of the airport, and Rick, in the passenger seat, struggled to leaf through their evacuation paperwork with his mittens. As they pulled away from the house, Alan tried to think of something to say, something to lighten the mood.

"What's wrong, Mommy?" Michelle asked.

"Hmm?" Katherine said softly. "Oh, nothing."

"But you're crying. Did you hurt your hand on the seatbelt?"

"Yes, dear. That's it."

"Okay. I'm sorry. I hurt my finger once on one of Grandpa's seatbelts too. It hurts."

"I've got an idea," Alan said. "Why don't we sing some Christmas carols? I think that would be a lot fun." He tried to sound jovial, but he knew his voice wasn't ringing true. "Jingle Bells, anyone?"

"Maybe we should focus on watching the road," Rick said. "There might be some crazies out there, and the autopilot doesn't always know what to do."

"I'd like to sing," Michelle protested.

Katherine sniffled. "Yes, let's."

"All right, fine," Rick said. "Just don't let the van drive too fast, okay? We have plenty of time. We don't need to hurry. Hurrying we'll just get us in an accident."

Alan felt his irritation rise, then let it go. He was amazed he could feel irritated even today of all days. He cleared his throat and began to sing with his scratchy voice, and Katherine and Michelle quickly joined him. Rick focused his attention on his papers for a few blocks, as if there was something there that he could have possibly missed, but soon even he was singing. And that's how they passed the time as they made their way along the slick roads, the vents blasting warm air, the tires sloshing through water, soon out onto the ghostly highway, hardly a car on it. So many people, already gone, and those that weren't had headed somewhere in the middle of the country, though he knew it could hardly help them. The asteroid coming their way was bigger than the United States.

When they finished that song, they launched immediately into Frosty the Snowman, then Silent Night, then Rudolph the Red-Nosed Reindeer. He couldn't remember them singing like this *ever*, and here they were singing fools. When they were nearly to LAX, he wondered if they should be talking more seriously, but he didn't know what the point of it all would be. What needed to be said had been said well enough in the previous months. Now there was only the parting.

The only person he *hadn't* talked to about what was happening was Michelle, and he wasn't sure he could bring himself to do that.

It wasn't long before they had reached the airport, navigated through three different checkpoints manned by soldiers, past tanks and jeeps with guns trained on them, down a special road to a gated area full of hundreds of cars parked in neat rows separated by red cones. Papers were checked, retinas scanned. At the last gate, they had to get out, and their car was thoroughly searched, their bags run through an X-ray machine before being tagged and dropped into the back of a pickup truck. In the gated area bright fluorescent lights mounted high in the air gave the place the feel of a sporting event. Hundreds of people were making their way slowly to the far end, where out in the middle of the tarmac sat the white transport plane, it, too surrounded by enough artillery and soldiers to subdue a small country. The transport ships, fat, white, and ungainly in appearance, had been nicknamed "spaceducks." Now, surrounded by all that army green, it seemed all the more like a duck—a duck sitting on a grassy bank.

For the past two months, all over the world, the spaceducks had been ferrying the lucky few up to *Little Earth.* And *that* ship, as big as a hundred football fields, with a self-contained ecosystem that could theoretically (but only theoretically) maintain itself indefinitely, would carry a little over ten thousand passengers and crew to *RNL-875*—a planet around a star much like the sun, some 157 light years away. The best scientists in the world had determined that planet, out of the hundred or so identified, to have the best chance of having an environment hospitable to humans.

Alan knew that scientists had pegged the actual odds at something like one in ten thousand, and that was mostly guesswork and wishful thinking, but nobody talked about that much. In any case, it would be hundreds of generations before the ship arrived.

They parked the van and fell in line with the others, heading toward the last X-ray and retina arch before the tarmac; a dozen yards beyond that were the stairs up to the ship. The snowflakes were gone now, the air thick with a wet mist that clung to his skin. Michelle took his hand. Her fingers were small but warm within his own.

"Why is everybody crying?" she asked.

Rick and Katherine trailed behind, and he heard Katherine start crying again, Rick shushing her. All around them, much the same thing was happening. The line was moving quickly. They would be to final gate in no time, Alan knew. He just had to keep moving. One foot in front of the other.

Alan swallowed. "It's hard saying goodbye."

"But they seem so sad," Michelle said.

"Yes."

"Are they sad because they don't get to go on the spaceship?"

He didn't answer. They were only ten or eleven people from the front, and a woman near the gate suddenly threw herself against the fence and was shouting someone's name, soldiers quickly pulling her back. Was it Frank? Or Hank? Watching this, Alan knew he could no longer lie to Michelle. The truth may have brought out some ugly things in people, but at least it was truth. When she was older, he knew she would mostly likely look back on this day with sadness, but he didn't want her to look back feeling betrayed.

"No," he said, looking down at her, attempting a smile. "They're sad because . . . because they're leaving. Leaving and not coming back."

He saw the skin underneath her eyes quiver. "What?"

"I'm sorry, honey. We didn't tell you until now because we didn't want you to be upset."

"But why?"

"Well, there's this asteroid that's heading toward Earth—"

"Jimmy across the street told me about that," she said quickly. "Daddy said they shot it down with a laser. They said it won't hurt anyone." Her grip on his hand tightened.

Alan nodded. "Your daddy told you that because he didn't want you to worry about me. You see, dear, I'm not going with you."

Michelle stopped, looking at him with an expression of shock and hurt he wished immediately he had never seen. There was only one group ahead of them, a family of five, and the arch beeped as each child passed underneath.

"I'm sorry," he said. "You see, only a few people can go on the ship that's going to take you to a new home. Old people like me don't get to go, but you and your parents are the lucky ones."

He was waiting for her to cry, but the tears didn't come. Instead she looked furious, releasing his hand and clenching her fists.

"But I don't want to go without you!"

"I'm sorry, dear."

"They can't make me."

Katherine touched her daughter's shoulder. "Honey," she began, but Michelle pulled away.

"No! I'm staying if Grandpa stays!" She grabbed Alan's hands and looked up at him with a pleading expression. "Please don't make me go, Grandpa! Please, I want to stay with you."

They were to the last arch; the plastic was bright yellow, like a children's playground toy. The soldiers waited silently, but he could see the impatience in their eyes. He wondered why any of them were even bothering doing this, then he knew that they must have also been lucky ones. They just had one last job to do before they got to board a transport ship of their own.

He bent down in front of Michelle and took her gently by the shoulders. "You know I love you," he said.

She swallowed. The tears still hadn't come, but he knew they weren't far away now. "I love you too, Grandpa."

"But you've got to go with your Mommy and Daddy. They need you very, very much. And I want you to grow up and be happy, and you can't be happy here with me."

"Yes, I can—"

He put a finger on her lips, quieting her. "Please, don't argue. Just go."

She nodded, though she now looked dazed. He kissed her forehead, looking away so he wouldn't see her crying. If he saw her crying, he knew his strength would desert him. He'd end up just like that woman throwing herself against the fence. He hugged Katherine, then Rick, said a few words of goodbye that had already been said, and then the three of them were ushered through the archway. Alan got to watch them for only a moment before a soldier escorted him out of the line and to a roped-off area where dozens of people stood along the fence. There were no lights in this area, and their faces were shadowy and dark. Alan wondered if it had been deliberate. He didn't want to see these people's faces.

He took his place along side them, and by then Rick, Katherine, and Michelle were entering the ship. He saw Michelle looking around frantically. He waved, but she didn't see him.

"Michelle!" he shouted.

She turned, perhaps not seeing exactly where he was, but definitely looking in his direction. Then she was in the ship. He knew he shouldn't have done it, but he wasn't the only one. Lots of people shouted. He heard a sound, a heavy thumping, and for a moment he thought it might be the asteroid crashing through the atmosphere, since he had no idea what that would sound like, and then he realized it was the pounding of his own heart. A few minutes later the rest of the passengers were in the ship. A woman in an orange jumpsuit was at the hatch, closing it. This is it, Alan thought. They're really leaving.

And then, before the hatch was closed, he saw the woman in orange stumble to the side. A figure emerged, short, dressed in a white jacket, running down the steps. When he recognized Michelle, he cried out, reaching as if he could grab her, his hand finding only the cold and damp metal fence. All around him others were crying out as well. It was as if she had fallen into an ocean full of sharks and they all stood helplessly on the boat.

The two soldiers at the bottom, who had turned aside, now turned back, but Michelle was already at the bottom. She ran for Alan. "Grandpa! Grandpa!" she cried.

She was surprisingly fast for such a little girl, so fast she may have surprised the soldiers, because she was halfway to Alan before they broke into a run. They gained on her quickly, but she was nearly to Alan already, slowing when she got close to the fence.

"Grandpa?" she said.

He hesitated for a second, but then his resolve broke. "Here," he said. "Here, Michelle, here!"

She dashed to the fence with the soldiers, two thin men with assault weapons slung over their shoulders, close behind. Other soldiers were also approaching. Alan bent down to meet her, reaching to embrace her, forgetting that there was a fence in the way. His fingers closed around the gaps, and then her smaller fingers were over his own.

"Grandpa!"

The light was bad, but he saw the grim horror on her face, the desperation. All of these soldiers here to prevent the unexpected, he thought, and all it took was a six year-old girl to disrupt them.

The first two soldiers grabbed her and began to pull, but she released Alan's fingers and grabbed onto the fence, screaming. Try as they might, they couldn't pull her away. They had her whole body in the air and still they couldn't pry her off the fence.

"Damn kid," one of them muttered.

"Don't hurt her!" Alan said.

"Grandpa! Grandpa!" Michelle cried.

The other soldiers had reached them now, a half dozen of them all looking the same in the dark. A tall, bald man with a silver mustache stepped between the two who were holding Michelle. "Put her down," he said.

The two obeyed, putting Michelle back on her feet. Her white-fingered grip on the fence didn't slack, and she pressed up against the metal.

"I won't go!" she said.

"Please, Michelle," Alan said.

"No!"

"If you don't go," the man with the silver mustache said, "you'll be left behind."

"I want to stay with Grandpa!"

"Don't you want to be with your parents?"

"I want to stay with Grandpa!"

"Oh, for heaven's sake," the man with the silver mustache said. "We don't have time—"

"Wait," Alan said. "Let me come over there. I'll walk her up."

The man with the silver mustache looked at him skeptically. All those guns, Alan thought.

"Please," he begged.

The man with the silver mustache looked at him a moment more, then nodded back toward the gate. As Alan ran, some of the soldiers on the other side jogged alongside him. There was a moment of fuss at the arch, a few words spoken on radios, and then he was ushered through the beeping mechanism, the soldiers on the other side guiding him back to Michelle. He was still a few steps away from her when she turned and threw herself into his arms.

"I don't want to go!"

He stroked her hair, feeling the warmth of her face through his damp sweater. He knew there was nothing now he could say to comfort her. The truth was what it was. With his own private army accompanying him, he turned and headed for the plane. Two people in orange jumpsuits, a man and a woman, watched him from the top of the steps. Michelle's body shook with each breath. The yelling and shouting from the spectators had stopped; he knew they were all watching. When he started up the stairs, feet clanging on the metal, the soldiers stopped and gathered at the bottom.

With each step, his legs seemed heavier. He wasn't sure he was going to make it, but then there he was, at the top, placing Michelle on her feet between the two people in orange.

"There now," he said, his throat constricting.

She looked up at him with wet eyes, cheeks glistening. He steadied her with a hand on her shoulder.

"Grandpa," she said.

"It's for the best, honey. Please do it for me."

"But—"

"I know."

"I want—"

"Yes, but you still have to go."

Her chin dropped, and she looked down for a moment before turning toward the ship. Then she turned back suddenly, her hand reaching into her jacket pocket and emerging with the amber-like keepsake. She thrust it at him.

"I want you to have this," she said.

"But it's yours."

"But I want *you* to have it."

He nodded and took it from her, kissing the back of her hand when he did so. She turned, not a trace of emotion on her face, and the two people in orange closed in behind her. He placed the keepsake in his pocket, then without waiting, turned and started back down the steps. He had to go quickly. He would not even wait for the ship to take off. He had to get out of there.

When the hatch clanged shut, he jumped. The soldiers watched him as if he was the walking dead, and he knew that to them perhaps he was. When he reached the bottom, a few patted him on the shoulder. The man with silver mustache personally saw him back to the viewing area, shaking his hand and saying something inaudible before turning and leaving. Some people in the crowd asked him questions, but he didn't listen. He moved close to the fence, pressing his face up against the cool metal, and watched the plane.

The regular engines started turning, rumbling; the plane lurched forward. Even where he stood, he felt the frigid air pushing against him. He knew when it was up higher, the rocket engines would take over for the last leg of the journey. Science, his old friend, would see his family into space.

"Some Christmas," he heard Janis say behind him.

The plane taxied along the runway, gathering speed. As he watched the ungainly white bird sail up into the darkness, he thought about Christmases past and Christmases future. He thought about a huge hunk of rock hurtling toward the Earth. He thought about little girls with microscopes and insects encased in amber. He thought about the meaning of the word hope.

"The best ever," he said.

Acknowledgements

THERE ARE MANY PEOPLE who have helped me with my short fiction over the years, too many, really, to list here, but there are a few I would like to single out: Kristine Kathryn Rusch, for both encouragement and unflinching honesty, a rare combination in a mentor, and for being the best example of professionalism a writer could ask for; Dean Wesley Smith, for not being surprised when I came back to writing much more seriously the second time; Stanley Schmidt at *Analog*, for seeing a spark in that first story he bought from me, and for being willing to work with a relatively new writer on it; Shawna McCarthy at *Realms of Fantasy;* Sheila Williams at *Asimov's;* Janet Hutchings at *Ellery Queen;* Peter Crowther at *PS Publishing;* Denise Little at *Tekno;* all the members of the Eugene Writers Workshop from 1991-1994; all the members of the Nexus Writers Workshop from 2002-2003; Kate Wilhelm and other members of her monthly workshop; all the members of the various *Oregon Coast Professional Writers Workshops* I attended over the years; Douglas Cohen and Warren Lapine at Fantastic Books, who believed in my work and shepherded this collection into print; and of course, my first reader and the love of my life, Heidi Carter.

About the Author

Scott William Carter's first novel, *The Last Great Getaway of the Water Balloon Boys,* was hailed by Publishers Weekly as a "touching and impressive debut" and won the prestigious Oregon Book Award. Since then, he has published ten novels and over fifty short stories, his fiction spanning a wide variety of genres and styles. His most recent book for younger readers, *Wooden Bones,* chronicles the untold story of Pinocchio and was singled out for praise by the Junior Library Guild. He lives in Oregon with his wife and children.

Visit him online at *www.ScottWilliamCarter.com.*

www.ingramcontent.com/pod-product-compliance
Lightning Source LLC
Chambersburg PA
CBHW020635260626
47157CB00008B/2747

* 9 7 8 0 6 9 2 2 4 7 4 4 0 *